The Turtle
Sang in the Land

About the Author

After taking a degree in English Literature, Dorothy Cadwallader became a teacher in secondary education, which she found engrossing, satisfying but totally time-consuming. Following their careers, she and her husband lived in various parts of the country, finally settling in the Lake District.

Early retirement enabled her to study painting with the O.C.A. She combined her love of painting and studying the history of Art with foreign travel.

She now also had time to write, which she had enjoyed since childhood. The discipline of producing poetry and short stories to fulfil the membership obligations of a writing group, led to her finishing the novel, 'The Turtle Sang in the Land' that she had begun several years earlier.

Dorothy Cadwallader

The Turtle
Sang in the Land

Olympia Publishers
London

www.olympiapublishers.com
OLYMPIA PAPERBACK EDITION

A CIP catalogue record for this title is
available from the British Library.

ISBN: 978-1-84897-699-3

(Olympia Publishers is part of Ashwell Publishing Ltd)

This is a work of fiction.
Names, characters, places and incidents originate from the writer's imagination.
Any resemblance to actual persons, living or dead, is purely coincidental.

First published in 2016

Olympia Publishers
60 Cannon Street
London
EC4N 6NP

Printed in Great Britain

Acknowledgements

I should like to thank Daniel and Karen Parker for their invaluable help, and Helen Delbourgo and Helen Bond for agreeing to read and comment on the novel as it was reaching completion.

I am also grateful to the artist Rolf Parker of Skylark Studios, Cockermouth, who painted the seascape used on the cover to illustrate a poignant episode in the novel.

I would like to thank The Literary Trustees of Walter de la Mare and the Society of Authors for their permission to reproduce an extract from the poem *Nod* by Walter de la Mare.

The Turtle Sang in the Land

'Now I saw in my dream, that by this time the Pilgrims were got over the enchanted Ground, and entering into the Country of Beulah, whose air was very sweet and pleasant, the way lying directly through it, they solaced themselves there for a season. Yea, here they heard continually the singing of birds, and saw every day the flowers appear on the Earth, and heard the voice of the turtle in the land.'

Extract from 'The Pilgrim's Progress' by John Bunyan (1628-88)

Chapter One

He stood deferentially in the doorway, tall, dark and slender.

"Sorry. I'm disturbing you," he said, "I'll come back later."

Half empty crates filled the tiny room. Books and files were sliding from every chair and the desk was piled high with massive tomes.

Margaret rose from the floor, her finger automatically marking the page in the book she had been reading.

"Come in, Mr .... er .... Forgive this mess. I ought to have been sorting this lot out, but you know how it is when you start unpacking books. You flick through a few pages, then start reading and before you know where you are, hours have gone by. I'll just remove these, then you can perhaps sit down."

She looked round vaguely, her arms full of books, then deposited them on the floor. She was trying to remember who he was. Not one of her students certainly, and not a fresher; his manner, although very polite, was too relaxed, and anyway she felt she ought to know him. There was something familiar about him.

She went on talking to win time.

"I was just glancing through Blake's epigrams," she said, indicating the book she had left open on the desk. "I remember when I was a student, I had one of those calendars with a proverb or quotation for each day that you tore off, and I used to hate throwing them away. It seemed faintly insulting to the writers. One I kept was Blake's. I've just come across it here." She picked up the book and read.

He who binds to himself a Joy
Doth the winged life destroy;
But he who kisses the Joy as it flies
Lives in Eternity's sunrise.

The fading light had left the greater part of the room in deep shadow. Margaret looked towards her visitor. He stood motionless near the chair she had cleared, attentive and thoughtful.

"Why did you keep that particular one?" he asked at last.

"Oh, partly for the elegance of the expression, but mainly, I suppose, looking back, that it justified a part of life. It gave to a passing affair a style that I thought human feelings merited. And of course it cuts out completely terms like 'promiscuity' that merely vilify and never describe."

"Will you read it again?"

Margaret smiled. "Yes, of course."

She began to read the lines again, more slowly this time and, knowing the passage by heart, raised her eyes from the book as she softly repeated the last two lines,

But he who kisses the Joy as it flies
Lives in Eternity's sunrise.

They looked at each other, each held by unspoken thoughts.

"What if the Joy doesn't fly away?" he asked.

"A piece of luck, indeed!" she laughed. "But it always does."

"Even for Romeo and Juliet?"

"They died, you remember."

"Yes. That was a silly example. What about Tristan and Iseult?"

"They were drugged."

He laughed, revealing white teeth of perfect shape.

"I'm obviously no expert on romantic lovers. But surely these affairs are sometimes lasting?"

She had suddenly remembered who he was when he laughed. I ought to have been a dentist, she thought, I have a perfect memory for people's teeth.

"Mr Lodge," she said, smiling her recognition, "I'm glad you came to see me."

He laughed again.

"I had an idea you didn't remember me. But thanks for the poetry lesson."

"I'm sorry. Really I am. My husband is always telling me I live in a dream world. But it is quite a while since June when we cast the play. Not that that is any excuse. And today, as you see, I have been changing rooms. Incidentally, how did you find me here?"

"I met the porter near your old room and he said you'd moved up to the fifth floor. He didn't remember the number so I knocked at every door in the corridor, cupboards and all."

She laughed and failed to ask the reason for his visit; after all, actors and producers naturally flowed together before the production of a play.

"I've been after this room for ages," Margaret told him. "It looks a mess now, but it's a beautiful room really. I feel I'm at the top of an ivory tower here - cut off from the petty world below, and yet able to see everything if I look down from my window. Come and see."

They stood together in the turret-like window watching the tiny figures that crossed from the Arts Block below them to the Science Block opposite.

Then she turned as if to go back into the room. He did not move but stood two feet away looking at her. Against her will she returned his gaze, wanting to discover the particular features that made so pleasing a whole. Black hair, dark eyes, a slightly aquiline nose and that remembered, beautiful smile, and withal something sad in the expression when the smile faded that melted the heart. She thought, I must tell Douglas how a beautiful young man searched for and found me in my little turret room, and how we read poetry and gazed soulfully at one another, before he went away.

"Have a drink," she said suddenly. "For you are the first that ever burst into this silent room. Now where in Hell's name are those glasses?"

She scrutinised the boxes.

"Ah, yes, I remember."

She unearthed a cardboard box with 'Hooch' scrawled across the side and began to draw bottles and tumblers from it.

"Now what is your favourite spiritous liquor?"

She looked doubtfully at a bottle of sherry.

"I suspect this is a cheap refill, we'd better have the Scotch."

She poured a generous amount into each tumbler in the reckless fashion of women whose drinks are usually poured for them. She handed him a glass.

"What shall we drink to?"

"To your little turret room, long sought and at last found," he said.

They drank and a peaceful ease grew between them. Shafts of golden light from the blazing western sky filled the window embrasure. It drew them together to gaze at the sunset.

"This is a good time of year," Margaret said. "I'm glad the academic year begins in Autumn. I always want to begin new enterprises now, meet new people, study new things. I like the touch of frost in the evenings, the misty mornings, the hot sun of noonday, the garish colour of the trees, the sunsets. I enjoy the approach to Winter."

She turned to her guest.

"We must also drink to a new venture we shall share. To 'Coriolanus'."

They raised their glasses and now each looked appraisingly at the other.

How would Mrs Gerrard direct, Lodge wondered. He could not yet imagine, yet felt a curious confidence in her. He was filled with excitement at the thought of beginning rehearsals. He longed to get to grips with the part, to prove himself. He had just begun to read 'An Actor Prepares' by Stanislavski and hoped he would not make the ass of himself that the student Nasvanov had done in his first endeavours. Margaret was searching his face again. Was the essential quality of a Coriolanus there? Did he have any of that central pride, immovable as a rock, without an understanding of which no actor could begin to play the part? Was he, she wondered, of the class that understood in its bones the patrician's loathing of the commonalty? In these so-called classless days, disdain was a trait well-hidden, but not infrequently revealed by small signs to the initiated. It would be interesting to find out.

Immersed in their thoughts, they gazed out over the lawns to the trees lining the main road, silhouetted now against a reddening sky. They drank, relaxed yet eager to stride over the brink into the unknown.

"We'll make a start on the play at the beginning of next week," Margaret said at last.

15

"Good," he replied and put the empty glasses on the table. "Thank you for the drink."

"Goodbye, Mr Lodge, until next week."

She remained leaning on the window sill, her thoughts divided between ancient Rome and the student who had just left. Eventually she noticed down below a running figure. It expressed the same *joie de vivre* that raced through her own limbs. Half way across the lawns the figure turned and began walking backwards. It seemed to be looking up to her window. An arm was raised in salutation. She smiled.

"A warm-hearted young man, our Coriolanus," she murmured.

She left the window and wandered about the room, opening books at random and flicking restlessly through their pages. The task of sorting out her books and bringing the room to some sort of order didn't appeal to her, yet the thought of meeting this chaos in the morning was so distasteful that she decided she must make the effort. She made a bargain with herself to work really hard for two hours, then go home. It was five p.m. She would stop at seven.

Within a quarter of an hour she was engrossed in the work. As the boxes were emptied she put them outside in the corridor. The cleared floor space made movement easier. The proportions of the room began to show themselves. The shelves, now filled with books, glowed with life. She unpacked a reading lamp and found a place for it on the desk. She switched it on and stood back to see the effect of its light on the room. It softened the glare from the bare central bulb and when this was switched off, the room was revealed as the intimate retreat Margaret had hoped for. She knew instinctively that here she would be able to work at last.

The last few years, although outwardly successful enough, had forced the realisation upon her that time was slipping away and her achievement was paltry. In five years she would be forty. She was already half-way through the allotted span and not one book had been written. For years she had postponed the serious writing that she had always known was to be her real work. At first she had done it consciously, feeling unready to commit to paper what she feared might be lost in the writing through her lack of skill. In the thick of life she might not be able to summon the objectivity that she believed the writer's craft demanded. Was it not often said that no one under thirty could write a good novel? She had felt this to be true, but there was something alarming, nevertheless, in the success that came now to the very young.

Until recently, Margaret had privately been affected by a deep diffidence, as if her youth were some sort of disadvantage. In her work as lecturer and teacher she had overcome it by scholarship, conscientiousness and sheer professionalism. In the study alone, however, with a blank sheet of paper before her, self confidence drifted away. She envied the cock-sure of her own generation in their ability to act, and yet, reluctantly, she had to admit she often despised their achievements. She knew she would be a writer, she had a lot to say, but it was in the saying that the truth could so easily be lost. For years she had been preparing herself. Now it seemed to be time to begin.

She had been approaching steadily for some time past a position in which the centre of her being, from which creation would spring, if it were to do this at all, would be impregnable. Her high turret room was just one of the superficial aids to this. Emotionally and financially secure, all she had to do was make a start.

Her determination to write released within her so much energy that she began to realise just how tightly she had reined in her own desires and ambitions. She had been concentrating first on her job and secondly on being Douglas's wife. Secondly - the word amused her. Many men would have hated to be given second-place in their wives' interests, but not Douglas. He saw all things as having their proper places and seasons, and understood, more than anyone she had ever known, that the shifting kaleidoscope of life now brought one element into the foreground of interest, then another. The pace and preparedness for life were what interested him. His own life was full and it never occurred to him that other people's lives might be less meaningful. He could not give the whole of his time to any single being and never expected the life of his wife to be centred on him. He valued her because she was a complete individual, dedicated to her teaching as he was to his work. And, if she were to achieve any success with her writing or anything else, she knew Douglas would be the first to congratulate her.

It was a good life, living with Douglas and teaching at the University.

Chapter Two

It was seven thirty when Margaret left the almost deserted University to drive the three miles home to the village of Covlington where she and Douglas lived. She felt pleased with what she had accomplished in so short a time. Her room was now habitable and fit to receive the first-year students who would be coming to introduce themselves and receive their assignments of work the following day. There would be no need to hurry tomorrow morning. The mess was cleared away, she need not arrive before ten a.m.

Covlington, she saw as she drove past the first of the Halls of residence, had again been taken over by the students. Lights blazed from the spreading wings of Thulston Hall, the largest of the women's halls. Dinner would be over by now and the late arrivals would be dashing about to find their friends, finish unpacking and to begin the talking, talking that never stopped. Margaret smiled remembering her own first hectic days at University. She had never understood Douglas's hesitation about living in Covlington in the thick of University life. She found the annual return of the students after the long vacation stimulating. It was convenient too to be able to walk to the meetings held on Sundays in the various halls; easy to invite students home for coffee.

Margaret lived in an old stone house at the far end of the village, overlooking the woodland that surrounded one of the men's halls. It was a long low house of pleasing proportions that had been altered and added to in the twenties by a stockbroker who, so local legend had it, alternated between extreme affluence and bankruptcy. Margaret was grateful for the period of affluence that had added oak floors, innumerable and ingenious cupboards and the balconies and conservatory, large windows and double garage to the house. She also loved the room that had been built on stilts and was set aslant to the main part of the house to catch the late evening sun. It was a home she had recognised instantly; a house to dream about and collect treasures for. Douglas liked the house too and spent hours in its large garden, simplifying its complicated plan by obliterating flower beds and creating neat stone walls to replace weedy rockeries.

Sometimes, she and Douglas would walk in the garden late at night, following the winding paths beneath the trees to the lily pond, from which they had a clear view of the house. Bathed in moonlight, the old walls seemed to be under a spell, held in the magic embrace of such benevolent spirits, that Margaret felt no real disaster could ever overtake one who lived there. They had often lingered in the garden, listening to the wind soughing through the topmost branches of the scots pines, delighted to hear the owls calling from the nearby woods.

As she drove towards the house she saw with pleasure that lights were shining from several of the rooms downstairs. Douglas was home. She drove the car into the garage and parked it next to his Land-Rover, then hurried into the house.

"Hello," she called, "I'm back."

"In the sitting room!" Douglas replied.

He was sitting in an armchair with magazines spread all around him on the floor. A large sheet of brown paper revealed several dark green folders. He was binding what looked like a hundred years' copies of 'Trout and Salmon', magazines that Margaret had banished to the junk room in the summer.

"Oh God," she said, flopping down in the nearest chair.

"What's the matter?"

"Nothing. But where are you going to put them? They'll take up more room than ever now."

"I'll fix up a few more shelves in the study."

"I'd like to know where. That study is just overflowing with books."

She watched Douglas sorting the magazines into years and shaking the dust from them.

"There must be something about the autumn," she remarked, "that makes people get cracking who can never be bothered to spring-clean. I've just been feet deep in a worse muddle than this. Old Jeremy has at last shifted out of the Art's Block so I grabbed his room while the going was good. I've been trying to get my stuff sorted out - that's why I'm late."

"I thought you must have got embroiled in rehearsals," Douglas mumbled, his pipe clenched between his teeth.

"Oh no. I haven't started yet. I'll have to get down to it soon. I thought I might reread the play this evening."

"You don't sound particularly enthusiastic," Douglas remarked.

"I had wanted to make a start on some writing I have in mind. And I'm rarely keen right at the start. There's something daunting about a play you are just about to produce. It's different later when you're in the thick of it. Then the difficulty is in stopping."

"Yes," Douglas agreed with feeling.

"Don't worry, I'm not going to get so involved this time. After all quite a few of these students are capable of putting a play on by themselves. I sometimes wish they would."

"I never thought I'd hear you say that. You always seem so keen and alive and... dedicated, when you're with a troupe of actors. It has even occurred to me that perhaps you missed your vocation. Why didn't your mother put you on the stage? Or you might have been a film director. You might have earned millions!"

She laughed. "I'd more probably have starved in some ghastly garret or had to play bit parts in a seedy rep. and when I think of the difficulties involved in getting intelligent people to act decently, I dread to think what it must be like to direct a dumb star, who may throw a tantrum if she is criticised half-honestly. You look surprised, Douglas. I suppose I'm getting old. Where is the enthusiasm of yester-year?"

"You don't look a day over fifty!"

"Thanks. Would you like a drink? How about a Scotch?"

"Fine. I've nearly finished this lot. Just one more year, 1970."

As she poured whisky for the second time that day, Margaret remembered the young man who had drunk with her earlier.

"One of my actors came to see me today," she told Douglas. "I didn't feel fifty, then."

He laughed, flinging an arm round her legs, as she gave him his drink.

"Never mind, I have always preferred the mature type of woman," he said with a gleam in his eye.

"You'd better join the Darby and Joan Club, then. I've decided to retreat to the age of twenty-nine."

"You could probably get away with it too."

22

"What do you mean 'probably'?"

Douglas had now finished sorting his magazines. She helped him to carry them into the study, where she was surprised to see a fire had been lit.

"How lovely. What a good idea, Douglas, to light a fire here."

"It wasn't my idea. Mrs Briggs lit it. I expect she thought you might do some 'studying' now the students are up again."

"And she was right too. What a treasure she is."

The furniture glowed in the firelight and the lavender scent of the furniture polish that Mrs Briggs used so liberally could be detected still beneath the more robust odour of chrysanthemums in a large jug by the window.

It was a peaceful room, papered in dark green with white paintwork. There were chintz covers on the odd assortment of chairs and a settee. The walls were lined with books and a desk stood in a large square bay with french windows opening on to the garden.

They put the magazines down and Margaret fetched the whisky from the sitting room. She sat on the rug before the fire, letting the warmth from the flames lick over her.

"How peaceful it is here," she said smiling at Douglas. "I sometimes think it is too good to be true. We are too much at ease. The gods may grow jealous, and take it away from us, or put it into our hearts to destroy what we value so much."

"How philosophical you are, this evening, Maggie," commented Douglas. He puffed at his pipe, then added, "I approve of the thought, however. It will prevent our sinking into complacency, and that's worse than anything your 'jealous gods' can send."

"I don't think many people are complacent today. Perhaps they would be improved by it. Most people are only interested in grabbing. I suppose I am as guilty of it as anyone but it's not so easy to recognise in oneself."

"I don't think you have it very strongly. I'm sure you never think of pay day. I doubt if you have any idea at all of how many hours you work each day, or of how much you earn in an hour. You just seem to enjoy it."

"I'm not so sure of that, sometimes I positively dislike what I do."

"Then it's possibly because you aren't functioning at that particular job as well as you would like to. It's an irritation you feel, like that of a child who knows he can shoot a ball into the net but through some lack of concentration misses it. You don't ever hate work, only your own performance of it."

"Is that supposed to comfort me?"

"No," he laughed, "I don't offer comfort."

"No. That's true. I wonder what you would say if, after a year's hard work, I suggested we took a sun-bathing holiday. Don't you think, Douglas, it's time we tried it?"

"I can just see you lying in a bikini with something like Richard Hooker's 'Ecclesiastical Polity' resting on your stomach!"

"Magnificent prose!" she enthused, laughing. "Now I'll go and see if the auto-timer has worked and cooked my casserole."

"Is there some doubt? And have you been calmly sitting here all this time without checking?"

"Yes. You don't keep a dog and bark yourself."

"But machines are different. They have no sense of responsibility. They are either switched on or off. It isn't a question of delegating."

After dinner Douglas had a batch of scientific periodicals to read. It was nine p.m., too late to begin writing a novel, she thought, so she went into the study to find a copy of 'Coriolanus'. She found the one she had prepared for the production with a clean leaf inserted between each page of the text for her own notes.

She began to read the play.

What an opening! What absolute certainty of purpose! Bare it was, lacking the imaginative intensity that in the greatest plays coloured every word, but the lines had a clarity that had a tremendous appeal. The play was swinging along in seconds. If its impetus slowed later the effect had nevertheless been made.

For two hours she read, seeing the play unroll in her imagination, testing, occasionally, the moves she had already planned and drawn out on the pages inserted in the text. Her concentration was absolute. The study grew dim and faded from her consciousness, and Caius Marcius, now taking the shape of Antony Lodge, bore on with excessive pride and defective judgement to his tragic end.

It was a taut bitter play. The last tragedy that Shakespeare wrote and the most sombre. What a bleak picture it gave of humanity. Plebeians, tribunes, patricians, senators, mothers - all were defective. One could identify with no one, for evil was everywhere.

The nobility of the hero, Caius Marcius Coriolanus, rested on his valour and prowess as a warrior and to a lesser extent upon a limited integrity that would not let him flatter those he despised for reasons of caste. Basically Coriolanus was the victim of that integrity, or patrician trustworthiness. That he was mistaken in his philosophy of life did however dim his brightness as a hero. His main fault, pride, whether or not the greatest of the deadly sins, was basically unlovable, and as a result the play had a coldness at its centre that remained unrelieved. Even the plebeians indulged in no horse play. A child pulled a butterfly to pieces, a mother gloried in her son's wounds and sent him proudly to inevitable death lest dishonour smirch his name. So Coriolanus, having returned to Rome as conqueror, was urged to save the city, that had banished him, by making a treaty. He did this and returned to Antium to meet his death at the hands of Aufidious, a man consumed by jealousy who plotted with conspirators to kill the man he was totally incapable of defeating in an equal struggle.

The justice with which the different opinions in the play were presented, the cold clear eye that probed the pettiness of man and the way the first three acts led up to the spine-chilling reversal of the fourth, these made 'Coriolanus' a masterpiece.

The uncompromising attitude of the characters also gave the play a surprising modernity. Margaret remembered clearly the television presentation. Its hard ruthless exposition perhaps appealed to viewers schooled in shots of Vietnam, Dallas and Northern Ireland. But the play was a bitter pill to swallow. Margaret longed for a Falstaff or Mercutio to set its values at question and relieve its gloom.

Why had they chosen this play she wondered as she put her copy away and went to make coffee.

Chapter Three

"Going to the rehearsal?"

Antony Lodge turned and waited for a fair-haired athletic-looking student to join him. It was Geoff Sloan who was to take the part of Aufidious.

"Five-thirty wasn't it?" asked Lodge, although he knew quite well when the first rehearsal of 'Coriolanus' began.

"Think so," replied Sloan.

"Have you been reading it?"

"What? Oh yes. I glanced through it last night."

They walked for a while in silence.

"Have you read it?" Sloan asked.

"I looked at it last night as well."

Lodge looked pale and tired as if he had not slept the night before. He had stupidly worked himself into a terrible state of nerves, reading and rereading his part, until he had convinced himself that he would never even be able to learn the lines. His worries had begun on the evening he had gone to see Mrs Gerrard. Talking with her had made him want to excel in this part.

It was the second week in October and the Shakespearean Society was to meet for the first time since 'Coriolanus' had been cast. Lodge and Sloan were surprised to find so many people they did not know waiting in the hall of the University.

The size of the cast had brought in new members and these students lent an air of strangeness to the gathering. The empty stage seemed to mesmerise several of the new-comers so that they sat silently watching that huge area where soon they would have to show their paces. Even those who had already taken part in earlier productions were standing in uncustomary silence in small groups, finding nothing to say that took away the empty, sinking feeling in their stomachs.

"Christ it's like a wake!" muttered Sloan.

They sat together at the end of a row.

"Do you think we ought to get started?" Lodge asked. "They look like a crowd of school kids."

He was glad when Sloan shook his head. For the moment he felt it was beyond his powers to organise anyone. He noticed Sloan was rubbing his damp palms for the fourth time on a creased handkerchief.

"Can't think why I was so keen to join this lot," Antony heard him say.

He looked with amusement at the solid figure beside him. To think of that superb physical specimen, sprinter and javelin thrower par excellence, worrying and sweating over a rehearsal, almost brought him to his senses. What after all was there to be nervous about? Lodge knew that Sloan, unlikely as it might seem to those who knew him only on the athletics field, was an able and sensitive actor.

The auditions last term had been very well organised. There surely was no cause for this despondency.

He heard the sound of someone walking in the corridor outside, the long easy paces of the unconcerned, wandering down to the library perhaps for a forgotten book, or drifting to the refectory for tea. Then the first of the swing doors opened and Margaret Gerrard stood in the doorway.

It seemed to Antony that it was an entrance she had made many times. She did not move for a moment, but looked round at the assembled cast as if pitying their fragile nerves, understanding at once just how most of them felt. Then she saw that Lodge at least had noticed her arrival. She looked at him for a fleeting moment before she smiled and moved round the group to stand with her back to the stage.

She wore a light blue tweed suit and looked composed and amiable. She smiled at them before speaking, a mocking smile that told them she understood exactly what they were feeling.

"Don't worry! We all feel the same!" she said and one or two actually laughed.

"If we hadn't got such cold feet, I think we'd all run a mile from the first rehearsal."

"I hadn't realised she was so kind," Lodge thought.

She turned to look at the vast stage with its thick velvet curtains drawn to each side.

"Forget it. By the time the play is to be performed you will all be so bouncy and insufferably cocksure that there will be no place in this college that can hold you except that stage! Until then let us not waste any energy worrying about the finished result. We must concentrate on the book."

She held up a copy of the play.

"Here's the bare text. Together we must perform that most exciting miracle - resurrect a living play from the page. Breathe life into these words. Lend our bodies, emotions, intellects and voices to these ancient Romans, so that they live again."

They listened as if she were revealing the secret of a success so startling that they could not afford to miss one word.

"Concentrate on the text. It's all there. Learn to understand it so that the words come as if from your own new-minted thoughts. Acting has nothing to do with loud words rushing out

29

of mouths in meaningless ribbons, it is to do with truth, emotional and intellectual. Cling to the truth and you cannot go far wrong. And remember, Shakespeare knew what he was doing. He was an actor himself, not a playwright sitting in a study devising torture for schoolboys at 'O' level. His plays come to life on the stage again and again. Those of you who haven't played in Shakespeare before will be delighted to see just how this is so."

She glanced round at the students.

"Shall we group the chairs in a ring so that we can all see each other?"

They did this.

"That's better," Margaret remarked. "Now a first rehearsal is really a gathering together to see if everybody is still with us."

Two students had been sent down at the end of the previous term so rueful laughter accompanied the grating of chairs as they settled down.

"The best thing we can do," she continued, "is to read quickly through the whole play. You will find who you are acting with and learn more about the play than you think, in this way. Try to read as well as you can but don't worry if certain scenes don't go too well.

"At the next rehearsal we'll plan basic moves on the stage, an act at a time. You will have to make a note of all the moves so be prepared to write quickly and remember everything that is decided. There will not be time to repeat a 'walk through'. Of course we shall have to change things that don't work out, but, after the first rehearsal, you will need to know exactly where you should be at any given moment."

As she spoke she drew them after her into the world across the footlights where everything was possible, if one only worked hard and gave generously of oneself, as she did. She offered escape from self into a disciplined world where rewards had to be earned but were infinitely worthwhile.

They read the text and soon a spirit of comradeship began to grow among them. As individuals they vanished. They cohered into a troupe. They grew to belong to their parts. They began, without realizing it, to gain an understanding of the play that their lonely readings had failed to extract. Some, at the back of their minds, even began to imagine the togas and sandals they would wear. They enjoyed themselves. They had been, they thought, let off, reprieved. No outstanding performance had been required of them, so, they worked hard, eagerly absorbing the atmosphere of the play.

Margaret saw how the mood had changed and as she listened to the reading she began to feel again a familiar enthusiasm rising for this play that, against all reason, she had agreed to direct. Almost automatically she reacted now, jotting down brief notes as she heard the hesitation that showed a lack of understanding, or drawing symbols to indicate where a reader had gone completely wrong with his interpretation. It came easily to her because she loved drama. She was a born director. Her sympathies flowed out to the actors, she rejoiced with them as they overcame difficult hurdles. She seemed to have an ear so attuned to each different voice that later it would seem to those taking part that she had listened to each of them particularly, as if their part were the key to the play.

Like many producers of plays she referred to each actor, during rehearsals, by the name of the character he portrayed. This was done with a purpose. The private personality was kept quite separate from the acted role. It helped to sustain the atmosphere built up in rehearsal, even when the director had to interrupt frequently. It helped the self-conscious also. Their own names were never mentioned. It was Menenius who waved his arms about meaninglessly, not David Rolston; Volumnia needed just a little more dignity, not Kate Sacher.

It was easy for the cast to forget that Margaret Gerrard was a professional teacher and not one of themselves. They accepted her as a keen knowledgeable director, an integral part of the troupe. She had started the ball rolling, now its own volition would increase daily until the play was performed. They would all be borne along with it.

The cast left their first rehearsal with a feeling of warmth towards her. She had been so kind to so many of them, encouraging to all. She had won their confidence. The play, they believed, would be a success. They were in good hands.

Margaret had the satisfied feeling that comes with a job well done. She had set them gently on the way. What praise she had given had been to encourage their efforts, to let them begin with some sense of achievement behind them. The next rehearsal building on this would be that much better. She had praised the actors in exactly those speeches where the right note had been struck. She left it to them to carry over this feeling into other parts of the play. She believed in letting the seeds grow at their own pace at first. After the detailed planning of moves in the next rehearsals she would begin to make demands on them. By then their confidence would have grown, they would be glad to accept challenges.

Her use of applied psychology had become almost automatic. She knew of course what she was doing, could have analysed the whole handling of the meeting, but her strength lay in the natural way she used this most important of a teacher's tools.

She had a natural objectivity which in a woman who seemed to give so much of herself was disconcerting, until she was known well. Now, she remembered what her brain had sorted out as being of importance in the production of the play. The rest she forgot. She would come to know the cast intimately as regards voice, accent, physique, emotionalism, intellect and imagination. She would know many of them better than they knew themselves. What she would not know was almost everything else about them. Even their names she might have difficulty in remembering. She would never know certainly whether they were first, second or third year students. She would have little idea what subjects they were reading. It is likely had she met them in a different context, even the following day, that she would immediately have been able to place them. And this was her strength as a teacher. She seemed to give all of herself to her classes, in fact she was playing a part.

In no sense did this detachment prevent her from enjoying the society of the students. Within the context of the play she liked most of them. She believed, however, that there was an invisible barrier round her as their teacher and that no relationship would ever breach it.

She had heard Lodge read with satisfaction. He obviously had an excellent control over his voice. He read with just the right clipped speech of a Roman patrician. Then in the bursts of fury from wells of emotion came a voice powerful in anger yet full of disdain. He had, even so early, caught the essential attributes of the character.

"You will be magnificent," she had told him, casually, at the end of the read through.

She had seen his eyes glow. The beauty of the young man moved her. She lingered to look longer, hearing his breathless murmur of thanks, as if from a distance.

"Have you done much acting before?" she asked.

"Last year I played a small part in 'The Rivals'. Nobody recognised me, though. I was Sir Lucius O'Trigger."

"Was that you?" she asked, laughing. "How incredible. I certainly didn't recognise you. You were very good and the Irish accent was most convincing."

"It was fun doing it," he said laughing as he remembered it.

"And you've changed your allegiance from the Dramatic Society to this. Weren't they sorry to lose you?"

"I don't know."

"Why did you make the change?"

"I wanted to act in Shakespeare. And there's a more serious attitude in this society. They messed about so much, I got a bit fed up. It was fun though."

"Did you act at school?"

He grinned sheepishly. "I was usually the lead."

"What plays did you do there?" she asked, genuinely interested to learn more about his background.

" 'Julius Caesar' and 'Serjeant Musgrave's Dance' "

"Really?"

"We had to cut out a lot of the foul language in 'Musgrave' but we had a pretty 'with it' English master."

"I'm glad you made the change," she said.

"So am I," he replied, looking at her with the long gaze of one who means more than he says.

The look was not lost on Margaret. She felt rather annoyed. She hurried away alone, conscious that he looked after her from the top of the stairs. Then she grew annoyed with herself. Had she been silly snubbing him like that? She did rather like him, after all. She could at least have walked across the quad with him instead of taking flight like a frightened virgin. Then she heard him whistling as he ran down the stairs and the carefree sound of it brought a smile to her lips.

Chapter Four

Throughout October and November Margaret felt a wonderful quickening of the impulse of life within her, she was able to complete an enormous amount of work each day, then turn with relief to her novel. As daylight faded she lit the lamp in her high room at the top of the Arts Block and began to write.

During these weeks writing came easily to her. It seemed that once having made the decision to start, all her inhibitions were washed away in the flow of ideas that came rushing into her mind. Page after page she covered in her large spreading scrawl, totally lost in this first painless creative spurt. She cast off her habitual critical attitude and wrote as if an inner voice were dictating to her. She hardly ever turned back to read what she had written, but with quiet delight felt the thickness of the block of pages she had already covered.

She told no one about her novel and secreted its pages beneath a file in one of the desk drawers she kept locked. The very isolation and privacy of the room worked its own cogent spell. She wrote nowhere else. Even at home there was not the absolute solitude and freedom from interruption that obtained here. Douglas would not of course come and read over her shoulder, but even a glimpse of him through the window, at this stage, she believed, could frighten away the Muse.

By the beginning of November the movements of each act of the play had been tested in rehearsal and approved or altered. Each rehearsal, now, seemed to urge the play forward in enormous strides. The actors felt themselves to be running headlong after the perception of the play that their director seemed to see so clearly. Occasionally they caught up with her vision and a scene would take fire suddenly. Then a stillness would fall upon the rest as they watched the players on stage.

The first time this happened was in a rehearsal of the fourth act when Coriolanus seeks out Aufidious in Antium after being banished from Rome. Summoned from feasting and merrymaking, Aufidious fails to recognise his enemy. He comments upon his grim appearance and wretched clothes but recognises an air of command and nobility. At last Coriolanus reveals his identity.

> *My name is Caius Marcius, who hath done*
> *To thee particularly, and to all the Volsces,*
> *Great hurt and mischief; thereto witness may*
> *My surname Coriolanus.*

This was the first scene in which Coriolanus and Aufidious meet away from the battlefield. Here the struggle is psychological. The cold calculating honesty of the Roman patrician sweeps away the ancient enmity of Aufidious in one audacious speech. He offers his 'revengeful services' against his 'canker'd country'.

> *But if so be*
> *Thou dar'st not this, and that to prove more fortunes*
> *Thou art tired, then, in a word, I also am*
> *Longer to live most weary and present*

My throat to thee and to thy ancient malice;
Which not to cut would show you but a fool,
Since I have ever follow'd thee with hate.

Lodge, in this speech, struck a relaxed note that in its weary undertones conveyed perfectly the last careless toss of the utterly despairing. It was ennobling and moving. At the same time, it engendered that dramatic excitement that makes Aufidious' emotional acceptance of his enemy both credible and inevitable.

Let me twine
Mine arms about that body where against
My grained ash a hundred times hath broke,
And scarr'd the moon with splinters; here I clip
The anvil of my sword, and do contest
As hotly and as nobly with thy love
As ever in ambitious strength I did
Contend against thy valour.

In the first rehearsals Sloan, in the part of Aufidious, had played this speech straight and soberly and in the previous rehearsal with the befuddled air of inebriation. Now he compromised and suggested a man who spoke from his heart with his habitual inhibitions merely reduced by alcohol. It sounded so right that Margaret could hardly refrain from jumping up and congratulating them. Her vision and the performance here at least were one.

When they reached the end of the scene, applause burst from everyone in the hall. Margaret saw Lodge's surprise then he relaxed and the Roman patrician was replaced by a grinning boy who bowed and grimaced at the audience. She felt irritated by his frivolity and surprised at the speed of the change from the acted role to the reality - if reality it was. For what was Lodge really like? Wasn't that grinning simpleton just another role to him? In fact his talents perhaps lay in playing comedy. His mimicry was superb. He had even caricatured her instructions once, until quietened by a sharp rebuke from one of the others, Pasco, she suspected. Margaret liked Pasco. He had an easy friendliness and maturity that she found relaxing and comforting during the long hours of rehearsal, when, often, he would sit two or three seats away from her, respectful and interested in all that went forward. He would occasionally slip away in the darkness to remind actors playing bridge in the green room that their cues were about to occur or quieten the girls who chattered too loudly in the wings. Pasco took the part of Cominius, the general under whom Coriolanus fought against the Volscians. He acted an undemanding part with intelligence, being as relaxed and easy upon the stage as he was off it. If as an actor he lacked the emotional force and power of Lodge, he was as a person much easier to have dealings with.

There were times, that she wished to forget, when she had been so annoyed by Lodge's foolery that she had lashed out with the sort of cutting sarcasm she particularly despised. Once sitting with Pasco over a cup of coffee at the end of one such rehearsal, she expressed her regret.

"I loathe people in authority who throw out such vile remarks. I feel awful."

"He asks for it," Pasco assured her. "He really is a fool at times."

She said no more, but watched her tongue afterwards, for she remembered the pain she could still see in Lodge's eyes when minutes later she looked at him again.

She began to watch over him, to clear away stumbling blocks to his progress, by rehearsing the other actors separately in odd moments so that his scenes might flow on and he might measure the pace and length of his role.

The rehearsals lengthened from two hours to three and then to four or five. They grew tired together with a weariness that sleep could never quite throw off, and suffered the same manic excitement engendered by the dramatic art. The stage, the play became the centre of their lives. Each of the main actors and those responsible for costumes, props and lighting grew a little light-headed, if not half mad and Margaret outwardly seeming the least affected, was perhaps the maddest of all.

Such was the turmoil in her brain that she began to suffer from insomnia, or, if she slept at all, she would leap awake after two or three hours with confused visions pounding through her brain. Sometimes she dreamt of disastrous failures, sometimes of dreary muddle and confusion that needed more energy than she had got, if it were ever to be sorted out.

"Blast this wretched play," she would mutter, making tea in the chilly sleepless dawn, but it was like a disease that relentlessly pursued its course to the crisis and would only then leave its victim pale and listless and empty of desires.

Even when the rehearsals lasted until nine p.m. Margaret persisted with her novel. She hurried across to the Arts Block with the same lithe stride that carried her, apparently tirelessly, through the day.

Pasco and Lodge had fallen into the habit of accompanying her from the hall. Pasco and Margaret discussed innumerable aspects of the play while Lodge mainly listened, perhaps silent as a result of fatigue. Once, standing in the window of her room before starting to write, she had seen them riding away together on bicycles. The lights streaming from the entrance hall illuminated them for about twelve yards and she saw that Lodge looked up at her window as they passed. She did not know if he saw her standing there or merely glanced up at the light, but she had the impression that it was not the first time that he had gazed at her turret window.

"He's very good, isn't he?" Pasco commented one evening as they watched the rehearsal together.

"Yes, very," she replied, and knew that he was voicing the opinion of the whole cast.

Lodge had become an inspiration to the others, not solely because he had the leading part, and that a dominant role, but because on stage he had a power and presence that demanded respect and often produced awe. Aggressive, proud, bitter and solitary as Coriolanus, Lodge off-stage had begun to retain a kind of isolation and separateness. He sat alone at the side of the hall when not required on stage, and only if she sought him out to suggest a change in his performance did he come near her. But always, when the others had gone and she and Pasco talked as she collected her belongings from all parts of the hall, he joined them. Quiet, reserved, modest, he waited.

"It went well, tonight, I think, Antony," she might say.

"Not bad," he would answer, as if he cared nothing for how the play was developing.

Then Pasco would refer to some point of Roman history or belief and the three of them would cross the lawns to the Arts block. There they might linger a while talking and always, before they parted, Lodge would smile as he said goodnight and she would reach her room with the sweetness of the moment still lingering about her.

In the third week of November, a raging toothache had caused Pasco to leave the Thursday rehearsal early. Margaret missed him as the others left and she prepared to switch off the lights herself in the empty hall. Then the doors at the front opened and Lodge came back.

"I'll switch the lights off," he said.

She remembered how rarely Lodge ever did anything helpful in a practical way. He seemed oblivious of what had to be done in this sphere, standing by quite happy to let other people move chairs from the stage or fetch coffee, even for him, from the machine outside. Now he had come back to switch off the lights for her.

"My word, I am honoured!"

The words were out before she realised just how rude they would sound. He looked at her with some surprise and she felt a sudden warmth spreading over her face. Angry with herself, she picked up her books hurriedly and left the hall.

The lights in the hall went out and she found herself in darkness. Some idiot had switched off the lights on the stairs. She heard the hall doors swing again and Lodge's steps drew nearer. She felt on the instant the comfort of the darkness with the two of them near together and alone. It wiped out the hurtful words and nullified the innumerable barriers there seemed to be between them.

When he found the light switch, she saw he held out her handbag, swinging it slightly and smiling.

"Thank you," she said taking it and they descended the stairs.

"I've an idea how we might advertise this play better than with the usual printed posters," she told him as they crossed the lawns. "We'll have a photographic session with half a dozen or so of the cast in full make-up and dress, then blow up the best of the photographs for play bills, with details of the times of the performances written on top."

"That sounds like a good idea."

"Have we any keen photographers in the society, do you know?"

"Roger Fielding has a good camera with flashes and all that kit."

"Good. I know roughly what I want, but I'd rather leave the actual clicking to someone more knowledgeable whilst I concentrate on the posing and lighting."

"One of the fellows was saying, the other day, we ought to make a cine film of this play."

"It's a nice idea, but I don't think we could muster enough lighting to film indoors."

"Have you taken any cine films?"

"No. I've taken slides for years but somehow I've never bothered with cine."

"I'm not so keen either. It seems rather a waste of money."

"Yes. For the kind of films some amateurs take. I think people with children like to keep a record of their development."

"I can see that. Children are so natural too. They would make good subjects."

"Did your parents take any films of you as a child?"

"No. I expect they saw enough of me without that."

They laughed, but Margaret felt a twinge of regret that his childhood should have gone unrecorded. She had watched him with pleasure so much of late on the stage, had seen his grace and physical beauty used so tellingly to portray quite other things than mere handsomeness, that she pondered gravely on the mother who had watched him grow to manhood and let his boyhood slip into oblivion.

"If I had a child," she said, and that was a thought she had never uttered before, "I should like to take films of him."

"Yes. I agree, or her," he added.

They walked for a while in silence.

"Are you feeling awfully tired with all this rehearsing?" she asked.

"I am rather."

"Perhaps we overdo it. It's nine-thirty now. We started about six didn't we?"

"I think so."

"Do you work after rehearsals?"

"Quite often. We're kept pretty busy in the labs. all day, so there's not much chance to work then. Not like the skivers in your department!"

"Oh, come now. They have a tremendous amount of reading to do - and don't forget they have to learn Anglo Saxon."

"Ah, yes, Beowulf! Could you recite a bit? I've often wondered what it sounded like."

"Heavens! At this time of night? Let me remind you that I specialise in modern literature."

"Just a line or two."

Margaret racked her brains. She had never liked Anglo Saxon. It had seemed, in her lazy undergraduate days, too much like hard work to learn by her own unguided efforts what was literally a totally different language from modern English.

"I'm sorry. I can't think of any."

He did not believe her, she saw that and somehow it mattered. So often lately when they had spoken together she had failed to let any friendliness develop.

"I have a copy of 'Beowulf' upstairs. If you have time and really want to hear it, come up."

"Yes," he said, gazing at her, "I want to hear it."

'Christ knows how it's supposed to be pronounced,' she thought as she led the way upstairs.

She found her copy tucked away on the bottom shelf of her bookcase, a thick brown text-book with six times as many pages devoted to notes as to text.

"What memories this brings back," she commented wryly, looking at the pencilled annotations that sprouted all round the text.

He looked over her shoulder. "Read it," he urged. "I won't ask you to translate."

"I've never read it aloud," she faltered. "I'll try to give you an idea of what it sounds like as poetry by bringing out the main beats and you'll notice the alliteration in each half-line. They used that instead of rhyme."

She began, sounding more confident than she felt. The broad vowel sounds felt strange on her tongue, but she was determined to give as good a performance as she could. Then, after she had read about ten lines, something very strange occurred. She seemed to hear an echo of the words from a distance, spoken in a low voice and with the tuneful intonation and confident pronunciation that an aged minstrel might use, as he sat in the flickering shadows of a fire, occasionally strumming on his lyre. She shook her head and continued, but the soft voice accompanied her. It seemed now to grow louder, nearer. What nightmare situation was being unleashed? It must be the result of overwork. Her ears were playing tricks on her.

She looked up from the page. Her eyes met Antony's. He was sitting on the edge of the desk, motionless, listening. The voice had stopped.

"Did you hear someone just now?" she asked in an undertone.

He nodded.

"Whatever was it?" she whispered.

"I don't know."

For several seconds they listened, speechless, in the tiny room at the top of the empty building. There was now no sound at all. Margaret took a deep breath. Her heart thumped inside her rib cage. She closed the book.

The voice began again. Louder now and clearer.

Him pa Scyld gewat to gescaephwile
felahror faran on Frean waere
hi hyne pa aetbaeron to brimas farope

Suddenly the door swung open and a tiny bent old man shuffled in, on stockinged feet, chanting the heroic verse and moving his fleshless fingers slightly to the beat of the lines. He wore an ancient gown, the black gone green with age, the torn hem trailing on the floor.

He beamed upon them. "A seat of learning indeed!" he said, breaking off as suddenly as he had begun, "when I am wakened from my slumbers to the ancient rhythms of a bygone age. But why did you stop, dear lady? For a while I lost the thread and could not remember how it went on. But I have not forgotten it quite. The loves of our youth stay with us."

He fluttered a hand at them, smiled gently and turned to go.

"Oh, please wait. Forgive my surprise, I had not expected that at this time anyone else was in this part of the building. I'm Margaret Gerrard and this is Antony Lodge."

"I'm delighted to meet so enthusiastic a pair of students. I'm Christopher James Dewhurst. I am here for a few weeks to be of what assistance I can to some undergraduates whose tutor in Old English has been overtaken by an unfortunate illness. I was looking over their work when I believe I must have dozed. I am so pleased, Miss Gerrard and Mr Lodge, to have met you. Perhaps I shall have the pleasure of aiding your studies. I hope so. And now, goodnight. What a delight to hear 'Beowulf' again."

From the doorway they watched him drift away and soon his voice reached them again as he recalled and lovingly recited the ancient words.

"What a wonderful old chap," Antony remarked when the old man was gone. "It would certainly be a privilege to learn from him! However old can he be?"

"I think I may be able to find out."

Margaret flicked over the pages of 'Beowulf' until she found the bibliography at the back. She ran a finger down the list of works headed, 'Literary Criticism, Fabulous and Historical Elements'.

"I thought so. Look!"

She held the book towards him and he read, "C.J. Dewhurst : 'The problem of Heorot'. 1913 English Studies. But that was published before the First World War!"

"Over fifty years ago. He must have been quite a young man when he wrote it."

Antony pursed his lips in an admiring grimace. "And he's still bubbling over with enthusiasm for the same poem!"

Margaret's lips curled upwards and as her eyes met his they both began to laugh. They grew a little hysterical as they remembered how eerie they had thought the disembodied voice was.

"The door must have been open," she said in a moment of calm.

"Yes, it was," he replied, then laughed again.

"Oh, do stop my sides ache!" Margaret begged. "Anyway, it's been a more memorable introduction to Anglo Saxon than most students get."

"Did you see his gown? I'll bet that saw him through the trenches."

"And he had no shoes on," Margaret added.

"No. I say, do you suppose he's gone home without them?"

"Sh. He might remember and come back for them."

"I'll shut the door."

He closed it and stood with his back towards it, suddenly serious. "He thought you were a student."

"In the widest sense of course I am. But if he did think I was an undergraduate, I suppose everybody under fifty looks young to him."

"You look young to me."

"Is that a compliment?"

"Not particularly. Being young isn't anything to envy. Although I'd rather not be decrepit."

"What's wrong with being young?"

He turned away and picked up a paper-weight from the bookcase near the door.

"I suppose it's the uncertainty, the inadequacy," he said gazing into the millefiori pattern.

"You feel that?"

He smiled. "Sometimes," he admitted.

"But never on the stage."

"You just pick up another character, then, whose life and words and actions are ready made."

"But doesn't your success in acting give you confidence?"

"Yes - to take another part. Although even then some roles scare me stiff. But after you've stopped being another character

47

and get off the stage, your own self seems, if anything, more a nothing than it did before."

"Tell me. Do you despise actors?"

He did not answer at once, although she sensed it was no new idea but one he had thought about.

"Acting is a pretty useless pastime," he said at last.

"But you are so talented."

"Yes, and I'm only an average chemist. Do I drudge away my life in industry or fritter it away on the stage?"

His tone was flippant but the question was real enough. Tiredness, she saw, had drawn a grey veil over his features. He looked older now in the harsh glare of the overhead light than he had done the first time he had visited this room, lit then by a glorious sunset.

"You paint too black a picture," she said. "I don't accept that actors, who give millions of people hours of pleasure and stir up their emotions, are frittering away their lives. After all, what is an important job? I suppose most people would say being a doctor. Curing bodies, in my opinion, is no more important than uplifting men's souls, and a good actor can do just that, given the right play."

"And if he doesn't make the grade, he becomes at best the idol of the local rep. acting in stupid plays, to a sprinkling of middle-aged ladies who are glad of a sit-down after shopping, on wet afternoons."

Margaret shuddered. "Say no more. I know. I know it all."

He was quick to notice the ill-concealed note of pain in her voice. "I'm sorry. I believe I've offended you."

"No. You have spoken only the truth, but I try to forget it. My father was, for a time, and they were the good times, just such an actor as you have described."

"Will you tell me about him?"

"Not now. Sometime, perhaps." She smiled to lessen the refusal.

"But I think, don't you, that whatever one decides to do in life, the really important thing that makes for happiness is human relationships."

He looked at her and seemed about to say something of great moment, then changed his mind.

"That at this time, I find no comfort at all," he said at last, and, putting down the paperweight, he wished her goodnight.

Chapter Five

The hall was in darkness apart from the spotlights that illuminated the characters posed on the stage.

"Hold it. I think this will be excellent! Can you get that, Roger? I hope you've set everything up all right." she added. Margaret spoke quickly and urgently in the shadows behind the spot lights to Roger Fielding.

"I have," he said quietly and bent to the position she indicated. Calmly he held the camera for a second or two and centred in the view-finder the figures transfixed in the glare of the spot lights.

Volumnia, Virgilia and young Marcius knelt before Coriolanus who held his mother's hand and bent towards her, his face bleak with anguish, his eyes glistening as if with unshed tears. If the shot turned out as she hoped it would, then the most heart-breaking scene of the play would be recorded.

"That should bring them in," she said cheerfully to Roger, behind the camera. "Everyone likes a good weep."

But beneath her levity she marvelled at their ability to produce, in this unnatural way, the high-lights she had selected to be photographed. Their professionalism delighted her. Volumnia had spent hours on her make-up, insisting on doing it herself, and looked uncannily like a well-preserved woman of about fifty, of somewhat forbidding aspect, bearing, even in her humble mourning garments and lowly position of pleading, the unmistakeable air of uncompromising nobility. Virgilia, devastatingly pretty with curls tumbling over her forehead, in the antique Roman style, symbolised subdued sweetness. Little Marcius, a four year old, borrowed for the evening from his parents, did exactly as he was told for the photographs, then dashed back to his Lego fort, that many of the actors were helping him to assemble. Margaret herself had put the finishing touches to Coriolanus's make-up. By emphasising the bony ridge of the nose and high-lighting the chin a subtle alteration had been achieved. He looked less sensitive, more the man of action, the soldier. Deeper shadows around the eyes and shading beneath the high-lighted cheek bones added to his apparent age. His hair recently cut, like that of the other actors, in a short Roman style, completed, with his costume, the transformation.

"We'll have one of Coriolanus and Virgilia together now."

The other actors moved aside and the two waited.

"Look into each other's eyes, a bit closer. Hold her on the upper arm. Now, Roger, can you be ready to take a close-up from about here. If you get it from just above Virgilia's elbow. How does that work? Do the figures completely fill the frame?"

"Not quite. I could get them well placed by cutting it off at the lower edge just on her shoulder."

"Yes. Try that. Now Coriolanus should be looking half-teasingly at his wife - remember she weeps easily - not at all the stuff his mother is made of. And Virgilia try to suggest through your tears and horror of war and wounds, deep thankfulness that your glorious husband is home safe. Have in mind the scene in Act Two. You remember Coriolanus first sees his wife after the triumphal entrance and says something like, "My gracious silence, hail!""

"Yes. I've got it," Coriolanus said and Virgilia nodded.

"Good. Turn your face a little more to the right, Coriolanus. Virgilia, chin down, just a fraction, eyes still on Coriolanus. Yes. Draw a little nearer. Fine. Hold it. Put the spot a foot or two nearer and can you get it higher? We must suggest daylight here. Righto, Roger, have you got it?"

Five days later, Margaret lay back in a deep arm-chair in the Senior Common Room with the strip prints Roger had just handed to her. Tiny as the prints were she recognised their quality with a growing excitement, as she studied each in turn.

Her coffee lay forgotten on the table before her.

That hectic evening's work had paid off. Something of the excitement engendered then in the dressing up, make-up and stage lighting had been captured by the camera. It had been exhausting work for her, thrust forward from her position in the neutral darkness to stand amidst the actors beneath the glaring lights, directing them from the closest proximity. She felt she trespassed on their ground, yet all the time was aware of their deference. The whole relationship had subtly changed. Their voices muted to the tones of normal speech took on in her ears a fearful intimacy. The expansive gestures and projected voices from both sides of the stage were now held in check, but the emotionalism seemed heightened.

Partly this was due to the use of make-up and costumes that brought the actual performance leaping nearer, and partly due to the demands made upon them. She saw more clearly the efforts they made and their seriousness, and knew that she herself was primarily the cause of such exertion. She felt humbled and wished to reduce the strain, to laugh and let them rest. But her role was drawn up too - they made demands on her. They expected to be driven hard, she saw. It was their drug, without it they would as actors fall apart, lose themselves and see the triviality of the grease-paint and draperies.

So from one scene to another they had flitted, seized the heart of each in poses and facial expressions, and waited in the glare of the lights for the word of approval and the click of the camera's shutter that would give them a brief immortality and a moment's respite.

What Margaret found most exhausting was her apprehension of the tensions, stresses and emotions of the cast. She began to feel that if she touched even a chair that one of them was sitting on there would be sizzling of burnt flesh and wood. And when she had been asked by Marion, the girl in charge of make-up to advise on Corilanus's make-up, she had gone reluctantly, her fingers icy cold. She took the stick of grease-paint and stroked on the high-lights, not really looking at him. Then she touched his cheek bone and smoothed in the colour. His eyes were lowered, their lids darkened, the long lashes emphasised by mascara. His lips were firm beneath the brown grease-paint.

It had seemed to her that all around them there was a stillness, as if they inhabited a magic circle. There was amazingly no sizzling of the flesh. She stroked on the make-up, studying, now, his face as if it were a picture she was painting. She noted his youth, his fineness, the clarity of his skin, the sweetness of his breath. Had not Shakespeare, himself, written sonnets to just such a youth?

Now, she gazed at his photograph, observing the strong neck revealed by the Roman costume, the unexpected breadth of the shoulders.

"I believe you're infatuated, Mrs Gerrard," a voice softly murmured in her ear.

She looked up, startled, and laughed when she saw Miles Radford.

"But isn't it a beautiful face?" she replied.

Miles sat on the arm of her chair and took the strip of prints. "These are good," he commented as he studied each one.

Margaret liked Miles. Young, eager and highly talented, he was a lecturer in Mathematics who one day, she expected, would leave teaching to devote all his time to painting. He had already had one exhibition in town which had aroused interest locally and in the national press.

"We are going to have one or two of these blown up so that we can use them as posters. I have been wondering if you would have time to do some lettering on them for us - only the name of the play and dates of performances and so on."

"Certainly. It will be a pleasure. Which have you chosen to enlarge?"

"This of Coriolanus alone. Our aim here was to suggest his prowess as a warrior."

"He looks aggressive enough. Yes. It's an excellent shot. Who is this taking the part?"

"Antony Lodge. He's reading Chemistry.

"Is he as good as he looks in the part?"

"Come and see."

Miles glanced at her. "You think he's very good, don't you?"

"He's the best I've seen." She said it as a statement of fact.

"You mean in amateur dramatics?" Miles asked.

"I mean anywhere."

Miles whistled.

"When are you starting to sell tickets? You've got me really interested."

"Oh, don't ask about tickets. When I think of how little time we have left to do so much, I start to get nightmares."

"Your coffee looks pretty foul. Shall I get you some more?"

"No, don't trouble. I didn't want it. I really must dash now. I have an eleven-thirty lecture."

Miles caught her arm as she stood to go.

"Loss of appetite is a sure sign," he mocked.

"You're mad," she answered giving him a push that sent him slipping back over the arm into the vacated chair. His coffee cup rattled violently in its saucer and Miles guffawed. Eyes were turned in their direction and Margaret left as quickly as she could.

After lecturing to the first and second year students on the Victorian novel, Margaret hurried downstairs intending to seize an early lunch before driving into town. It was Wednesday so there were no lectures in the afternoon. That evening she and Douglas were entertaining friends and she felt like buying a new dress, something fashionable and interesting. She might also have her hair done if she had time. The Foyer was crowded. As she made her way slowly to the door she rummaged in her handbag to ascertain whether she had her car keys before leaving the building. She collided violently with someone.

"I'm so sorry, I wasn't looking . . . Oh. It's you."

"My fault," Lodge said. "I was walking backwards."

"For Christmas?"

"Be Jasus no. I'll not be crossin' the Oirish Sea for a while yet."

"It was not the Irish accent that made Margaret laugh so much as his immediate recognition of the Goon song and quick reply.

"I have the photographs here," she told him, forgetting she had been in a hurry. "Perhaps you would like to see them?"

55

She handed him the strip of film. He took it and studied each shot with an eagerness similar to her own. They found themselves marooned in the centre of the hall by a crowd of students surging past. He seemed quite oblivious of them and took his time.

"Some should be worth enlarging," he said at last, returning them.

"Which do you think?"

"The one of Volumnia and Coriolanus and this, I guess, is perhaps the best."

He indicated the shot of himself. There was nothing conceited in his choice she was sure. He had excellent judgement in matters concerning drama.

"I agree, that was my choice."

She looked at it again as she took it, marvelling at the power of personality that even in such a tiny print blazed from the face. Where did such power in an actor come from? What else could channel out that tremendous inner energy other than a part in a play? Was the Lodge she saw merely a shadow of the person other people knew? Quiet, reserved, diffident, or else almost childishly frivolous - these were the faces he turned in her direction. And yet, remembering the night when she had read 'Beowulf' in her room, she recalled his questioning of the value of acting that hinted at the doubts of a deeper personality altogether. He had a complicated nature that he perhaps hardly yet understood himself. In his attitude to her she sensed a vulnerability that she wanted to protect, just as a mother must feel tender concern for her son when she senses the danger he seems bent on embracing.

They stood together speaking casually of having enlargements made and of other trivialities that crop up in a production and need to be settled. It seemed to both of them that they had all the time in the world to stand idly conversing whilst all around people hurried to and fro.

After a while they seemed to realize that they were gazing rather too much into each other's eyes and first Margaret then Lodge would make an effort to look away. Then neither of them made any effort to dissemble. They continued to talk but concentrated less now on the words they exchanged. Their eyes sent quite other messages. Sadness preponderated at first. Then came recognition, but, more disturbing, because less in the control of either, was a flicker that grew, as they gazed, into a glow of unbridled joy.

Lodge had no idea how long they stood there, nor how they moved, when the crowd diminished, through the swing doors and out into the fresh air. They negotiated a flight of steps and still talked in the yellow autumn sunlight while a breeze drifted through their hair.

Suddenly she asked, "Do you play any games on Wednesday?"

He laughed, "I'm sorry, I don't understand the question."

Oh, dear, Margaret thought. Either my brain or his has become affected. "I mean," she said, unable to stop the laughter that would bubble up. "I mean, do you play rugger or squash or something on the Wednesday half-day?"

"Yes. I do. I play rugger."

"Well, I have an idea that some of your friends are getting a little impatient."

He turned and saw that a coach had drawn up ten yards away and Sloan, among others, was leaning out of a window gesticulating wildly. They were too polite to shout whilst Margaret was there but, as she walked away she could hear low murmurs and whistles then cat-calls as Lodge ran grinning back into the foyer, presumably to fetch his kit. He had put it on the floor when he took the photographs from her.

She chose her lunch without knowing what she asked for. She sat at an empty table at the far end of the dining room next to the window. The low sun set the dew on the grass a dazzle and lit up large spider's webs on the window panes. She ate slowly. She was not hungry. She sat for a while unaware of the passage of time. She knew now that what she had suspected was true. Poor Antony. There were three weeks to go before the play went on, then they would not see each other. It was really quite simple.

One of the serving women approached.

"Thank you, no, I won't have any pudding, but I should like a cup of coffee - black, please."

She stirred her coffee, concentrating on the dark, hot liquid through which she could faintly see the sugar swirling about before it melted.

Her thoughts wandered after him on the coach trip to . . . ? Wherever. 'What was he thinking?' she wondered. Not of her. Of that she was sure. These infatuations were very slight things. A lot of immature young men thought they were in love with older women. It was part of the long process of growing up.

She went out to the car-park. It was half-past two. Where had the time gone? She would have to hurry.

As she drove along the well-known route into town she noticed the bright yellow leaves still clinging to the trees and smelled through the open window the strong odour of chrysanthemums planted in the flower beds on the traffic island. Autumn was a lively time of year. She put down the swelling happiness of her heart to the season; she had after all always loved this time of year.

Chapter Six

It had been a successful shopping expedition. Margaret studied her reflection in the glass with approval. Dark green suited her - it emphasised the green of her eyes. Cat's eyes she had always called them privately, but she knew their power. The dress was well cut. Its flared skirt and closely fitting bodice effectively enhanced her neat waistline. Lately she had become more interested in her appearance, taking greater care with her make-up and always having her hair cut and re-styled before it needed it. She found herself at odd moments gazing into mirrors, weighing up her good and indifferent features. Ruthlessly she discarded clothes that she thought were dull or shapeless. She concentrated on an image of youthfulness and dashed through her daily routine with an impressive vitality. Her face seemed to be lit up from within. Her skin glowed with health, her hair crackled with electricity when brushed. The most striking of her features were her eyes, fringed with thick black lashes that held perpetually in their depths a glint of amusement and revealed an uncompromising intelligence.

As she finished dressing, she heard Douglas's Land Rover tearing up the drive. She stepped through the glass doors on to the covered veranda to look at the night sky and the garden and to watch Douglas emerge from the garage. It was frosty, the dark blue sky was a-dazzle with stars. Burly, in a sheep-skin jacket, Douglas strode across the yard and entered the house by the conservatory. She heard him hurry through the house, making for their bedroom and left the verandah just as he reached the bedroom door.

"Sorry I'm so late. I couldn't get away."

He gave her a long appraising look. "You're looking rather gorgeous tonight. Is that new?"

"Yes. I bought the dress this afternoon. I went on a shopping spree - shoes, new perfume and a book for you. It's the one you wanted on Richard Burton."

"That's marvellous. Where is it?"

"Downstairs in the study, and you're not to have it until you've showered and dressed for dinner. The Clifts will be here soon."

Margaret went downstairs. She switched on the lamps in the blue and gold drawing room, altering the shadows cast by the fire, on which she threw a few more logs. She drew the dark blue velvet curtains then poured herself a sherry. She felt too restless to sit down. She crossed the hall and went into the study. The curtains were already drawn here. She sat on the edge of the sofa and picked up Douglas's book. Flicking through it she found that a corner of one of the pages had been torn away. On one side was a map of the Nile and on the other the opening of a new chapter. Almost intact at the top of the page under the missing chapter heading was an extract from Richard Burton's Journal dated 2 December 1856.

Of the gladdest moments in human life she read, *is the departure upon a distant journey into unknown lands . . . man feels once more happy, the blood flows with the fast circulation of childhood . . . afresh dawns the morn of life . . .*

There is something tremendously compelling about snippets of books casually read in idle moments. Margaret felt that she had been meant to read those words, but only the accident of the torn off fragment had led her to them. She forgot her irritation at finding the copy damaged and concentrated on the words. They were so exactly in tune with her own feelings of late. Her own blood seemed flowing again with the fast circulation of childhood, she too longed to break free of the fetters of habit. What had gone wrong with her life that she felt this urgent need to escape? Was it part of the aging process, a kind of rebellion against the inexorable flow of time? In her own case she seemed to have returned to the emotional turmoil of adolescence. She felt she was drifting anchorless on an increasingly turbulent sea. Perhaps the middle-aged and old never did feel calm and rooted as she had believed; perhaps upheavals of the spirit were common to all ages.

"Heh, you're reading my book." Douglas playfully snatched it from her. "I'm reading it first."

"I've just read a snippet of Burton's journal. I must say the language was a bit flowery, but not, I guess, unusual for a Victorian translator. Have you read his translations of 'The Arabian Nights' and 'The Kama Sutra'?"

"No. I stuck to his explorations in Africa and the East, including how in the guise of an Arab he penetrated the shrines of Mecca, forbidden to unbelievers."

There was a knock at the door and Douglas moved to answer it, still talking. "He was a wonderful story-teller, one of the first anthropologists, an excellent swordsman and... altogether fascinating."

Margaret followed him into the hall to greet their guests. The Clifts were ushered into the drawing room. Margaret had known Elaine for over ten years. They had taught at the same Girls'

Grammar School when, as recent graduates, each had drifted into teaching. Almost immediately they had become friends and their friendship had never grown cold. Margaret delighted in Elaine's pungent Northern wit and found endearing her occasional bewildered inability to cope with both practical matters and affairs of the heart, that is before her recent marriage to Jonathon. Now, after removing her coat she held up her gloved hands.

"Dear Margaret, have you any nail varnish remover? I painted my nails whilst Jonathon got the car out and forgot they were still tacky when I put my gloves on." Elaine grinned in an abashed manner, as her friend led the way upstairs.

"Come into the study, whilst the girls mess about up there," Douglas invited Jonathon. "I particularly want to ask you about your time in Africa. I'm planning an expedition in March to the lake regions." The men went into the study where Douglas kept his maps. From the half-open door the murmur of their voices and the crackle of the new maps being opened followed the women upstairs.

"I say, this room looks delightful. When did you move to this end of the house?" Elaine asked.

"About two months ago, just after we'd had the new bathroom put into that little box-room next door."

"Oh. do let me see!"

Still wearing her gloves Elaine went into the bathroom and examined the new fittings, praised the colour scheme and generally delighted her hostess with her comments and exclamations of admiration.

"Now I must try to drag these gloves off," she said with a grimace. "Gosh, my nails look sort of furry."

Margaret provided her with nail varnish remover and cotton wool. As Elaine rubbed at her nails and gossiped, she wandered about the room until she was brought to a standstill by her reflection in the glass. There her eyes met Elaine's.

"Would you like to use this colour?" she asked hastily, conscious that her self-scrutiny had been observed with interest.

"Do you think I should bother now?"

"Why not? The whole evening is before us. I know the men will be quite happy on their own for a while."

"Come and sit beside me, Margaret, you're as restless as a cat on a hot tin roof. There's something different about you. You have something on your mind. I caught your expression in the glass. It was interesting and a little disturbing. Tell all whilst we're alone."

Margaret laughed. "There's nothing to tell! Or shall I invent something to prevent your disappointment?"

"No. I want the truth!"

"What can I say? I just feel restless. Overworked perhaps - resenting the daily drudgery."

"Then why not plan to do something exciting when Douglas is away? You could take a trip to the States or Iceland or somewhere."

"I don't think I want to travel - not physically anyway - perhaps in the mind. That's if I ever get going."

Elaine waited for her to go on.

"I've begun to write you see. At first, after I'd actually made a start, it went swimmingly. I had planned to write a novel, a sort of comedy of manners, in which I hoped to present a true picture of people in an enclosed society - a university - as they actually were during the period covered by the novel. I wanted to cut, as it were, a chunk out of their lives and examine it under a microscope - just as a biologist might take a square yard of a meadow and give a full description of everything he found growing or living there."

"And what happened?"

"One of the main characters became more and more dominant and took on so many of my own preferences and prejudices that it became uncomfortably like a self portrait."

"And didn't you like what you suddenly recognised?"

"It wasn't that. What happened was infinitely more disturbing. The character demanded a past. It insisted upon becoming three-dimensional in time as well as space. It wanted a past - my past- and demanded, needed a future. Night after night I wrote at college, pushing on with my original plan, and then as I drove home, images would swim into my mind of events and people I had thought were forgotten. You remember how one felt in adolescence, when absolutely everything was of such importance that it was soul-shattering? Well I seem to be suffering from a second dose. I find myself almost wallowing in the miseries and degradations of the past. I don't want to remember them. I certainly don't want to write about them."

"They say writing is therapeutic."

"I've found it soul-destroying!"

"You say your main character also demanded a future. Surely there everything could be plain sailing. You could let your imagination rip!"

For what seemed a long time, Margaret looked aghast. Then when she saw Elaine's surprised expression, she began to laugh.

"What have I said?"

"Oh, dear, dear Elaine, I think you've put your finger on the trouble. I find myself quite unable to let my imagination, as you say 'rip'."

She returned to the glass and checked her mascara carefully. "What an age we have been. Are your nails dry yet?"

"Margaret, you are hedging! I know something's amiss and you have avoided telling me anything."

"I'll tell you something funny instead. You know I'm producing 'Coriolanus', well, guess what? One of the cast has a crush on me!"

Even as she spoke, she was dismayed at her cheap remark. It was too late to retrieve it.

"Male or female?"

"Oh, Lord!"

They recalled the dreadful episode at the Grammar School when a fourth-former had developed a passion for Margaret that was either a symptom or cause of the girl's nervous breakdown. Elaine's amused laughter ceased as memory passed beyond the inconvenient phone calls, the constant secret surveillance and the embarrassed attempts at communication to the real tragedy behind it.

"I wonder whatever happened to Cynthia."

"Her treatment was prolonged, but, I suppose, she was at a difficult age. I expect she's married with a large family by now." Elaine's common sense was a comfort to Margaret.

"I expect so. And we old crones are still childless."

"Is that your trouble?"

"Heavens no! You know what I have always thought about having kids."

"I know what you have always said, but minds can change."

They went downstairs. Margaret led the way into the sitting room. "Let's leave them to their maps for a while. I want to hear all your news, before the men join us."

Elaine settled herself comfortably on the chesterfield and looked appreciatively round the room. The Canaletto reproduction was still there and the thick gold carpet but the lamps were new. Some had gold shades others were the palest blue. The whole room was furnished in blue, white and gold with touches of green and rose in the predominantly blue loose covers of the sofas and easy chairs. Its elegance and refinement provided a fitting background for their owner. Margaret was pouring drinks.

"She's more attractive than ever," Elaine thought as she watched her friend. She reminds me of a line in Eliot about a flower that knows it is being looked at. She looks as if every movement she makes is calculated to enchant the observer.

"Are you having an affair?" she asked bluntly, watching to see the effect of her question.

Margaret turned her head slowly and the green eyes seemed filled with laughter.

"Should I be?"

"No, but I think you may be, or else you're hovering on the brink."

Margaret smiled as she carried over the drinks, her eyes lowered over the pale gold liquid in the heavy glinting sherry glasses. "No," she said softly, "there can be no affair."

"A pity. It would have made an interesting story to tell your old friends in a few years' time."

"Are you assuming it would have ended by then, and that my marriage would have survived it? Can such assumptions be made?"

"Knowing you and Douglas and being occasionally privileged to enter the warm ambience you create around yourselves, can I doubt that your marriage is impregnable?"

"Let's find the men and then go and eat." suggested Margaret.

After dinner they returned to the sitting room. They had been talking about Paris so it seemed natural, when they wished to listen to some music, to play Edith Piaf's "La Vie en Rose" followed by her raucous song of triumph, "Je Ne Regrette Rien". Douglas handed whisky round.

"This is just the sort of sleazy evening I hoped to have." Elaine drawled. "Have you any of Frank Sinatra's?"

"How about 'Something Stupid'?" suggested Douglas.

"Great!"

Margaret seized Jonathon and they inched about on a square yard of carpet, giving a reasonable imitation of an infatuated couple lost to the world.

Douglas came and sat by Elaine. "You're looking marvellous," he said. "Marriage obviously agrees with you."

"I'm glad I took the plunge at last. It gets harder you know, the longer you wait. I'd grown so accustomed to my independence that, I admit, there were times, before we married, when I feared to lose it. But once wed, I never looked back. Do you like Jonathon?"

"Yes. And I think he's right for you."

Elaine could not resist glancing at her husband who held Margaret closely and danced with half-shut eyes. Douglas looked vaguely embarrassed. He got up as the record ended and refilled the glasses.

Gershwin followed Sinatra, the whisky flowed and their laughter grew heartier. Logs were regularly thrown on the fire which also consumed the pips of grapes and skin of tangerines. At twelve Margaret swayed down the passage to the kitchen to make black coffee. At one their guests departed. At two Douglas held his wife in his arms and she clung to him as a defence against the inner turmoil that nothing could calm. Dreams came in the early hours, that he could not banish, when she drove through a dark wood on a track that twisted and turned. In the thickest part of the forest she stopped the car. She turned to face her companion. It was Lodge. She had known throughout the drive that it was he. Now as their eyes met in her dream, the air seemed to be filled with a sweet perfume and a joy so pure filled her heart that the whole scene began to tremble and evaporate with delight. She clung to his image, even reaching out her arms to catch and hold him, but instantly all around her were the bare branches of the trees and the light that had bathed the scene in a silvery glow faded. She awoke to such a loss that she could not hold back the scalding tears that had begun to flow as the dream ended. "Oh God! Oh Antony!" she breathed into the pillow.

For the first time she seriously acknowledged what her subconscious had known for weeks, and what jocularly she had dismissed as a passing fancy, whenever she had been forced to form some mental impression of her feeling. At thirty five after ten years of happy marriage and complete fidelity to Douglas she had fallen in love with someone else. What was so horrifying to her, as she considered it, was the glaring unsuitability of her heart's choice. He must be fifteen years younger than she, a mere student, a callow youth. She tried to picture him as he might be in twenty years' time - thicker in build, more assured with skin coarsened, perhaps wrinkled . . . but she was so sickened at the imagined alteration that she quickly emptied her mind of the impression. It was Antony young that she loved, the Antony of today exactly as he was now. Half-sick with fancies, she softly slipped out of bed and went to stand on the balcony. The stars were less bright now. The branches of the Scots Pines, outlined against the sky, moved uneasily as the wind rose.

Chapter Seven

It was strange that the success they had all hoped for in performing the play should, in the event, take them so much by surprise. 'Coriolanus' had not been a popular choice but the audience throughout the performance was peculiarly intent upon the play. Its intelligent sympathy seemed to lap up to the very boards on which the actors strode. It was uncanny yet exhilarating. Inevitably the actors drew on feelings that had never been plumbed in rehearsal and a stately calm seemed to govern the later action so that entrances were timed to perfection and the lighting flowed and ebbed, as if automatically linked to the unfolding text. To have called it professional would have been to praise it but weakly. There were certainly no amateurish gaffes but it surpassed many West End productions in that every part was played intelligently, every actor was dedicated, strung to the exact pitch his part required. They were all young and sensitive to the context of their playing. The movements that Margaret had blocked using chess men, so long ago and indefatigably rehearsed them in, now blossomed into actuality, and gave the actors a secure basis upon which their own emotional contributions could be built.

What was it she had said at their first rehearsal about Shakespeare's plays? That only in the actual performance did his real genius shine forth and only then did the actors appreciate his enormous stagecraft, that shoved junks of history across a stage in three hours, and delved into the heart of human affairs in a language both exact and beautiful. So right was it all that memory did not need to stretch and fumble; the thoughts came straight from the heart as Margaret had foretold.

If Antony, before his first entrance, shook in the wings like a colt with the bit for the first time in his mouth, none were aware of it when he stepped across the threshold that divides the dark obscurity of the wings from the blaze of the footlights.

> *What's the matter, you dissentious rogues,*
> *That rubbing the poor itch of your opinion,*
> *Make yourselves scabs?*

Shakespeare wasted no time in revealing his character's basic qualities.

Margaret knew she was indulging herself as she watched Antony from the wings, but excused her self-gratification with the knowledge that this was the last time she would see him perform as Coriolanus in her production.

As always she was astonished at the minute attention each member of the cast gave to his dress, the props he carried, the exact second when he took up his cue and entered. It was as if the audience out there were a monster demanding perfection, or, rather, as if it were a royal assembly to which they were graciously pleased to offer their utmost. They were so practised as they stood togaed in the wings. Had they been like that when she alone had been out there? She remembered storming at them for missing their cues, or for wandering in as if they had come from nowhere. Now she could only stand aside and admire their achievement, feeling her own part had been nothing in comparison with this.

But Antony's performance engrossed her. He had become Coriolanus. She knew now exactly how the cast had felt about him. He was separated as far from them as he was from Antony Lodge. It was a style of acting that demanded total identification with the part. Here was no minor talent for the techniques of play-acting. He was no player who having learnt his lines and movements went through his tricks on the stage automatically. He had changed identity and could not, as did Pasco, slip off his role as he left the stage. He came off laden with the problems of Coriolanus and stood brooding restlessly in the darkness, hardly able even to sit as he waited for the action to flow on to his next entrance. He was unapproachable. Quietly served with the things he needed, his concentration was never impinged upon. If someone dropped a dagger, he looked as blackly at the culprit as a Roman patrician might at a worthless slave.

As the play progressed Margaret knew, as they all must, that they had a rare and wonderful actor in their midst. She felt as if she were seeing everything through a nostalgic haze of separation in time. This play would be remembered as one of Antony Lodge's early successes. She thought that in years to come she would be able to picture this stage, this fierce white lighting, the white pillars and platforms, the costumes, everything. And she would be glad that she had been able to help provide a fitting background production from which this actor could blaze forth.

In the interval coffee was brought to the Green Room for the cast. They jostled together happily, their faces witnessing that lightening of the spirit that being in the thick of a successful enterprise always brings. Margaret passed among them welcomed by smiles, sharing their jokes, enjoying the euphoria that more than anything else they would miss after it was over and long quite desperately to renew. She herself was hardened to that sense of the staleness of life when the play was over and simply filled the vacuum quickly with other things.

Pasco, as usual, sought her out, "How do you think it's going?"

"Extremely well, of course," Margaret replied laughing at his naivety.

"You aren't surprised?"

"No. I think we are very lucky with our audience, they seem to be in exactly the right receptive mood."

"And lucky with the leading man?" Pasco's look belied the frivolity of the phrase he used.

"Why, yes." Margaret glanced at him enquiringly.

"He's got everything, hasn't he?"

"You mean as an actor?" Margaret asked carelessly, irritated by the vague phraseology of the question. She began to look for Antony among the cast crowded into the Green Room.

"Are you looking for someone?"

"I was wondering where . . . "

"He's over there, trembling like a leaf, I shouldn't wonder."

Automatically she turned to the corner he had indicated and registered a fold of white cloth, the only visible evidence that someone leant against the wall within the recess. She was sure it was Antony. She wanted to go over to him to say how well the play was going, but first she must deal with Pasco. Her eyes had lost their habitual glint of amusement and looked dangerously black as she turned.

"I don't like your tone."

"I apologise. It must be blamed on the green-eyed monster."

The green-eyed monster? What nonsense was this? She had neither the time nor inclination to consider. There could be only about three minutes or so left before the curtain rose on the fourth act. She struggled through the crowd to the recess. It was empty. She went into the wings and waited. Why had Pasco been so deliberately infuriating? She couldn't fathom his reason and she felt her anger evaporate. Across the stage she saw Volumnia and Virgilia joined by Coriolanus and others. The stage lights altered, the curtain rose and the actors slowly processed towards the gates of Rome, bidding goodbye to Coriolanus.

In the wings Lodge took off his toga and was wrapped in the dark mean apparel that constituted his disguise in the scene in Antium. Lodge and Margaret waited in the wings. She moved nearer to whisper, "It's going extremely well."

He smiled and nodded and she crept back to the place where she had been standing. From there she could see the front eight feet of the stage. Lodge followed and watched over her shoulder. His loose garments swayed and she felt the rough cloth on her bare arm. She moved and he put out a hand as if to steady her. He held her arm gently. She kept still in the darkness and he did not remove his hand. They watched together like two children peeping into a lighted room where all was familiar and safe and they outside in the dangerous dark. How easy it would be, how simple and natural to turn and let his arms slip round her. How impossible! She was being reckless enough to let one hand rest on her arm. Soon this scene would be over. Already his concentration on the scene was increasing. The balance of his body changed. She felt a slight pressure on her arm and he slipped past her. She watched his profile silhouetted against the lighted stage then he pulled the hood of his mantle over his head and seconds later he was Coriolanus in Antium.

"A goodly city is this Antium."

A sweet longing swept over her. What was this feeling that had grown between them? A strong infatuation? A mere physical attraction? She had been insane to let it develop so far. So far? That was a ridiculous thought. It had not developed at all. Not a word had been exchanged between them. The whole thing amounted to nothing more than a hand laid on her arm for a minute or so as they stood, director and actor, silently, in the wings. There had been nothing. She admired his talent for acting, she liked his face- he was incredibly good-looking. He had a pleasant voice, a cultured accent, beautiful teeth and eyes that spoke. But what his eyes seemed to say she must not try to interpret. Nothing after all had happened.

She crept away, back to the Green Room. The scene with Aufidious was too full of emotion for her present mood. She would not watch it.

"Is there any coffee left?" she asked, not noticing who was there. She sat on the steps leading down from the stage area. She ached with tiredness. "I must look awful," she thought. A cup was handed to her.

"May I sit with you?" Pasco asked.

She looked up and indicated with a half hearted gesture the place on the steps beside her.

"You look tired," he said.

"Yes. I feel I could sleep for a week when this play's over."

"I'm sorry about . . . earlier."

What was he talking about? Margaret felt she could not even make the effort to try to remember.

"I've forgotten it," she said evasively.

"It's just that all of us have become very fond of both of you. And there can't be any future in it for anybody can there?"

"Are you trying to say something to me?"

"I think you know. . ."

"No, on the contrary, I haven't understood a word of it."

"I hadn't realized you could be so defensive. I spoke with the best of intentions."

"Oh, yes," she said with an unpleasant laugh. "That is your great strength, good intentions. Christian charity. What makes you think I need any of it?"

He stood up. "I'll take your cup back."

"Thanks."

From the hall came a burst of applause and seconds later the door of the Green Room burst open and Sloan and Lodge came in radiant with the success of their scene.

"They suddenly started to applaud," Sloan announced astounded.

"They think we're a music hall turn," laughed Antony, slapping him on the back.

There was laughter, hastily stifled. The two young men, flushed with success, smiled at each other. Enormously attractive they held all eyes captive. Exulting in their triumph, they might let the play slip through their fingers. She feared the frivolity of youth could let the clapping of hands disperse the vast seriousness of endeavour. She slipped back to the wings. She knew Lodge watched her go. Oh, what a great night for him! Everyone was at his feet he would think - including her. How could he get back into the role of tragic hero now?

She went into the dressing room to check her makeup and hair. Both surprisingly were immaculate. She walked to the end of the corridor, down the narrow staircase and out into the dank night air. She felt almost feverish with lack of sleep. There was a fine mist of rain. She closed her eyes and lifted her face, hoping the cold damp air would restore her equanimity. Coatless she walked slowly round the building, through the quadrangle and up to the hall. She slipped in through the rear door. The fifth act had started. She watched, impatiently waiting for Coriolanus' entrance half way through the second scene. When he came with Aufidious she noticed a stir in sections of the audience. After a long speech from Menenius pleading for Rome, Coriolanus, constant in his desire for revenge, rejected his pleas and left with Aufidius.

In the third scene of the fifth act his wife, mother and son come to the tent of Coriolanus in the Volscian camp outside Rome. Having already dismissed his old friend Menenius, he now faces a more severe test. Moved by their pleas, particularly those of his mother kneeling before him, he agrees to spare the city, knowing that in doing so he is likely to lose his life.

> *O my mother! mother! O!*
> *You have won a happy victory to Rome;*
> *But for your son, believe it, O! believe it,*
> *Most dangerously you have with him prevail'd,*
> *If not most mortal to him.*

Rome rejoices at the good news and welcomes the return of the women with the sound of drums and trumpets.

The perfidious Aufidious waits in Antium for the return of Coriolanus. He rages against him, jealous of his fame and popularity with the Volscians. When Coriolanus offers him the peace treaty signed by the consuls and senate of Rome, Aufidious calls him a traitor for giving up the city the Volscians had won, to his wife and mother.

He whin'd and roar'd away your victory.

Inciting him further he calls Coriolanus' *'a boy of tears.'*
Predictably, Coriolanus' anger explodes.

"Boy!' False hound!
If you have writ your annals true, 'tis there,
That like an eagle in a dove-cote, I
Fluttered your Volscians in Corioli
Alone I did it. Boy'!

Aufidious' supporters draw their swords and kill Coriolanus. Aufidious stands on his body- an ignominious act that horrifies the lords, who had begged for calmness. Then Aufidious pretends to feel grief and speaks the eulogy over Coriolanus and with three chief soldiers bears off the body.

"Though in this city he
Hath widow'd and unchilded many a one,
Which to this day bewail the injury,
Yet he shall have a noble memory."

The curtain fell. The applause was deafening. Curtain call followed curtain call. The audience, now on its feet, seemed unwilling to stop clapping and calling out its appreciation. The whole cast appeared again and again to bow in acknowledgement of the applause. Again and again the main characters walked forward hand in hand to bow and smile. Then Antony stood alone as the others stepped back, and took a final bow. The applause increased. Smiling slightly, he stood immobile, dignified and remote. Then as if to put an end to the adulation he raised an arm to salute them and walked off the stage. The curtain was lowered for the final time.

An impetuous crowd of students forced its way into the area backstage eager to find Antony. Screaming and pushing they surrounded him. For a moment Margaret feared an unpleasant scene as she hurried backstage, but with a commanding presence Antony managed to defuse the situation and, after speaking briefly to them, courteously excused himself. It was an admirable performance. He saw Margaret and, watched by them all, joined her to thank her for directing the play. The cast applauded, the intruders smiling left.

Antony and Margaret stood facing each other, half smiling, grateful to be together.

"We did it!" he said. No other words seemed to be needed. Reluctantly he left her to go and get changed, the others calling to him to hurry.

"The party can't start till we're all ready!"

Margaret moved among the others, welcoming the sanity of being able to talk calmly to jolly young people without the fever of the blood that came when she was with or even thought of Antony.

When he returned the others welcomed him warmly. He joined Margaret's group and although others came and went they stayed together, as if by the common consent of every one in the room. The cast seemed to be conniving at their relationship, as if it were obvious what was growing between them.

It was one of the warmest parties Margaret could remember after a play. They drank and ate, played records and some danced. She and Antony ate and drank what was offered them and stood together, not talking a lot, but often looking at each other. Both were exhausted, Margaret after weeks of pulling the play together, whilst at the same time wrestling with her novel and carrying a full time table of lecturing, and Antony exhausted with the performance into which all his nervous and emotional energy had been poured.

Chapter Eight

It was a colourful procession that at the end of the party streamed out of the building.

One strummed on a guitar, others carried banners that they unfurled, the rest like a band of travelling players followed, laughing, singing and jostling. Antony and Margaret got caught up with the rest. They passed through the deserted quadrangle and crossed the lawns to the Arts Block behind which were the car-parks and cycle sheds.

As quickly as it had formed the procession now dispersed. There were quick calls of goodnight and then cycling figures shouted to each other and rode off into the dark. Margaret and Antony walked alone to the edge of the car-park where three cars remained, one of them hers.

They stopped, silenced by the magnitude of the things to be said. Instinctively each shrank from first putting into words what they both knew. There was a sort of safety in leaving everything unsaid. It was cold. There was a limit to the time they could stand there, weak with tiredness, aching with longing, half-way between his cycle and her car. She shivered, and he heard the jangle of keys when she put her hand into her coat pocket.

"Let's walk, for a while," he said, desperately trying to postpone their parting.

Slowly they went past the laboratories and reading rooms and other prefabricated buildings into areas where neither of them had penetrated before. Their feet crunched on the cinder path with an abnormally loud jarring noise in the dark, against which it seemed impossible to talk. They cut through the huts, then wandered aimlessly across a playing field. The Union building loomed to the left, its windows blank and sightless. They passed on until they reached the road that bounded the university land. Margaret stopped at the gate.

"We could go on walking all night, but morning would surely come at last."

"Don't go just yet," he pleaded.

"I don't know why I've come so far. This is quite ridiculous."

"Is it? I thought it was ridiculous before. Let us at least be honest now!"

"What is the use?" she asked and there was anguish in her voice. "It would make it worse, harder for you. It will be easier to forget if nothing is actually said. Leave it, Antony, leave it."

"Haven't I bottled it up long enough? For weeks I've lived through a sort of fever, longing just to see you - even at a distance - on days we didn't rehearse. I began to think I should go mad with holding in what I felt. I was afraid I might suddenly stop in the middle of some speech and yell out from the stage, 'I love you,' so that everyone would know it."

She leaned wearily on the gate looking down at her clasped hands.

"I love you," he said quietly, leaning beside her. "It's a fact of my life. How can I forget it? To forget that would be to forget you and I want to remember for always what I know about you. Please look at me."

Reluctantly she turned her head and raised her eyes. He gazed at her with such intensity that she thought she would never be able to look away. Her self possession ebbed. He raised a hand at last and touched her cheek, drawing her nearer with his other hand. She tried to turn away but he held her steadily.

"If there is no future for me, haven't I the right now, at least to tell you how I feel?"

"I can't listen. Don't say any more. You forget every thing that should forbid you even to think as you do."

He laughed. "Oh, how can you? My first clear memory of you is linked to that poem of Blake's that you said you liked because it expressed the dignity of human love wherever it turned up. What was important was not to imprison love. You seemed then so free, so bold. Don't build up barriers to keep us apart now."

"I'm merely recognising that they are there." Her voice was calm, but he detected a note of regret.

He let her go and stood thinking.

"Which is the strongest barrier?" he asked, then, as if fearing the answer, added, "No. Don't answer if you'd rather not. I have no right to ask."

"There is a very apparent objection that you know as well as I do and I'm not referring to the other equally strong objection that I am married."

He looked at her thoughtfully. You mean I'm too young?"

She said nothing.

He smiled. "Time will cure that."

"Oh, yes. Everything is cured in time. The grave yawns for all of us."

"Then let's be happy while we can."

Even as he said it, she heard the great torrents of Marvell's verses pouring through her brain. English Literature gave no encouragement to the chaste.

"The Grave's a fine and private place,
But none methinks do there embrace." she
quoted.

Surprise and delight were in his face.

"There is no argument, "she explained, "on that ground that
I am not a past master in."

Suddenly they were closer in feeling than they had been for
weeks. She was after all what he had supposed. It wasn't glib
hypocrisy that opposed him, he was sure. So they would be
able to talk. As if sharing his feeling, she asked, "When did it
begin?"

"That afternoon, I think, when I found you buried in books
and first noticed that your eyes were green and sparkling with
life. You were the first really alive person I'd ever met. It was a
remarkable experience, like suddenly finding a new species of
humanity, only you were of course the only specimen. I went
away changed somehow fundamentally. Your high room
became for me a sort of symbol of bliss, like a tower in a fairy
story, where great treasure lies, and upon it were focussed all
my dreams. I didn't then even know you as a person."

"And when you did," she interposed, "the tower rapidly
came tumbling down!"

He smiled. "Then, I became obsessed with the desire to
excel in acting. What I felt for you most strongly then was
respect and admiration - as, I think, they all did. When you
seemed satisfied I was extremely happy, yet, all the while,
feeling I didn't deserve it. The praise, I mean. I thought you
gave it too easily. I wanted a more difficult test."

"You shouldn't have been so good then," she remarked.

"You make me sound conceited. It wasn't that I didn't value your judgement, heaven knows we all learned a tremendous amount from you. Rather I wanted you to make impossible demands upon me so I could prove . . . oh, it sounds rather silly now."

"What did you want to prove?"

"My worth, I suppose."

"How do you mean?"

"I didn't want you to think I was really as idiotic as I must sometimes have appeared. I think for a while you actually despised me. Then you seemed to change - to treat me as a special case, as if you had been told to protect me. Not me, but the actor, who, as it were, hadn't to be crossed lest his performance should be spoilt. That was queer. I felt unreal. I could never think of anything to say to you. You had really got me tied up."

"You are more perceptive than I thought."

"Was I right in sensing that you felt something for me too? I couldn't believe it at first. I don't know if I should believe it now."

She said nothing.

"There was a day," he continued, "when you stood with the wind blowing through your hair. The sun caught red and gold glints in it where it curled over your forehead. Your face was lit from within with a sort of joy and you were looking at me. I couldn't even listen to what you were saying, but I dared to believe what your eyes showed. Was I right to do so?"

"I don't know. I remember that day. I suppose what you saw was there."

"What sort of answer is that?" Hurt and exasperated, he asked.

"What sort of an answer can you expect? Think for a while of the situation. All there can ever be between us is already

83

finished. We did a play together. We liked, even admired, each other. That is all. There can be nothing else."

"But there is something else. There is!" he cried.

"I blame myself more than you can know for letting you speak as you did just now. I should have stopped you. I know that. Try to forgive me. I've been stupid and weak. I know how I've looked at you and thought of you. I know what I felt."

"And now, Margaret, tell me!"

He seized her hands as he spoke and gazed with such yearning and love that despite everything her heart leapt in delight to know of his passion. Was it right to refuse to admit what she felt when admission had gone so far on his side? Yet what did she feel? Thirty-five was not twenty. There were reservations, doubts and uncertainties in her every thought of him. How could she force the parting that was essential for his sake? Would he accept that nothing could come of it? Could she rely on his discretion?

Her silence was already having its effect on him. He released her hands and moved a little away.

"I see," he said, after awhile. "You don't trust me.

"It isn't a question of trust," she replied wearily.

"Of course it is. What else would stop you telling me what I know to be true already. All right, keep it to yourself and may your heart wither up with the knowledge of it. Oh, you can be generous enough in theory, you can spread a philosophy of freedom in love, but when it comes to giving a breath of hope, you are as..."

"Hope? You speak of hope? What hope can there be?"

"Finally perhaps none. I'll face that when the time comes, but now, in this godforsaken spot, when everyone is asleep and we are alone, what harm can there be in just enjoying one brief moment of honesty?"

She watched him, hunched in his navy duffle coat, his eyes dark shadows, his voice tired.

"It would mean so much to me."

She felt drained of emotion, utterly empty, adrift in vacuity. Tomorrow seemed a very long way away.

"Yes. It's true." The words slipped out unbidden, almost irritably.

Motionless, he stared at her. The flat statement then took wings. He laughed and lightly and gaily out tripped the endearments that intoxicated both of them. His arms were about her in the tight hold of one who finds after long seeking. The sweetness of the embrace dizzied her senses. She wanted Time to stand still so that forever she might remain in his arms. It felt so right, so innocent to be there. He didn't need to say over and over again, "I love you," for her to feel the truth of it. His lips brushed her cheek, her hair, then reluctantly he moved back just far enough to look at her.

"I can't believe this is happening," he said and grasped her more fiercely as if he heard a distant baying of hounds that would drag them apart. The clinging together generated its own delirious joy, no dread of the future could stem the tide of happiness that rushed to engulf them both. Their lips met in a cool chaste kiss that lingered on warming and intensifying until oblivion threatened. He held her face then between his hands. "I'll love you for always," he said, holding her close.

She stiffened and gently pushed him away. He hadn't after all accepted that for them there was no future at all. At once his face was troubled, he knew instantly what was in her mind. There was a dreadful silence between them. She reached for his hand, a lean hand with long fingers.

"Dear Antony, it's got to be like this."

He stared at the ground.

"I can't let it drift on making your life a misery and believe me that is what it would do."

"Oh, please." He turned away from her.

She moved along the fence and realised how cold her feet were in the thin shoes she wore. When she looked back she saw he was watching her from the gate.

"I don't want to avoid the misery if that's what I have to pay for seeing you. We can't just cut off our feelings like that. I've got to see you again, talk to you. You must see that. I don't want to be told what is for my own good. Christ, I love you."

"And I'm old enough to be your mother . . . "

"You're not! And I wouldn't care if you were."

"Also I'm married," She sounded so exasperated that Antony began to laugh.

"You don't sound very happy about it."

"I can do without cheap remarks like that," she said. "I'm frozen. I'm going home."

He followed her and they walked back across the field.

"I'm sorry. I really meant nothing more than a comment on your tone of voice. I would never infer anything seriously about your marriage. You must know that."

"Yes. We are both so tired I think we hardly know what we mean. But believe me now. I cannot meet you again. Whatever our feelings we must not risk destroying our lives by letting them develop further. I am married, you are young with all your life ahead of you. Don't make the mistake of taking this too seriously. Please forget me."

He had always known theoretically that she was married, but until tonight the unknown husband had remained in the shadowy background of her life. For months they had worked together in a closed tightly knit group where no one's outside life impinged on his role. They all existed for each other only within the group coming from and returning to a vacuum. For the first time he thought seriously about her husband, but having no foundation of fact as a basis, his thoughts remained unanchored. He wondered if the marriage was successful. He believed it could not be. Obviously there were no children or she would not spend night after night rehearsing. Could it be happy if many nights, even after the cast had gone home, she stayed working at college. He was intrigued by her situation. Even tonight, when a husband might be expected to put in an appearance, she remained alone and in no hurry to leave the party. Finally there was this between them. He had not dreamt the kiss.

They reached her car sooner than either believed possible.

"I'll drive you to Covlington," she said. "It's too late for you to cycle back, tonight."

"Thanks."

She unlocked the door and he climbed in beside her.

As she drove she remembered the dream she had had two weeks before of driving through a forest with someone beside her. And she recalled the sweetness when she had turned to find it was he. It was all happening but the sweetness was all behind them. They sat silently, engrossed in thought. She drove past her house towards his hall of residence and stopped where he indicated there was a layby.

"How will you get in?" she asked.

"No problem. My room's on the ground floor and the window's always open."

"Things don't change much. What about the wall?"

There was an eight foot wall around the grounds.

"It's easy enough."

"I hope you aren't caught. What's the time? I've got a torch here somewhere."

He struck a match and looked at his watch.

"Two-thirty. It can't be! Oh well, everyone will be sound asleep by now." He hesitated. "What about you?"

"I keep the hours I please."

He registered the non-committal reply.

"Well, thanks for the lift."

He made no move to open the car door. She knew he was watching her, waiting. She switched off the car lights and plunged them into total darkness.

"Tell me one thing," he said. "Are you happy with your husband?"

She laughed. "What melodrama are you quoting from?"

He began to shake in his seat as he tried to stifle the laughter that somehow he felt was indecent. Margaret, always prone to fits of hysterical laughter, was affected. Somehow the darkness made it worse. He controlled himself sufficiently to get out of the car and say, "Goodnight," then ran across the road and fell against the wall, laughing out loud even as he heard her car drive away. He couldn't stop laughing even then.

"But, Christ, it's curtains," he thought and hardly had the strength to leap for the top of the wall and haul himself over it.

Chapter Nine

Ten hours after leaving Margaret, Antony opened his eyes to find sunlight shining into his room. His whole being was filled with a delicious, yet indefinable, feeling of peace. His sleep had been profound and he awoke with no memory of the usual tormenting dreams or restless turning in the night. A slight noise made him realise he was not alone. He sat up and saw Sloan sprawling on the floor in the act of pouring boiling water from an electric kettle into two mugs.

"At last!" Sloan commented as he handed Antony a mug of steaming coffee. "Thought you were never going to wake up. We hammered on your door at about ten, we'd brought you some breakfast, but you were so sound asleep you never even stirred. So Dick ate it. Then at eleven Steve came and called you, he wanted to borrow your bike. I stopped him shaking you and said he could take it, but no one could find it."

"Thanks. This coffee's great."

"Where did you get to last night?"

Antony drank his coffee as memory flooded back. "I went for a walk," he said.

Sloan laughed. "Who with?"

"Alone."

"Where's your bike?"

"I left it at college."

"Ah, ha, so someone gave you a lift home? Such as our charming Mrs.G?"

"I told you, I walked."

"Come off it, Antony, its common knowledge you're stuck on her and she certainly seemed rather encouraging when . . ."

"Oh, shut up, Geoff!"

Sloan grinned. As he drank his coffee, he watched Antony from the foot of the bed. The weariness of the last few weeks seemed miraculously to have cleared from his face. Sleep had restored the glow of youth and there had been added to his features an inner happiness that shone most obviously from his clear dark eyes. It was impossible for Sloan not to speculate on Antony's movements the night before. At one a.m. that morning his room had been empty and then that unusually profound sleep certainly led one to suppose . . . Yet was it likely? Older and more experienced in the ways of women than Antony, Sloan had known for some time that Margaret singled Antony out for special regard. There was about her an unmistakeable sexuality, never blatant, but to be read quite clearly in her eyes. They were laughing eyes with dangerous glints. There was a sinuous grace to her body suggesting the ease with which it might be roused to passion. But she was after all married and a lecturer, would she be silly enough to risk an affair with a student?

"Be careful, old son," he said with feeling. "It's stupid to mess around with... fire"

Their eyes met for an instant then Antony looked away, irritation hardly concealed in his voice, as, getting out of bed, he said dismissively, "I'll see you at lunch," and reached for his dressing gown.

Sloan made no effort to move, so Antony left him there and went down the corridor to the bathroom.

Alone, Sloan glanced round his friend's room. Apart from variations in the patterns of the soft furnishings, the study bedrooms were identical. Some students added individuality to their rooms with posters and pin-ups, cushions, ashtrays and trash gleaned on away matches to other universities. They moved their furniture around and seemed to compete in reorganizing the space allotted.

Lodge's room was quite undecorated. Only the crowded bookshelves hinted at its owner's individual taste. There were the usual standard Chemistry textbooks, more than the average number of novels in paperback editions, an Oxford Shakespeare, several modern plays and half a shelf full of poetry - Hopkins, Donne, Yeats and Auden seeming to have been most used. They were like the shelves of a student of English Literature rather than of Chemistry. Tucked into the top of the bedside cabinet were a battered copy of 'Coriolanus' and a translation of 'Le Grand Meaulnes' by Alain Fournier. Sloan read the blurb on the back of the cover. 'A masterly exploration of the twilight world between boyhood and manhood with its mixture of idealism, realism and sheer caprice.' Published in 1912. He flicked through the pages idly, remembering how Antony always seemed to have read whatever book was being discussed and could comment on it intelligently and with discrimination. How did he know what to read?

Once they had wandered into a market in the old part of the city and found a book stall. Sloan, seeing nothing but battered copies of Dickens and ecclesiastical works was about to walk on when he saw that Antony was engrossed and soon had an armful of books that he delightedly purchased for almost nothing. Later he showed him what he had bought. Among them were: 'The Leopard', 'The Screwtape Letters', 'The Goshawk' and Boccaccio's 'Decameron'. He seemed to find 'such treasures' unerringly as he moved quite quickly round the stall and knew at once what he wanted to buy. Only once had he hesitated over a copy of 'Wuthering Heights'. Its back hung loose and its pages were yellowing. Lodge looked at it regretfully. "I've got a decent copy at home," he remarked, "but I should have liked to have one here." He turned the pages stopping to read paragraphs here and there and at last reluctantly replaced it on the stall. "It's a bit too battered," he said, and Sloan was surprised for no one seemed less concerned about the shabbiness of the books he read than Antony usually was. "Ah, but it's "Wuthering Heights", he replied to his friend, as if this should have explained his action completely and resolved all Sloan's doubts.

As he replaced 'Le Grand Meaulnes' Sloan noticed the corner of a piece of paper sticking out of the book. He idly opened it, thinking he would read the part Antony had reached and marked. It was a plain post-card on which there was a drawing in black ink. It was the face of a woman caught in a masterly economy of line. Idealised, yet tainted, it expressed both the nobility of brow, eyes and nose and the curving cruel mouth of Margaret Gerrard.

It was Antony's work unmistakeably. He remembered how easily as far back as the Fourth Form he had drawn caricatures of the masters at school on the blackboard, capturing exactly in a few deft chalk strokes a bulbous nose or more cruelly the scars of war. But this drawing delineating so clearly the individuality of a face with regular well-proportioned features was masterly. The eyes even mocked one from the picture. Was such an honest drawing possible from an infatuated youth? With Antony he had to admit it was. He had never known anyone more uncompromisingly honest. Even love would not close his eyes and would, after all, be a splendid aid to memory. He slipped the drawing back between the pages and replaced the book. He had not meant to pry. He respected Antony's deep reserve too much to do that and had spoken of Mrs Gerrard earlier to clear away his own doubts and concern more than to satisfy curiosity.

He hoped, now that the play was over, that Antony would put all thoughts of her out of his mind, but he feared that would not happen. Having reached the age of twenty heart-whole he was more than ready to fall in love. Always courteous and kind to girls, Antony had steered an unwavering course through the teenage turmoil of broken hearts, apparently untouched. One girl recognising her fate all too clearly had remarked to Sloan, "I think he likes his dog better than anyone else. God help him when he falls in love because he's going to fall hard." And they had watched him through the dusty windows of the pavilion at the tennis club playing with Ross at the edge of the courts. The red setter was a beautiful animal, sleek and shining, noble in appearance, loyal and obedient but, like many of the breed, over excitable and nonsensical. One of Antony's endearments for him was Old Looby, and much time was spent in extricating the dog from foolish scrapes. Ross could not abide being chained up so a run was made for him in the garden. This proved largely effective, but at times his free spirit rebelled and he would leap over the six foot fence and go in search of his master. He had a peculiar dancing gait that with his rich copper red colouring made him instantly recognisable when he appeared to Lodge's horror on the school playing fields or at the bus station where, dicing with death, he jumped on and off buses, searching for Antony with gay abandon and apparently complete confidence in success. Through the holidays the youth and his dog would go delving into the woods or tramp the hills, delighting in each others company. There was a playfulness in Lodge that seemed echoed in the dog's nature and perhaps accounted for his closeness to and affection for the animal. When the dog died part of his youth ended and for a long time afterwards, although Antony never referred to Ross, habit made his friends look for the dog dancing beside him, until they remembered. It was not easy to accept the sudden termination of so much liveliness and beauty. Ross's death was a too cruel end to his zany adventuring. It had occurred in the last week of an extremely hot September a week before Sloan returned to university and Antony had begun his last year at school.

They had met by prearrangement at the river just after four p.m.. In the shadow of the bridge they had flung off their clothes and scrambled into trunks. A few yards below the bridge was a deep pool. They plunged into its grateful coolness and idly floated turning their faces up to the hot sun. By one of those ghastly chances, Sloan caught a glimpse of a red-gold tail flickering above the long summer grasses where the road began to rise towards the bridge.

"Old Looby's here", he remarked to Lodge.

Idly, without bothering to look, Lodge shouted, "Ross, come on in, boy!"

Seconds later they both saw the dog magnificently outlined against the sky on the parapet of the bridge, his jaws open, his bright tongue lolling out of the side of his mouth, his tail swaying slowly from side to side.

"Get down, boy!" Even as Lodge called out, Sloan heard the heavy vibration of a lorry revving up as it approached the bridge. Ross paused, whilst with agonising helplessness, they waited, hoping the dog would not jump back into the narrow road. He barked once, the deep joyful note with which he invariably greeted Antony, before he leapt into the river thirty feet below. He landed short of the pool on the dry rocky bed which gave precarious footing. There was a single yelp of pain. Horrified they lifted the dog to the bank. He died that night of internal injuries. Lodge never kept an animal again.

Whatever grief Antony felt at Ross's death was kept to himself. Without the dog his detachment seemed perhaps a little more evident in the essentially gregarious group to which he belonged, albeit haphazardly. He gave the impression at that time of leading an extremely rich private life, from which he could spare only a few hours for social contact with his contemporaries. If he had been carrying on a secret love affair, or beginning some artistic enterprise (such as seriously practising drawing) his other life could not have pulled him away more completely, for he went to it with all the eagerness of a disciple to love or art. What he actually did was simply explained by him. "I was reading," or "I walked in the hills." Adolescence was for him an enlarging and developing of the spirit and mind. Physically he had become remote. There were times when Sloan wondered if he would become a priest so rapt had he become in his secret meditations so oblivious to the attractions of girls and the attraction he held for them.

He raised the question one Christmas on his return from University. Early one morning Antony rousted him out insisting they should not waste such a glorious morning indoors. Amused Sloan had wolfed down some toast and gone, still half asleep, into the dazzling brightness of the sunny frosty morning. Lodge's infectious gaiety soon affected him. They scampered like schoolboys down the crisp frost filled lanes to open country and reached the wooded slopes of the hills breathless. Sloan leaned on a fallen trunk, ready to enjoy the view below that had been transformed by frost and sunlight into a glittering, fairy tale landscape.

Antony now embarked upon an enthusiastic description of a film he had seen the week before. Its photography had been superb, he said, its direction meticulous and subtle. He remembered camera shots, dialogue, pauses in the action, close-ups of the actors and what their expressions said. The torrent of words, the power of description, the animation and brilliance of his visage astonished Sloan. He gazed at his friend only half hearing what he said, overcome by the impact of his personality, the fierce dangerous attraction of his glowing eyes, the carriage of his head, the powerful voice. Sloan felt himself swept along by the stream of words, half aware of a dangerous undertow of feeling that he had forgotten in his term's absence. An uncomfortable suspicion began to grow in him. He desired this youth. He looked away, gazing across the stiff white grass to a broken down fence and the trees that bordered a glassy stream. The morning had suddenly darkened for him. It was a wish perhaps to put Antony at a distance that led him abruptly to ask.

"What are you going on about a wretched film for? You don't live in the real world. What are you going to do with your life? You seem to show no interest in chemistry, physics or maths. Do you ever do any work? Do you expect to walk through your exams?"

Lodge was silent. Hurt filled his eyes, he could not reply until he understood the reason for the harsh interruption.

"You never socialise. You don't have a girlfriend. Perhaps you should enter the church. You have a spirituality about you at times that should go well with a dog collar, and by God your zeal and fire in the pulpit would carry them away. Ladies would faint with desire . . . for God."

"What is it, Geoff?" Antony's voice had lost its richness of tone and had become a hoarse whisper. "Why are you so angry?"

"You ought to harness your enthusiasm to something worthwhile. You go on about movies like a sick girl!"

"I'm sorry. I thought you were interested in acting." He paused. "I can't understand why you think I should enter the church. I'm the last person to do that!"

"The last? Why?"

"I don't trust or believe in God."

They had begun to climb.

"Shall I tell you why?"

"Yes."

"Or perhaps I'll bore you again."

Sloan turned and held out his hand. "Forgive me. You are never a bore to me. It was something else."

Antony returned his grasp and put his hand on Sloan's shoulder as they looked down through the trees at the sleeping white landscape.

"I used to love God. I think I saw him in everything good and beautiful, once. It was the Ichneuman fly that suddenly showed me the obverse side of creation. I was in the Biology Lab. watching some furry caterpillars, delightful creatures with faces resembling kittens. I forget their name. We were expecting them to change any day into chrysalises. Then, suddenly, yellow maggots began to pierce the sides of one of them and writhe out. It was so unexpected and so revolting, I did not know what to think. Mr. Watson came over and told us they were maggots of the Ichneumon fly that deposits its eggs on or in the larvae of other insects. They batten on the host whilst it grows apparently normally. Mr Watson was profoundly interested, even pleased; it was an exciting scientific phenomenon to him, being acted out

97

there in his lab. We stayed to watch. Soon there were so many of the yellow maggots that they completely hid the remains of the body of the caterpillar, and almost at once that writhing mass wove around themselves golden thread that would harden into chrysalids. I was absolutely shocked and sickened at the device of using any creature's body like that. It seemed to be the work of the devil rather than a loving creator. A rose may appear more beautiful and poignant because we know it will fade. I can accept that life has more form and shape because it ends in death, but I can not worship a creator for his manifold blessings whose ingenious contrivances depend, as they often do, on the suffering of the innocent. That sickens me."

"Your God seems to be essentially Old Testament. What about Christ's teachings?"

"I have no quarrel with his code of conduct - who could? It's the worship of God I can't accept."

"What about life after death?"

Antony grinned. "Who knows? But I'm not hoping. What about you?"

Sloan sighed. "I haven't thought about it much, but I believe there must be a purpose behind everything."

This stereo-typed non-committal reply had closed the subject, but Sloan could not shuffle off so easily the self-questioning that that morning's meeting had evoked. He came to accept the pleasure and excitement he felt in Antony's company as inevitable reactions to his friend's attributes. He acknowledged that physical admiration might have a part in all close friendships, but were his feelings for Antony deeper than that? He recalled some of the scenes in 'Coriolanus' where, as Aufidius, he had embraced Antony and uttered, with genuine feeling, a depth of love comparable to that of a bridegroom for 'the maid I married'.

Standing in Antony's room, he acknowledged how deeply he cared for his friend and stared for a long time at the book where he had found the drawing of Margaret. He left then, closing the door softly behind him.

Chapter Ten

After dropping him off Margaret turned the car and drove back to her house. It was in total darkness. She had forgotten to leave any lights burning when earlier she had left for the performance of 'Coriolanus'. Douglas was away, the house was empty and silent. She entered and moved through the rooms switching on the lights. In the kitchen she poured a large whisky and took it into the study. She sat on the sofa and took a long drink.

Her thoughts were confused. She was both happy and sad. But one thought dominated her mind. She had been a bloody fool. She should never have admitted that she cared for Antony. She should certainly never have allowed him to kiss her. She remembered the kiss vividly. She felt again the pressure of his lips on hers and how he held her so tightly and how the kiss had developed from a gentle sweet touching of the lips to a passionate dangerous intensity. And she remembered how she had clung to him and how their bodies fitted so neatly together, perfectly matched in height and size. His body was slender but hard, his arms strong, his hands gentle. She longed to hold him again, to hear his words of love repeated and repeated.

'God help me,' she whispered. She took up her glass and drained it and sat for a long time letting her thoughts drift back over the long evening. She recalled their first physical contact when they had stood in the wings with his hand on her arm as they waited in the dark and how his touch had thrilled her and disturbed her. At the party they stayed close to each other only partly aware of the music, the talk and the laughter.

At about four a.m., making an effort to dismiss him from her mind, she went to bed and sank exhausted into its yielding softness. Mercifully sleep came quickly with its blessing of oblivion.

Her deep sleep had rejuvenated her, but had not weakened her feeling of guilt.

Had she stressed sufficiently the obstacles to their relationship and that as lovers they could never meet again? Had she convinced him that she was too old for him? Had he appreciated fully the fact that she was married? She should have stressed the fact that her marriage was happy, successful.

Surely in the cold light of day he would see there could never be a future for them. He must forget this infatuation or whatever it was. She wondered if she had been adamant enough.

He had said he did not want to avoid the misery he might have to endure for seeing her, and that they could not just cut off their feelings. He had insisted that he loved her. His certainty was worrying.

And then as they parted there was that sudden burst of laughter when somehow they seemed to have reduced their situation to a scene from a melodrama. How had that happened? She worried that their laughter had negated all the serious misgivings she had raised.

She wondered, not for the first time, how she had become so obsessed with Antony. She was after all genuinely happy in her marriage to Douglas. He was an ideal partner and an entirely admirable person. Intelligent, witty and caring, he had in many ways transformed her life. When she was younger, despite her success and achieving the independence that had been for years her long-term goal, there had been times when feelings of desolation had overcome her. She felt then that somewhere within her there was a desperate emptiness that only with effort could she keep under control. It was like a pernicious vacuum that threatened to undermine all her achievements and end her happiness.

Douglas early became aware of these periods of despair and as he learned more of her early life, linked them to the misery she had borne silently and alone for years. He made her realize that life could be lived in the present. Moment by moment could be lived happily and usefully. Regret for the past need not dominate one's days. No one could alter the past but one could control the future to a certain extent. It had seemed to Margaret a healthy attitude to have and with Douglas she believed she had achieved it. She anticipated his home-coming for Christmas eagerly.

Yet for all her determination to forget him, Antony still held a central position in her thoughts. Unbidden he imposed himself upon her mind. Lately when reading she might reach the bottom of a page without knowing what she had read. Her mind had been elsewhere, her companion a tall dark young man with shining eyes and a beguiling smile. And the face was so well-known, so familiar, his presence so comfortable on these occasions. Yet when she actually thought of Antony, he was different. Part of his glamour was that he was largely unknown – a stranger whose life was still a mystery to her. He was a romantic figure in her eyes. She had perhaps desired him more because she had decided she could never have him. But when she had taken delight in thoughts of him or woken enchanted by dreams, the reality of her meetings with him had become cooler, crueller as a result. But if their one brief embrace had been meant as a climax that closed their short encounter with finality, it held one danger. It had given actuality to the longings of each and made further physical contact between them so much more likely. Although Margaret would not admit it the barrier had come tumbling down and Antony ranged free to drift away or come and take. No matter how she avoided him now, she could never regain the impregnable position she had held during the long rehearsals. It was not so much her admission in words but the fact that she had been held in his arms and kissed, to the verge of swooning that would bring them together again.

Her will however took her back to her desk, where she read and reread the first half of her novel. It seemed a strange, alien piece of writing that she found difficulty in connecting with herself. Parts of it she read with real interest as if she had forgotten what she had written. Parts of it she liked. A felicitous turn of phrase even aroused her admiration, but she could not imagine how she would ever finish it. How could she adopt that particular tone of voice again, that cool, analytic, amused attitude? There were evenings when for hours she sat at her desk and wrote no more than ten lines. At other times she slumped in an armchair, a glass in her hand dully staring at the walls, as if she had been recently bereaved and were in a state of shock.

A print she had bought a few months before of Marini's 'Riders and Horses' seized on her imagination and, again and again, drew her fascinated gaze. She would sit and look at it, tapping her teeth with her idle pen, letting time flow by unheeded. The picture seemed to express the sordid basis of the life of the professional performer, embracing not only the physical conditions in which much of his life had to be passed but something deeper. It told of the dust and ashes in the player's soul. It spoke of lives wasted in the tinsel frippery of entertainment. It whispered a dreadful warning about the gaping emptiness hidden from the player by the glare of the footlights. It said that the raging maw of the world's audience would suck him dry and leave him a faceless puppet, dangling from limp strings.

Pacing up and down, Margaret tried to throw off such nightmarish thoughts, assuring herself that Antony would not meet such a fate, should he become an actor. Perhaps he never would choose that vocation. His startling talent, which seemed to her to make a career on the stage inevitable, he might choose to ignore. She remembered what he had said about it. 'Do I drudge away my life in industry or fritter it away on the stage?'

He had been tired when he spoke these words, but she remembered how he had had a very clear idea of the misery that failure in such a profession could lead to. From her own life she could offer little comfort.

'I must not concern myself with his future,' she vowed. 'The play is over. Nothing will remain of these foolish feelings.'

Chapter Eleven

Antony loathed the bright spring days of early March that seemed so at odds with his mood. February rain he could cope with, but bird-song and sprouting buds twisted the knife. He craved the sympathetic background of overcast skies and early darkness.

He hid his grief as if it were a disgusting disease and tried to appear normal to his friends. He knew they now regarded him as dull company and he found it easier to drift away for long lonely spells to his room or the sodden walks to which he was becoming addicted. Only at ease now when alone, he was sometimes led by a perverse instinct to seek the very company he despised when found. He argued even quarrelled ridiculously with people he hardly knew, and would then leave them abruptly. His habitual gentle politeness had vanished, he was avoided now for his irritable arrogance.

Occasionally, one of his friends would speak of the change in him, saying that his portrayal of Coriolanus the previous December, had strangely influenced his behaviour since, implying that, having found a role to suit him, he clung to its essential characteristics. Unhappy and uncertain as he felt, Antony half welcomed these blunt comments and both dreaded and longed for them to talk further, perhaps even mention Margaret Gerrard. No one ever did. This amazed him, for her influence upon him had been so profound. How could they forget her? How was it possible that anyone close to him could be unaware of her invisible, encircling presence, while all the time his being trembled and jangled with love and loss?

Once he had read an article in a glossy women's magazine about unrequited love and being jilted. The writer put forward the view that the suffering entailed was akin to being seriously ill, or else bereaved, and yet no sympathy was offered and no care given to the one bereft. To Antony, at that time heartwhole, the article had seemed sensible enough in its suggestions. Now it seemed to have told but half the truth.

Naively, he had returned to university after the Christmas vacation a day early, hoping to meet Mrs Gerrard in college. He had ridiculous ideas about what he would say, and even half-planned asking her to have dinner with him. Ironically, that Christmas had been the happiest he had ever known because of the tingling joy within him. Sitting by the fire, idly looking at the Christmas cards and holly that decked the room, with no trace of Margaret's existence in the house, he felt her presence there more definitely than the heaped up cushions he lay on or the floor beneath his feet. 'Be absolute for Love'. That was not the actual line but it expressed his commitment admirably. His happiness seemed to grow and flower, filling the room with a quivering glow of intense joy. No doubts about the future had any power over him. Obstacles lacked all ability to distress. Margaret's presence, beautiful, intelligent, artistic, filled his soul. He was intoxicated with love for her.

In early January, a day before lectures began, he returned to University. Half-sick with expectation, he cycled down to College. First he went to see if there was any mail for him. There were two library reminders and notice of a cancelled rugby fixture, which he had forgotten about in any case. The

Foyer was moderately busy. He greeted one or two students and hung about looking nervously at the wide staircase. At last he decided to go up to Margaret's room. Halfway up the first flight he began to run. The staircase divided. Up to the right he ran, a short way along a corridor, then up narrower flights that led to the second and third floors. He negotiated two more narrow corridors and found the stairs that led, by the shortest route, to the top floor. He nearly collided with the History Professor at the top of the stairs on the fourth floor, but then the way was clear to the fifth floor. At last he reached her door and knocked.

"Come in." That was her bored voice, in a casual and automatic response. He smiled and opened the door. Margaret was sitting at her desk opposite a girl student. He had not considered the possibility of her not being alone. He glanced at the girl's back, then looked again at Margaret.

"Good morning, Mr Lodge, have you had a pleasant vacation?"

"Thank you, yes," he said, his eyes beseeching her over the head of the girl to help him.

"What can I do for you?"

He knew it then by the heavy pain that settled near his heart. Those six words did for him. He held on to the door and without moving his eyes from Margaret's face, realised that the girl had turned and was staring at him.

"I, may I... may I come back later? When you're free?"

"I shall not be ready to discuss future plans about the Shakespearean Society until sometime next week. Perhaps around Thursday. I'll let the secretary know. So glad you had a good Christmas."

With compressed lips he nodded and with an effort drew his gaze a few inches from her face, then looked at her again. She smiled without opening her lips. Her eyes were cold and empty, like the glinting green eyes of a cat. He stepped back and closed the door and wandered down the corridor. Coming to a small window, he sank down on the wide sill, looking out at the houses across the college lawns. Their chimneys seemed ridiculously tall and out of proportion. He blinked hard and began to count the decorative bricks that outlined the stuccoed walls. For a while it worked then he pictured Margaret and tears flooded his eyes.

Behind him a door closed and footsteps approached. He rubbed the back of his hand across his eyes and fled. The girl student, coming round the corner, saw the gesture and stopped. Without looking at her, Lodge hurried away. She followed him and began to speak but he did not seem to hear.

"I'm sorry I didn't catch him," the girl told Mrs Gerrard.

"Thank you. It is of no importance," Margaret told her. "Let me know if you find that book helpful, Miss er . . . "

She stood by the desk until the girl had gone, then went to the window. 'Surely he will come back anyway,' she thought, but continued to watch the broad path below her window to see him emerge. It was half-past eleven. How long would it take him to descend from the fifth floor? She needed a drink but couldn't risk moving from the window lest she miss him. At twelve she glimpsed him right below her window. If she had written a note she could have thrown it down. Just one word, "Come" and he would have understood. She then saw he was talking to someone - she saw the edge of a blue jacket. Could it be Miss whatever her name was, delivering her message? If only she could see a little more of her. It must be she; she was wearing a blue jacket, wasn't she?

"Oh, Antony, come back!" she whispered.

He was moving away from the girl, further out on to the path, replying briefly, she thought. Then he walked away. Not fast, not slow, he walked away. Was that the girl? Had she given him the message? Yes, if that was the girl, she must have passed on the invitation to return. And he had walked away. Margaret poured herself a whisky and sat on the edge of the desk, remembering the first time Antony had come to that room. What had they talked of? Romantic love wasn't it? She remembered saying that Tristram and Isolde loved because they had drunk a love potion. She and Antony had drunk together, and, even then, something had begun to grow between them. But it was ridiculous. She was thirty-five, nearly thirty-six, and he was a mere twenty. There could be nothing between them. It was fortunate that that girl had been with her when he came, otherwise . . . God, it would be like hiring a gigolo. She remembered the night, after the play was over, three weeks, a month ago? Had she really let him kiss her? It had been very sweet, but very foolish. She must not see him again. Not until it had all died down, until they had both forgotten. She would avoid him, and, after all, he had not come back.

He thought he heard a girl speak, but could not turn lest she see his eyes. There must be a cloakroom somewhere in this wretched Arts block where he could wash his face. He found one on the second floor and saw with shame, in the mirror, the greenish look of his skin. As he bent to splash his face at the sink, his body heaved and retching, he realised what the pain in his stomach had meant. What a snivelling wretch he had become, spewing up his guts because . . . Shaking uncontrollably he went into one of the cubicles, leant against the wall and wept.

He emerged at five to twelve, controlled, pale and wanting only to escape from the building, to be quite alone. He hurried down to the ground floor, grateful at finding the foyer almost deserted. He pushed open the swing doors and felt a hand on his arm. For an instant he dared to hope that Margaret had followed him, but rejected the idea even before he turned. It was a girl wearing a blue jacket. He looked at her coldly.

"Excuse me, but aren't you Antony Lodge, the one who took the part of Coriolanus in the play?"

"Yes."

"I was wondering if they needed any help with the next play. I thought I might help with something behind the scenes - make-up or scenery or something."

Antony looked at her closely as he replied. There was something he didn't like about her. She seemed to be smirking secretly, to be putting on a face. He could not tell exactly what it was that made the word 'sly' come into his mind. Perhaps it was his face she was smirking at. He moved through the doors.

"The Shakespearean Society has nothing planned for this term."

"Are you sure?"

"Perhaps you would be better suited joining the Dramatic Society."

"Oh, but Mrs Gerrard just said . . . "

He winced, but stared blankly at the girl.

"She just told you that next Thursday they would be making plans."

He realised that this girl had been the one sitting in Margaret's room. Unconsciously he moved further out on to the pathway.

"No. You are mistaken."

"But she just said . . ."

"There are no plans," he said and walked away, hating the girl's intrusive vulgarity, hating himself, yes, hating because of the cruelty of the rejection, Margaret Gerrard.

As the days and weeks went by, the pain hardly seemed to lessen. If he did forget her for a while and go to bed free of anguish, the next morning he was bound to wake full of inexplicable grief. He tried to go on sleeping to avoid the pain of awakening but the anguish just grew clearer, its source well-known, familiar. January and February crawled past. Antony realised how badly he was working and would have thrown up his course had he not been overcome by inertia. There were days when he wondered if he was ill. and one weekend he went home and slept deeply and peacefully, grateful for the healing kindness of his parents' love. He longed to stay there with them and never left the house over the whole weekend. He read in his mother's eyes concern for him when he surprised her anxious glances. The evening before he left, she said, "It might help if you thought you were able to talk about it." He got up and kissed her hair, and half-choking, whispered, "Not yet. I can't, but don't worry about me."

That night as he lay in bed, he acknowledged at last the necessity of taking positive action to cure himself of love. With this determination still strong he caught an early train the following morning and reached the University in the early afternoon. He spent two hours in the Lab. catching up on practical work, then went down to the canteen with Sloan at five p.m.

"I'm in funds, tonight," Sloan told him. "Fancy putting in a couple of hours here, then going to the Warrior's Arms? It's only cauliflower cheese in hall tonight, so we'll be missing nothing. I had a red-hot tip for the three-thirty at Beverley today. Came in fifteen to one."

"Great!"

"How are the folks?"

"Fine, thanks."

"Did you see any of the old crowd?"

"No. I didn't bother to look anyone up. I heard that Jack was getting married soon."

"Oh, yes? To Jean I suppose?"

"I suppose so."

"Nice girl."

A nice girl. A nice girl. And Jack had settled for a nice girl. A dull rather stupid, nice girl. A girl with an accent you could cut with a knife, whose hips were already spreading, who knew nothing of politics, literature or music. A nice dull girl.

"Yes," said Lodge, "I suppose."

"Don't you like Jean?"

"She's nothing to me."

"I think she's all right, Jean. Good sport. Doesn't mess around with other blokes. Jack's jolly lucky."

"Is he?"

"Oh come on! Look I know she's not Raquel Welch. I know she's not got an I.Q. of 135, but she's not bad. She's a nice girl!"

"All right. She's a nice girl. Jack is lucky. But thank God I'm not in his shoes!"

"And whose shoes would you like to be in? If it's not a rude question."

Antony stopped and bellowed at Sloan, "No one's. No one's bloody shoes! Have you got that straight? Have you got that through your thick thatch? No bloody person's shoes at all. I'm free and no bird is going to get me tied up and reduced to imbecilic domesticity. No bloody thank you!"

"Hey, wait!" Sloan shouted as Lodge walked off. "I was making a civil enquiry about the type of girl that would turn you on. That's all. OK Let's forget it."

The canteen was half-empty. They sat alone at the bottom end near the windows. Black clouds rolled down from the north and drew their gaze skywards. Silhouetted against the vast windows, they watched silently, waiting for thunder. The rain when it came gushed down the window panes in torrents. It was after six before they left the Union building and ran through the last light rain to the Library. Inside they separated after arranging to meet and leave at eight.

Lodge found it surprisingly easy to concentrate and time slipped away in the dim bay he solely occupied. He experienced again the quietness that had begun to work its soothing spell on him at home. The hectic clamour of the blood seemed to be settling at last. At eight when Sloan appeared, he wished he could have stayed there alone, but he knew he must start to care about and cultivate his old friends. He regretted the recent lapse. He smiled a welcome and Sloan raised a thumb and left.

The Warrior's Arms was crowded. A noisy contingent of celebrating Freshers dominated the main bar, so to avoid their puerile wit, Sloan and Lodge made their way through to the rear quarters where there was an old fashioned conservatory with large plants in pots on stands and garden figures of stone. After the rain it was damp in places and chilly. They drank whisky, treating Sloan's winnings as a bonus deserving respectful treatment. The land-lady came in and lit a stove and asked what else she could do for their comfort. Her smiles and endearments and Sloan's sudden theatricality indicated a bond of friendship between them.

"My friend and I, Madam, having an urge to celebrate, and the funds wherewith to pay, beg the charming hostess of this ancient hostelry to please bring us a bottle."

"Split infinitive," thought Lodge.

Her plump face dimpled. "At cost price too I shouldn't wonder?"

"Madam, your perspicacity is stunning."

"And how about a snack?"

"A snack!" repeated Sloan scornfully. "Just bring the aqua vitae."

To Antony he remarked, "If we're lucky, we'll have this place to ourselves." He settled himself more deeply into a vast old cane chair.

In the heat of the stove, steam began to rise from their damp jackets and trouser legs. They drank steadily, saying little, but falling into the pleasing old companionship of former days. Sloan kept refilling Antony's glass, delighted to have his company in a setting so congenial. Before long they started on another bottle. Antony seemed oblivious of the amount he was drinking, aware only of a lightening of his mood. He felt less depressed, able to view his situation with philosophical detachment. Wasn't his after all a common predicament? And wasn't it better to sit cosily drinking here with an old friend than to trudge gloomily about in solitary misery? He drained his glass and met Sloan's glance of surprise.

"Sorry I yelled at you," he said. "Thought you were making inferences. Not that that would matter. Forgotten all about that."

Sloan nodded and stretched, then reached for the bottle to fill their glasses. He raised his own and looked through it quizzically at Antony. "I hope you have," he said.

A noisy group of students burst into their quiet sanctum, quickly filling the available seats and then crowding up to their table, sitting on the wide ledge that ran round the conservatory at the base of the glass. Looking to his left, Antony found himself face to face with a girl who said "Hello," as if she knew him.

"How's life?" he mumbled, reaching for his glass.

Sloan had been drawn into an argument by the group to their right. Antony leaned back and blinked hard. The room seemed blurred and alternatively far away then altogether too near. The girl at his left seemed to have her eyes glued to his face.

"Have I, excuse my asking, have I got something funny on my face?" His voice sounded ridiculously loud against the babble of voices. The girl smiled and as he concentrated on her face, wondering if he should know her, someone sat on the right arm of his chair and nudged him nearer to her.

"S'getting too crowded," he said. "Do I know you?"

"I think, perhaps, you don't remember me," she said.

"I don't know many women," he commented, emptying his glass.

She had an insinuating look that he couldn't understand. He didn't know whether she was ugly or just had an unfortunate expression.

"You have a gloating look!" he remarked loudly.

Sloan poked him in the back. "Steady on, don't get insulting!"

Insulting? No, he didn't want to insult anyone. Sometime later he realised his hand was being held and someone else had an arm round his shoulders and was sitting half on the arm of his chair, half on his right leg, now almost numb. It was all rather jolly. Sloan was singing with a group in the far corner. The girl on his knee was handing him a light and he realised, as it approached, that a cigarette was hanging from his lips. Later he became aware of a voice, urgent and insistent by his left ear. He began to listen but could make nothing of what was being said. Someone seemed to be apologising. A month was mentioned. January. That was ages ago. It was March now, or was it April? But windy too. January?

"It can't have been important," he said magnanimously.

This seemed to occasion vast relief in the speaker. A kiss was planted on his cheek. Then he and Sloan were on their feet, leaving, but his hand was held and proved an embarrassment as he tried to squeeze after Sloan, through a crowded smoke-filled bar. Outside he flung back his head and the rain ran, like a blessing, down his face and it was hilariously funny to find an equally wet face next to his, and cold, soft, yielding lips under his own. Lips that were wet and exciting and vastly accommodating. Arms encircled him, and a body was curving in a liquid fashion into his own. Some sickening hurt, he did not quite know what, seemed to drift away and in an alcoholic haze he accepted the favours so eagerly offered by this new companion.

Chapter Twelve

Fornication is cheaper than alcohol and its effects are not dissimilar. Like strong drink it contains its own oblivion and equally the morning after there follows a similar despair. It became for Antony addictive and, as he sank in his own estimation, for a time he relished his perversity. Her name he discovered was Susan but her identity escaped him. She was a conglomeration of features, experiences, snippets of family history and garments that would never jell to produce a wholeness that was a girl called Susan. He knew her body better than he knew her mind, in which basically he was not interested. Her body was infinitely sinuous, yielding and demanding. For most of their meetings they were locked in intimate embrace or hurrying to and from the lonely places in which their liaisons seemed wholly to be carried out. He hardly ever thought of her unless it was to prod himself into trying to remember exactly when it was and where they had arranged to meet. He worked harder than he had ever done, finding in the hours of study a calmness he had hardly known before.

"You may get a good second," his tutor one day wryly remarked, "if this fit persists. On the other hand you've probably left it too late."

"I expect so," he replied and wandered out across the quad, where daffodils in bright blue tubs nodded and agreed.

There was an air of festivity in the posters and paper flowers decking a stall below the library steps. The Spring Ball was exercising the ingenuity of the Entertainments Committee. They accosted everyone entering or leaving the Library and hailed by name students crossing to the archway that led out of the quad.

"Come on Antony. You'll want a double ticket this year. Just three pounds to you. We've only got six hundred tickets left."

Antony grinned, "Too broke!"

That evening he was disconcerted at Susan's determination to go to the Ball with him.

"But we must go. It's the Spring Ball! All my year will be there."

"Well, you go, if you like!"

"I can't. I can't possibly go alone!"

"Why not? You know loads of people who will be there."

"Yes, but at a Ball a girl needs an escort. You must come, Tony, please!"

"Really, I'd rather not."

"But why?"

"I don't care for dancing. I don't really like crowds."

"Oh, that's ridiculous. You'll enjoy yourself once you're there. Every one goes. All the Profs. and lecturers, every other finalist will be there. You will be thought an old swot if you stay away."

"All the lecturers?" It slipped out as with a pounding heart he thought of seeing Margaret Gerrard there. But, no. She wouldn't be there. Or would she? He hadn't seen her for weeks. Would she be there? Would she? Would he see her? Be able to speak to her? Oh, Margaret! Margaret!

Susan's voice went on but he heard nothing of what she said.

"Shall I go?" he asked himself, knowing that nothing would keep him away.

He took Susan home early that night and withdrew from her clinging embrace as swiftly as he could. He wanted to be alone and so urgent was his need to be gone that he did not see the look of panic that showed in her eyes. Suddenly, his flesh was cool again. Empty desire had had its day.

He walked back to his Hall of Residence slowly, savouring the scent of the flowering cherries that arched over the pavements and filled the air with beauty and fragrance. He paused to watch a tiny tree-creeper busily searching the bark for invisible insects. Suddenly his heart seemed to surge upward and a sense of freedom and happiness filled him. Whatever happens, he thought, wherever I go, whatever I do, I have known what it is to love another human being truly and absolutely. Joy filled him, enriching the whole evening. Perhaps such moments as these were God-given, even akin to religious ecstasy. Do I believe in God after all? he wondered. Was it possible that the mere thought of seeing her again would banish the bleak despairing horror of the past three months? Was he cured of that desolation of the soul that had numbed his essentially moral nature and let him carelessly take part in what he now shuddered to think of?

He followed the route that led past Margaret's house. Pale flowers glowed from the dusky bushes that surrounded her garden. No lights were showing from the house, that stretched long and low at right angles to the road. The gates were open. He paused and looked into the garden. There he saw a figure walking slowly past a low stone wall towards a garden urn which seemed poised as if waiting. Leaning on the gatepost, his arm resting along the top of one of the open gates, he gazed at the palely gleaming form. At times it was hidden by the

119

thickening growth of Spring leaves, then it reappeared as the path turned. It was a female form, dressed in a pale garment with wide sleeves and a long skirt. The woman stopped as if listening, then turned to look towards the gate, as if she had heard someone call to her in the silent air. Antony, hardly breathing, stared into the deepening gloom. He did not move. She too remained motionless.

"Whether she goes or stays really does not matter," he thought. "The moment is all. I should like to cease to exist at a time like this, so that the last image registered by my eyes might be Margaret clad in a flowing robe, standing alone in her garden." As they stood the dusk deepened. From a nearby tree a bird called and the wind rippled the grass and set the daffodils in motion - pale blobs of light bouncing in the near dark.

Immobile, enchanted they stood. Time seemed irrelevant. The only sound now was the distant murmur of an engine. A vehicle was approaching. They still waited, denying the interruption, unwilling to accept that the blissful interlude was ending.

The light changed. The upper boughs of the trees were lit by a vehicle's headlights. Against the glow from a distant street lamp a Land Rover was silhouetted, slowing down as if about to turn. Antony smiled and continued on his way as Douglas's Land Rover swept through the open gates.

Chapter Thirteen

Until the day before the Spring Ball Antony did not communicate again with Susan, then he telephoned her to say he had bought their tickets and had booked a taxi to take them to the Town Hall where the Ball was to be held. Although happy to hear the arrangements Susan could not disguise her irritation.

"Where have you been all this time? I haven't seen you for ages. And why didn't you let me know earlier that you would be getting a taxi?"

She had spent several anxious days fearing that Antony might not honour, or even remember, their very casual arrangement to go to the Ball together. She had wondered if she should go with girlfriends, something she felt would be a personal defeat. Sounding rather bored, he gave the usual excuse of pressure of work.

"If you've made other arrangements, that's OK," he said.

"No! No! I haven't. I'm looking forward to seeing you tomorrow - about eight?"

She wore her new blue ball-gown and silver sandals and hoped that her appearance would please her escort. She took especial care with her make-up and her nails and was gratified at her reflection in the glass.

The ballroom filled with the scent of flowers and lit by eight glittering chandeliers provided an elegant background for the occasion.

When Antony and Susan arrived a few couples were already dancing on the vast freshly polished floor; others were standing near the bar. All wore evening dress. The young women, eyes shining, hair newly curled and knowing how charming they looked in their long full skirted dresses glowed with anticipation. Every year the girls, as expected, looked pretty and desirable. But, perhaps more striking were the young men who had exchanged tweed jackets and baggy flannels for that most elegant uniform of dinner jacket, crisp white shirt and beribboned trousers.

Knowing how thrilled Susan was to be going to this her first university ball Antony   intended to make it an enjoyable occasion for her. They had a drink at the bar, where the rugby club already drinking copiously greeted Antony with enthusiasm and threw a few appreciative or curious glances at Susan. When the music began again, Antony took her hand.

"Let's dance" he said.

He held her close as they glided on to the floor.

"The slow-foxtrot has all the best tunes," he said.

Susan easily followed as he guided her round the floor. She was filled with joy and pride and believed she had never been happier.

"You said you didn't like dancing. How is it you dance so well?"

Antony grinned. "We were forced to learn at my school so we would not make idiots of ourselves at the end of year dances with the Girls' School."

"I think you have had a bit more sophisticated tuition than that."

"Yes. My parents believed there were certain social graces that all young people should be trained in. Hence the tennis club, the swimming and diving lessons, even horse-riding. Ballroom dancing was of course one of the tricks."

Susan listened, fascinated, wondering when she might meet his family. What he had just said was more revealing of his background than anything she had heard before. She wondered how rich his family was, what sort of house they lived in, whether he had ever told them about her.

They danced waltzes, quicksteps and took part in a snowball dance, then thirsty, they returned to the bar. Sloan had arrived unexpectedly, having driven from London in his recently acquired Ford. Delighted to see each other, he and Antony began exchanging news and jokes. Susan felt excluded. One of her year appeared and invited her to dance, politely asking Antony if he might take her away.

"Sure," Antony said.

Dances were in sets of three so Susan would be occupied for some time. Glad to have time with Sloan, Antony drew him to an area where small tables provided a quieter place where they could sit, drink and talk.

Sloan had joined a firm of London solicitors and regaled his friend with some of the minor, funnier cases he had been dealing with. They were engrossed, forgetting for a while where they were. The bar was becoming crowded and soon their table was hidden from the dance floor by groups of new people who had just arrived and were standing together drinking and talking loudly.

"How's the Chemistry going?" Sloan asked.

"I'm getting down to it. Guess what? It has been suggested I might get a 2.1."

"That's great! I knew you could do it if you put your mind to it!"

"I always could remember stuff. I only wish it was a bit more interesting."

Something behind Antony attracted Sloan's attention. He stood, then smiled and moved to the side of the table, holding out his hand.

"Good evening," he said.

"Why, hello! How lovely to see you. How is life treating you?"

The voice was unmistakeable. So lecturers did come to the balls. Antony rose and turned and gazed.

Seeing his friend was speechless, Sloan effortlessly rescued the situation.

"We've been having a good time catching up, Antony and I. It seems ages since I was here."

"Hello, Antony," she said.

She wore a dark red, low-cut taffeta gown. Diamante earrings dangled from her ears and a sparkling necklace clasped her throat. She looked stunning.

"Hello. Will you sit down?" He offered her his chair.

"May I buy you a drink?" asked Sloan.

"Thank you, I would like that. A gin and tonic would be nice."

"And what will you have, Antony? Same again?"

Sloan made his way to the bar. Margaret took Antony's proffered chair and he sat opposite. Their eyes met. Neither spoke.

"Oh, God, let me think of something to say! Please put some words into my mouth!" Antony pleaded to the God he didn't believe in.

"The – er – b – band is pretty good," he stammered. "They have a good sense of rhythm." What a fool he was. Of course they can play with a beat, they are after all professionals.

"Yes, indeed," Margaret agreed. She smiled. "How are you?"

"Fine – er – yes. Working pretty hard!"

"Oh, yes. It's your final year."

They sat in silence for a long time.

"Did the Druid ever appear again?"

Margaret laughed, tried desperately to stop, but couldn't. Her laughter was infectious as both remembered the old man quoting Beowulf and how they had thought he was a ghost. The tension between them was gone. By the time Sloan returned with the drinks they were happily talking about Shakespeare's History Plays and whether Henry 1V Parts 1 and 11 were his greatest achievements. Sloan had recently seen the plays in London and was as enthusiastic about them as they were.

"Those plays are just so full of marvellous characters - Falstaff obviously, but then there's Hotspur and Glendower and in Part 11 Doll Tearsheet - the name alone is perfect and hilarious," he enthused. They listened to his account of Justice Shallow's superb antics in the orchard and revelled in his description of the ancient lawyer's reminiscences of the 'bona robas' and 'hearing the chimes at midnight'. Both of them deeply regretted missing these performances.

"I sometimes think how wonderful it must have been to have gone with Shakespeare and his friends eating, drinking and talking in one of the ale houses after the play. What a ready wit, what hilarious company he must have been." Margaret smiled at her companions. "And it's so good to meet like this with you two enthusiasts."

The evening took on a glamour that she felt she would remember forever. They continued to talk, forgetting the crowded bar, the music. They congratulated themselves on the fact that the friendship that had grown strong during the production of 'Coriolanus' was still alive and firm. At ease and happy, laughing and remembering they talked on, not noticing that the crowd in the bar was diminishing and only occasionally glancing at the dancers, now visible from where they sat. Engrossed, they were only vaguely aware of the shadowy couples moving to the sentimental strains of the musicians. Sloan thought Antony had never looked happier. He seemed more at ease with Margaret than he had ever been during rehearsals. Perhaps that unfortunate passion had diminished and a calm friendship had grown between them. He looked from Antony to Margaret. What a beautiful couple they were. The age difference was not apparent. Antony, whom he had not seen for several months, certainly seemed more mature. He was less exuberant, calmer. He couldn't imagine his indulging now, in those sudden mood changes that had worried Sloan in their last days together before he left for London. Margaret and Antony were now laughing and looking at him; Sloan realised his thoughts had drawn him far away, he hadn't heard the last part of the conversation at all.

"How about another drink?" he suggested, rising.

"No. It's my turn," Antony said. "Same again?"

He went quickly to the bar where he was accosted by a young woman in a blue dress. Sloan had a sudden recollection of Antony dancing with a similar person, earlier in the evening, and simultaneously he knew that his friend had ungallantly forgotten her.

"Excuse me," he said getting up, "I think Antony might need some help."

Susan's fury had contorted her features to an ugliness that shocked Sloan. Her voice, shaking with anger, rose to a pitch of despair that was both pitiable and frightening.

"You bastard! You brought me here and deserted me. You left me to wander about looking for you everywhere. And all the time you were hiding . . ."

"Susan, stop it. You're making a scene." Antony's voice was flat and calm.

"I don't care. I'll make a scene. I can see now where you were. With that woman that you used to dote on. That married woman!"

"Be quiet. You are behaving like a fool!" was Antony's angry response.

Sloan grasped Antony by the arm and drew him away. Speaking firmly, he addressed the girl. "Susan, let me buy you a drink. And let's all sit down and be civilised."

"What? Sit down with her?" she shrieked flinging out her arm towards the table where they had just been sitting. "Oh, she's gone! Where is she?" Susan almost ran towards the floor.

The barman approached Sloan. "I'd get her home, sir. She's had quite a few drinks and seems rather upset."

Antony lent against the bar, his hand supporting his forehead. "Oh, God!"

"I'll go after her," Sloan said, "and get her home."

"Thanks."

Antony had turned white, "Get me a whisky, please," he mumbled to the barman. He could still hear Susan's voice and the low reasonable tones of Sloan urging her to leave with him.

He had behaved appallingly. His gross neglect of her sickened him. It was a feeble excuse, although true, to say that he had forgotten her and had not meant to hurt her. Their whole relationship had been sordid. He had never even liked her, but he had used her. God, why had she forced her way into his life? Why had she clung to him when it was obvious he was indifferent to her? He remembered being drunk and how she had . . . He did not want to remember. Then there were all those times when, utterly miserable, he had sought oblivion in the demanding kisses and caresses she had smothered him with. All those nasty assignations he had been too weak and unhappy to resist. He had been an absolute shit. He would write to her. He would apologise. But he was resolved never to see her again. He was filled with self disgust. Seeing Margaret again, so beautiful, cultivated, intelligent, intensified his shame at his appalling lapse into the behaviour of a lecherous lout in the past weeks. He felt unclean and worthless. Whatever would Geoff think of him now? And worse, unbearably worse, what would Margaret Gerrard have gathered from that appalling scene?

He finished his whisky, fighting against the temptation to order another double and another, to seek oblivion, for he remembered how it was a drunken orgy that had landed him in this mess. He remained leaning against the bar. The band was playing a medley of the sophisticated songs of an earlier age. Tunes popular in America in the twenties and thirties. Rodgers and Hart's 'Blue Moon' soothed him and seemed to caress the dancers with its sad haunting tune. He tried to remember the words.

> *You saw me standing alone*
> *Without a love of my own*
> *Without a song in my heart.*

This was a melody Antony had listened to at home. The house had always been full of music. His parents particularly liked jazz and the music of Gershwin, Irving Berlin and of course Rodgers and Hart. Now the band began to play 'Night and Day'. Its relevance to his own situation was almost too much to bear and yet the familiar song eased and comforted his tormented spirit.

The bar was almost deserted now. The few sitting there were talking softly, sitting down to recuperate their energies and rest their tired feet.

A bank of scented flowers screened a corner of the bar from the dancers. Margaret on her way to the cloakroom, hesitated there when she saw Antony standing just a few feet away by the bar. Withdrawn and grave, his isolation permeated the air about him. He looked older, tired and sad. She wondered exactly what thoughts took him so completely from the present. She gazed, not for the first time at his beautiful countenance and the elegance of his form. A sort of spirituality overlaid the sadness of his expression. Fearing to intrude, she nevertheless remained there watching him. "I can't bear to leave him," she thought, "he looks so unhappy." Then slowly he turned and looked directly at her. His expression did not change. She wondered if he had actually seen her. She stretched out her arm, "Come!" she said, and with his hand in hers, they left the ball-room.

With ease they found her car, and she drove slowly and quietly to her house. No words were spoken as she parked the car, led the way to the house, took out her keys and unlocked the door. They entered and went to the drawing room where several lamps were lit. She brought white wine in long-stemmed glasses and they drank, sitting side by side in the elegant room furnished in blue and gold.

When Margaret rose he followed her up the wide staircase into a bedroom perfumed with roses. Slowly they drew the curtains at the two windows and stood, each looking at the other, marvelling at the grace that against all odds had brought them together there.

Their hands touched first and then softly their lips. With arms encircling each other they seemed for a time to lose their separate identities. Gently, slowly, they helped each other to undress, leaving the warm garments on the floor.

"You are beautiful," he said.

"So are you," she replied.

Lying between the crisp lavender-scented sheets, they gazed at each other, slightly surprised to find themselves together thus.

"I love you," she said.

He gasped. "I can hardly speak," he said.

"Just kiss me then," she murmured.

His hand in her hair, he drew her nearer and his lips met hers in a kiss that developed from exquisite tenderness to ardent love.

His hands stroked her body, his lips touched her breast.

"Oh, my America, my new found land," he whispered in her ear.

"I 'licence your roving hands'", she replied, "and more beside,"

And slowly, gently, they became one continent.

Chapter Fourteen

Daylight glowed through the curtains that stirred gently in the morning breeze. Petals fell from an overblown rose, its scent filling the room. Outside birds sang and a dove cooed, a sound redolent of summer and peace.

Margaret opened her eyes. She lay motionless for a while, then turned to look at the youth who lay by her side. He slept. His black hair was tousled, some locks covering his forehead. His eyes were closed; the long lashes gently touched his olive skin. His full lips were firmly closed.

"I'm glad he doesn't sleep with his mouth open," she thought, "although, even then, could he ever look ugly?"

She slipped out of bed, put on a silk robe and tip-toed out of the room. As she went downstairs the thought crossed her mind, with a pin-prick of disquiet, that the young tended to sleep longer and more deeply than older people. How long should she let him sleep? It didn't matter. It was Saturday. No one would come to the house.

In the kitchen she poured a glass of orange juice and wandered into the conservatory to drink it. The garden beckoned. The air was warm. Overhead swifts, outlined against a cloudless blue sky, glided with spread wings in wide circles. She loved watching them, thrilled by their speed and acrobatics, always delighted by their annual return. She did not linger for long in the garden; the thought of Antony drew her back to the house. After she had dressed, she made tea and carried it upstairs. He slept on, lying as she had left him. She put down the tray and sat on the edge of the bed. She touched his hand. He stirred and opened his eyes. His smile enraptured her.

"I'm sorry you woke first," he said.

"I've made some tea."

"How marvellous!"

They drank the tea then Margaret began to pick up their discarded clothes. When she held up his black jacket, the same thought hit them simultaneously. How would he get back to his hall in that outfit without causing comment in such a closed community?

He laughed. "I guess the Warden might put two and two together if he saw me dressed in those togs this morning."

"I doubt it would bother him. It won't be the first time someone has rolled up in conspicuously unsuitable clothes after staying out all night."

"Actually, from what I've heard, the Warden is pretty good at turning a blind eye."

"It isn't the Warden that concerns me. I'm bothered more about gossiping students. However, I have a solution, just give me a minute."

She left the room and Antony put on his shirt and trousers.

On her return, "Here we are," she said and tossed him a sweater. It was grey and had a polo neck. It concealed the shirt, but the trousers still looked rather unsuitable. It was strange, she thought, to see Antony in one of Douglas's jerseys. It was rather too large but inconspicuous enough to let someone wearing it pass unnoticed.

"Do you mind wearing something of Douglas's?"

It was the first time he had been mentioned.

"I'll pretend it's from a charity shop. Pretty good quality too!"

The light-hearted reply relieved her as he had hoped it would. Within he felt a dull but insistent discomfort. The absent husband had insinuated his presence into the idyllic morning. He caught a glimpse of his reflection in the glass; the adulterer dressed in the clothes of the cuckold. Then he dismissed the thought as ridiculous and melodramatic.

"I'll go down and make breakfast. Come when you're ready. Have a shower if you like."

Ten minutes later, freshly showered, he went downstairs. The appetizing smell of bacon welcomed him into the large sunny kitchen, where a table was set in a windowed extension. White china, silver cutlery, tall glasses of orange juice and a basket of warm rolls were spread on a chequered table cloth. How different from breakfast in hall, where you queued for mass-produced food served on thick pottery plates.

"This looks great," he said, when Margaret placed large china plates laden with bacon, eggs, tomatoes and sausages at the two places set at the table by the window. "I think I've landed in paradise."

They loitered over breakfast, exchanging looks and smiles at first, then talking, at ease with each other. Time floated by. They drank coffee and still sat at the table, luxuriating in the warmth of the sunlight and their memories of the night before.

"May I see your garden?" he asked, and they went through the conservatory and followed a paved path to the round pond at the far end of the garden.

"I once stood at your gate," he said, "watching you walking here. Just the sight of you made me deliriously happy. I even thought it would be bliss to die on that instant."

"It was about a month ago, wasn't it? I remember feeling very restless that evening, impelled to go outside. After I had been in the garden some time, I felt I was being watched. It wasn't at all threatening, I remember, but rather like being watched over, blessed in some way."

"And you looked towards the gate. I didn't know whether you saw me, it was growing dark. Then a Land Rover was driven up the road and I left, when I saw it was about to turn into your drive."

"I didn't see you. I just felt a presence."

Antony took her hand and they wandered back to the house.

"I'll have to go soon," he said. "There are some things I'll have to clear up."

"I know."

He took her in his arms. She wondered if they would make love again and was glad when he planted a chaste kiss on her forehead.

"Shall I telephone you?"

"Yes. This evening."

Now he had to find Geoff Sloan. He rather dreaded meeting his old friend, who had so gallantly saved him from the appalling situation of the previous evening. He deserved any harsh words that Sloan might care to throw at him, but he also wanted to forget the whole thing. He didn't want to remember what he had done or hear how Geoff had managed to get Susan away. He just wanted to think of Margaret and recall all the details of the past eighteen hours; to remember their arrival at her beautiful house, to recall the elegant rooms and Margaret herself, gorgeous in her dark, red dress, drinking wine. Then the dizzying memory of their embraces caused him to pause and for a while he stood, looking back and longing to return to her, to run all the way and to hold her again. He forced himself to dismiss such a plan and continued on his way.

There were few students in the building on such a fine day. He avoided speaking to anyone and hurried to his room where he took off the sweater, black trousers and white shirt. Dressed in casual clothes he went in search of Sloan. After checking the Junior Common Room he made his way to the grounds at the rear of the building. They extended over many acres, laid out with beds of flowers, lawns and woodland. To the side of a beautiful meadow that rose gently to the furthest reaches of the grounds was a lake where wild duck nested in Spring. This was a likely place to find Geoff, but he was not there. He wandered back towards the Hall and hearing on the way the sound of rackets on balls, made his way to the tennis courts. All the courts were in use and several groups of students, dressed in white, sat on the grassy banks surrounding the courts, waiting for a game to end.

"Hi, Antony, Geoff Sloan's been looking for you!"

"Oh, do you know where he is now?"

"On the far court."

He threaded his way through the groups sitting and lying on the grassy slopes.

Geoff was playing with three other men in a game that was fast and furious. Unnoticed he sat on the grass to watch. They played well. Two of them had impressive serves and all of them were quick and agile. He recognised one of them who had been in Geoff's year reading law; the others were probably from the town - perhaps solicitors. It was a good game, appreciated by the watchers who sometimes applauded a long rally or a particularly clever return.

The warm afternoon drifted by and the game ended. The four, chatting and laughing, left the court, draped in white

135

sweaters and lugging sports bags. Feeling like an intruder, yet knowing he must greet Sloan, Antony stood and waited for the group to approach. When Sloan saw him, he stopped speaking, hesitated, then excused himself from his friends. "Sorry, give me fifteen minutes and I'll see you in the pavilion."

Calmly he walked towards Antony, hiding the annoyance that had clearly spread over his features on first seeing him. Hardly breaking his stride, he flung an arm across Antony's shoulders to turn him and together they moved away from the courts and the people surrounding them.

"I don't know which to do first - apologise or thank you. I'm so sorry for landing you in that mess and I can't begin to say how grateful I am that you took her home."

"I'd like to know how on earth you got mixed up with her. She's a pretty unpleasant person and I think quite dangerous. I had a hell of a job getting her home. She was filled with fury, really nasty, wanting to damage you in any way she could. After I got her in the car, she became tearful and although I tried to shut her up, she insisted on giving me a detailed account of what she called your 'affair'."

"I'm so sorry. Sorry you had to hear all that. It's so sordid. I hate myself when I think about it. Even more now. I've been trying to break off with her gently. She desperately wanted me to take her to the dance, so I did all I could to make the evening pleasant for her."

"Oh God! Don't you see that your tactics were ridiculous. She told me that *you* persuaded *her* to go with you to the dance, behaved like Prince Charming for the first part of the evening, then, like some bumpkin, you dropped her and went off drinking with your pals."

"I expect she blamed you for that."

"Oh, yes, I came in for some stick, but," he hesitated, "what is worse, she is convinced that you are having an affair with Mrs. Gerrard."

"How dare she bring her into it?"

"Well, she has. And what is more, she's planning to take some action."

"She wouldn't dare!"

"Antony, the girl is mad. You may be lucky not to be charged with rape!"

"I don't believe it! She absolutely threw herself at me. I could say she raped me!"

"What is important is for you to calm her down. And you must make her see that it would be disadvantageous to her to make her sore feelings public. She's obviously in a state. She thinks she has been jilted for no reason, out of the blue. She is madly infatuated with you. She dreams of marrying you. It seems your behaviour, dancing with her, as you did, talking about your family, led her to believe that you returned her feelings."

"I was only being polite."

"The thing is, Antony, you are a charmer. You just don't know how attractive you are."

"Oh, shut up, Geoff!"

"OK But you'd better not see her alone. She is in a nasty frame of mind and disturbed. Who knows what trick she might pull. I really think you need somebody with you, somebody she knows. Because she was so frank with me last night, I think she might accept me as a responsible witness."

"You sound like a lawyer. I'm not a child. I should sort out my own messes."

"Antony, I'm serious. She has to be stopped now. If I'm with you she will be more controlled. By yourself you might unwittingly give her the impression that you were there to appease her, to make up. She would probably go through all the rigmarole she subjected me to last night. She would work herself up into a fury. She would probably start to weep." He smiled. "She might even try to rape you."

Bad as the situation was, Antony had to laugh.

"I bet you are wishing you had a nose like Cyrano de Bergerac's."

"Not quite."

"I'll have to go now. I arranged to meet Luke and the others at the pavilion. After they have gone shall we try to get in touch with Susan and see her this evening?"

"Must it be tonight?"

"The sooner the better. Why?"

For a moment Antony nearly blurted out the arrangement he had made to telephone Margaret, but quickly realised how appalled Geoff would be to hear of this latest, even more outrageous, development in his life.

Chapter Fifteen

After a long wait, whilst some unwilling but dutiful student, who had answered the telephone, went in search of Susan and summoned her to the phone, Antony was finally able to speak to her.

"Hello, Susan," he said. "I'm ringing to apologise for my behaviour last night. I can't believe I was so thoughtless and rude. You were justified in being extremely angry."

"Oh, I'm glad you see that," she said pettishly.

"What I propose is that we meet and talk the situation over calmly. Shall we call for you at about half-past-seven?"

"What do you mean 'we'?"

"Well, I shall be with Geoff Sloan - we are going on somewhere together, after you and I meet, and so he'll be with me."

There was a long silence.

"Susan, are you still there?"

"Yes."

"I'll see you at half-past-seven, then, outside your Hall?"

She made no reply. Antony quietly put the receiver down.

He did not know whether she would come, but he and Geoff waited until 7.45p.m. when she came slowly out from the students' entrance.

Antony moved towards her. "Shall we walk for a while?" he asked and slowly they sauntered past the long West Wing of the students' accommodation. Sloane remained behind reassured by Susan's quiet demeanour. She still looked angry and aggrieved but she no longer spoke in the hysterical manner of the previous evening.

Antony did not know how to begin. He hated the situation he found himself in. He knew he had acted badly the night before, when he had completely forgotten her. His meeting with Geoff had been an unexpected pleasure, and when she was taken off his hands he had been glad to be relieved of her for a while, so he could talk to his old friend. Then when Margaret had appeared all his attention had been given to her. Now, he loathed his behaviour in the previous weeks when he had allowed Susan to insinuate herself into his life. He had never even liked her. When he thought of how their relationship had begun, he cursed his stupidity in getting drunk with Geoff, who was spending his winnings on whisky. With horror he remembered Susan clinging on to him and, how, in his drunken stupor he had accepted her embraces and sought oblivion in sex. How stupid he had been. How could he atone for such behaviour?

"Last night," he began," and I am more sorry for it than I can say, I just had a mental blockage. I forgot I was with you, after you had gone off to dance with...whoever it was."

"Oh, thank you, that's very flattering."

"It was a dreadful thing to do. Please try to understand. I did not mean to be rude, but I had not seen Geoff for ages and we had so much to say to each other. I just forgot time was passing and I did not realise you might be looking for me."

Susan stopped and her knowing, spiteful expression made her look ugly. He guessed what she was thinking and

140

anticipated what she would say. With the memories of the heady hours he had spent with Margaret fresh in his mind, he could not bear to think of what she might utter to defile that blissful time. He walked on.

"It wasn't Geoff that occupied you. It was that foul woman..."

"Say no more!"

"You're besotted with her. And she's old enough to be your mother!"

Antony continued to walk away. Susan had to run to keep up with him which infuriated her. He could not bear to hear her thoughts about Margaret. He felt she contaminated everything she spoke about.

She yelled at the top of her voice, "You are a stupid fool. She doesn't give a fuck for you. She may have flattered you to get you to perform for her, in her precious play, but I know, I saw how she gave you the brush off when you came sniffing round her after the play was over. She sent me after you and I saw you crying for her, snivelling because she'd sent you packing."

Antony stopped, "What did you say? She sent you after me?"

"Yes."

"But why?"

"She wanted you to go back, I expect. She was sorry she had hurt your precious feelings."

So that girl in Margaret's room had been Susan. "And you never delivered the message?"

She shrugged, "Why should I?"

He remembered his anguish at the time and the weeks of misery that had followed. He thought of Margaret thinking he had received her message and believing he had refused to return. And what had she thought when he had not appeared at the casting session for the next play? He had heard later that she was not directing it but acting in an advisory capacity. The students, she had said, were quite capable of producing their own play. He wondered if his absence had had anything to do with her decision. It did not matter.

"Look, Susan," he said wearily, "we have come to the parting of the ways. You're angry and you're sick of my behaviour - with every right. Now let's just call it a day. There is absolutely no point in our going on meeting."

He could hardly believe the sudden agony of her expression. She seemed unable to find words to express her thoughts.

"Don't be upset. It's not worth it. You'll find someone else..."

"I don't want anyone else."

"You will soon forget me. We were never really suited. It was not a deep relationship."

"I thought it was! I love you."

Her compressed lips and closed eyes aroused his pity, but he was determined not to comfort her, nor to touch her.

"Susan, I'm so sorry. I have not behaved well. But I never really encouraged you to think . . ." he broke off. "It was never serious for me. I mean my feelings were never engaged. I just went along with it. I am to blame. But it has got to stop now."

"Why?" she cried.

"I've got to get my head down and work. Finals start soon and I've loads of stuff to catch up on."

"But afterwards?"

"No."

"Promise me this has nothing to do with her," she insinuated.

Antony hated her at that moment. He took a step back as if he meant to walk away. "You are a fool," he muttered, angrily.

Then he realised that in saying those words in that tone, he had revealed more feeling than anyone disinterested would ever have done. He tried to cover his tracks.

"What on earth can you mean? No. Don't answer."

She was smirking now. "I wonder what the Prof. would say if he knew Mrs Gerrard was carrying on with a student, her favourite actor?"

"What makes you think he'd listen to your foul accusations? You'd better watch your tongue."

Geoff approached. "We are due to meet Luke at eight thirty. Do you mind, Susan, if I take Antony away now?"

He was offering her a way out of the rapidly deteriorating situation. She could leave with dignity, bottle up her emotions and retain some pride. Had Antony been alone she would have exulted in savaging him with her envious and embittered accusations until she made him admit his feelings for 'that woman'. Then she remembered last night when Geoff had taken her home. She recalled his calming words. She had sensed his strength. She knew he would be a formidable opponent if she devised any scheme to harm his friend. She also felt very tired and heart-sick. She had never seen Antony look so angry. He seemed to hate her. Since she had known him it had been obvious that he was desperately unhappy. Weeks had passed when he never seemed to be truly with her. He was always forgetful, weary even. But there had been a change. After not seeing her for a while, he had taken her to the Ball and was happy, talkative, courteous, the ideal escort.

"Susan," Geoff said, "we must go now."

"Yes. Goodnight," and without looking at Antony she walked back the way they had come and entered the hall of residence.

They watched her as she went.

"Do you think she will go to Prof. Hutchinson?"

"I don't know. I think she will calm down. But as there is no truth in what she says, she can't really do much harm. It will just be rather embarrassing."

"For whom?"

"Well, for her, mainly. No one could blame you or Mrs. Gerrard for having a drink together at the Ball and I was with you, remember!"

"Yes, you were."

They walked back towards the village to meet Luke. Geoff hoped that after a few drinks Antony would cheer up and put this unpleasant episode out of his mind. Apparently this was not to be. Whatever Geoff said was met by silence or else his companion's mumbled answers came after such long intervals and were so vague or inapt that it was obvious he had barely heard what had been said. Geoff stopped.

"What's the matter with you?" he asked. "Your mind is miles away. Are you upset?"

He could hardly believe that Antony cared sufficiently about Susan's unhappiness to make him so obsessive about the recent scene that he could not think or speak intelligently.

"The girl will get over it."

"I'm not worried about her. I can't stand her. I loathe myself for ever having anything to do with her."

"Then why on earth did you go out with her at all?"

"Because she offered sex on a plate for weeks and I was too miserable to stop it. It started that night we got drunk. Somehow it freed me from remembering, and I was able to work. God, it's so awful."

The bluntness of this outburst silenced Geoff for a while.

"I hate to see you like this. Don't go off by yourself. Come to the pub. and have a drink. Surely that will cheer you up."

"Sorry, I can't."

"Why not?"

"I'd just be a bore - you will enjoy yourselves more without me."

"There's something else going on. What is it?" He felt very worried about him. "Antony, tell me what is the matter?"

He returned his friend's gaze. He was tempted to confide in him, to admit his passion for Margaret and how he had spent the night with her and how desperate he was to telephone her and arrange to meet her again. But the moment passed. He touched his friend's arm. "I would trust you with my life, but I can't explain. I can not tell you what you want to know. It's private and must be secret."

Hearing these words, Geoff suspected what obsessed his friend and a cold feeling of dread filled him. He foresaw a very unquiet future. He watched him as he hurried purposefully away.

Chapter Sixteen

An hour later Antony cycled up the drive of Margaret's house. And there she was in the garden, standing by a blossoming apple tree near the boundary wall. He dismounted, left his cycle and strode towards her. He took her hand which felt cool in his hot fingers.

"I didn't believe you could get here so fast!"

He smiled, "There was nothing to detain me."

They drifted slowly down the path towards a group of birch trees where they paused, exchanging smiles.

"I have missed you so much," he said.

"Yes. It has seemed a very long day."

"What did you do?"

"Oh, I read the paper. I messed about, did some dead-heading, nothing of any consequence. And you?"

"I found Geoff who, predictably, was pretty annoyed with me." He paused. "Then I apologised to Susan who was also, predictably, pretty annoyed with me."

They looked at each other and laughter bubbled up, overcoming any reservations they might have about the situation of the previous evening. Their delight at being together again obliterated Antony's deeply felt guilt and made Margaret forget that ugly scene and what it suggested of her lover's previous behavior. Their arms were about each other as they wandered further down the garden and paused at the pool where the water-lilies grew.

"God, I love you!" he said.

"I know," she whispered and drew him closer.

Their lips met in a kiss exquisite and prolonged. They held each other tightly.

How long they embraced neither could have said. To each it seemed a coming home as if after a long absence. Near them the delicate branches of the birch trees stirred. Eventually they wandered back towards the house.

"I'd better move that bike," he commented. It lay across the drive where he had left it, conspicuously abandoned.

"It might be a good idea. Put it in the garage."

The developing air of secrecy persisted as they slipped into the house through the conservatory. Margaret went ahead lighting lamps and led the way into the study. As she drew the curtains against the rapidly fading light, he gazed at the book-filled shelves.

"What a super room," he said, drawn to look closely at the innumerable volumes that were arrayed around the walls.

"Yes. I like this room."

It was more intimate than the sitting room where they had drunk wine, the previous evening. It had an atmosphere of quietness and calm. It was a room conducive to the exchange of confidences where any subject might be discussed.

"Would you like a drink? I have whisky, wine, gin and tonic, or coffee?"

"Whisky, please." His choice was perhaps surprising after so regretting drinking it with Geoff. "That's what we drank in your turret. I'd like a reminder of that."

"An excellent choice."

There was a decanter and glasses on a table in one of the alcoves.

"Would you like to do the honours? Be generous in your pouring!"

He remembered how Margaret had sloshed whisky into two tumblers on their earlier meeting and grinned at her. "Do you always like a full glass?"

"Why not? Anyway these glasses are smaller and thankfully rather less crude than those awful tumblers we used."

He poured generous measures into the glasses and carried them over to a small table by a sofa on which she sat. He chose a chair opposite from where he could gaze at her face and see its changing expressions. She raised her glass.

"To absent friends," she said, "and may they stay away."

It was a provocative remark, conjuring up various people that she might be thinking of. He wondered guiltily if she was referring to Susan, or even Geoff. But the wish might equally apply to any of the actors that, after all, were the main 'friends' they had in common. Insinuating itself into these thoughts, however, was the idea that she might be referring to someone else entirely - her husband. She waited, her glass raised, for some response. Without speaking, he raised his own glass, then blurted out, "Where is Douglas?"

For what seemed a long time she looked at him, then her lips twitched into a rueful smile. The question, although sudden, was not unexpected. She tried to read the expression on his face. It was difficult. There was no answering smile. His look was blank and controlled. He waited for her answer. She rose and crossed the room to where an old, framed map of the world hung. The cartographer had depicted the then known world in a manner quaint to modern eyes, but the continent she pointed to, although strangely distorted, was, nevertheless, the recognisable shape of Africa.

"He is there," she said.

He looked over her shoulder.

"He is taking a trip down the Nile, following in the footsteps of Burton and Speke. This is an expedition he has been planning for several years. He left in March and will be gone for another two months at least. He intends to write a book on how Africa, in that area, has changed since the nineteenth century, when Burton and Speke went in search of the sources of the Nile."

Gazing at the map Antony felt humbled. Her husband came alive to him as a formidable adventurer, an august personality, whilst he was a piffling student. He searched the map for the Nile, or whatever was depicted, or guessed, of its position. He was fascinated, impressed and full of self-doubt.

Margaret's eyes were on him, trying to imagine what he might be thinking. She picked up her glass and deliberately speaking in a light-hearted manner said, "And a toast to all free-spirited adventurers who cannot be tied down to the prosaic way of life enjoyed by most human-beings."

They drank and their eyes met.

Then, summoning up as much courage, or bravado, as he could, he added, "and also to those that 'kiss the joy as it flies'."

His sudden smile bewitched her.

She sank into the depths of the accommodating sofa. She was determined not to be dragged into the morass of guilt that, moments before, seemed to be threatening them. Their love she felt was so true, so deep and tested by their months apart, that she believed it was also pure and strangely innocent. So a looming obstacle to their relationship had been adroitly diminished by Antony's confronting it.

He fascinated her. Every time they met a new different facet of his character revealed itself. There was a strength in him that in the early weeks of their association she had never suspected. She realised how little she knew about him.

"I'm glad you asked about Douglas- although your question took me by surprise. In fact you are always surprising me. I realise how little I know about you. I don't even know where you live. I should like to know all about you."

"Are you sure? Most of it is pretty boring stuff."

"Not to me."

"Where shall I start? There are no dramatic events surrounding my birth. I was not 'born with a caul' and denounced by an eccentric great aunt on account of my gender."

"Nor, I imagine, sent to a blacking factory by a cruel step-father?"

"No, certainly not. I can't entertain you with any villainous forebears. My father is a barrister with a practice in London - so at least he is on the right side of the law. You might call him an intellectual. He has wide interests. He reads everything. I'm afraid he doesn't suffer fools gladly. I suppose he is a bit other-worldly. He's not exactly a warm person, but his integrity is absolute."

"I'm impressed," she said, thinking there was no chance of such a father condoning his son's relationship with a married woman.

"My mother everybody likes. She is an artist, painting mainly in oils. She is always visiting galleries and buying pictures and reading about art. She is an enthusiast and is warm and loving. I'm sure she would like you and I'm sure she would understand what I feel about you and why."

He squeezed her hand. "I have no brothers or sisters. There are a few aunts and uncles, a full set of grandparents and three cousins."

"Tell me about your mother's work. What kind of pictures does she paint?"

"Probably her favourite subject is the sea, with mists and rocky shores and lighthouses. Her landscapes drift towards abstraction. There's a sort of mystery, or spiritual quality in her best work."

"You must have had a very happy childhood with parents like yours."

"Yes I did. They gave me a lot of freedom too, trusting me to behave responsibly, and that was a precious gift. I was fortunate, perhaps undeservedly."

"Why do you say 'undeservedly'?"

"Because I took it all for granted. I never had to drag myself out of bed to do a paper round. I lived in a beautiful house, in the lap of luxury really. I went to an excellent school, where I was chosen to play in various teams, like rugger and cricket, I found the work easy. As you will guess I was given parts in the school plays and I never did anything to pay back. I was pretty selfish and shallow. I dreamed my time away, and for a while I did the minimum amount of work."

"But aren't all boys like that?"

"Yes, I suppose they are." He smiled remembering. "But I had in Geoff an example of such moral superiority and dedication that I was always made aware of how much I fell short. We were of course at the same school."

He was silent, remembering how the older boy used to lecture him about his lack of seriousness.

"I think he is very fond of you."

"Do you? Yes, well we're friends."

Margaret remembered how well Geoff had suggested the homo-erotic aspect of Aufidious in 'Coriolanus'. She had suspected then that she was not alone in feeling the immense physical attraction of Antony in the leading role. Geoff had never let this feeling appear except on stage so she had put the thought aside, but now that she knew them better it was less easily dismissed.

"He's older than you?"

"Yes. A couple of years."

"I enjoyed meeting him again, yesterday. Was it just a day ago?"

"It was. But it's hard to believe, after our momentous encounter, last night."

Their eyes met. He moved across to sit beside her on the sofa.

"Last night was magical. I felt I was being drawn into a fairy tale by a beautiful enchantress. Everything was perfect. I was even glad that it had been so long since we had seen each other. The time lapse added to the glamour."

"And you were surely the romantic hero, passing from a tragic forlorn figure of remorse to an ardent lover quoting metaphysical poetry, as he seduced the enchantress."

Their laughter filled the room. They chatted on and time sped by.

"Would you like another drink?" she asked.

Antony, wondering if he might be taking advantage of the situation, asked quietly, "Ought I to be going? It must be quite late."

"I'd like you to stay if you are able to and wish to."

He wondered how his heart could continue to beat at a normal rate. If he wished to stay? Joy filled his being.

"I should love to stay, if you're sure."

152

She smiled, rose and poured the whisky.

"There is a test, as in all fairy stories. I'm going to recite a verse and you must guess who wrote it and where it's from. If you succeed you will be welcome in the enchantress's boudoir."

"I can't believe this. Are you a naughty schoolmistress or a wicked witch?"

"A bit of both. Now listen:

> *'What is love, 'tis not hereafter,*
> *Present mirth, hath present laughter:*
> *What's to come, is still unsure.*
> *In delay there lies no plenty,*
> *Then come kiss me sweet and twenty:*
> *Youth's a stuff will not endure.' "*

"I'm not sure. I think it's Shakespeare. It's obviously a song. I'm fairly sure it's not 'A Midsummer Night's Dream'. Is it 'As You Like It'?"

"No."

"It's not bitter enough for 'Troilus'. It's not a drinking song, so not 'Othello'. Probably one of those jesters sang it at some court."

"Yes, you're nearly there!"

"A clown who is pretty cynical, who is perhaps making a point, a clever clown. Oh I know. It's Feste in 'Twelfth Night'."

"Excellent. It starts, 'O, Mistress Mine, where are you roving?' I'm really impressed by your knowledge of Shakespeare."

"Thanks. But it's a bit selective. I know the tragedies and the Roman plays best, but it was certainly not 'Julius Caesar' nor 'Coriolanus'.

153

"That would have been too easy for you. It certainly was not 'Coriolanus'. You know that's the first time either of us has mentioned that play. Do you ever think of it, now? You must have whole chunks of the text still in your mind."

"Yes. I suppose it's all still there, but quite a time has gone by since then. If you gave me a cue, I could, I suppose, still rattle it off."

"Don't worry, I won't ask you to."

In the silence that followed, each remembered the hectic weeks of rehearsals and the gradual growth of feelings between them. Margaret recalled sitting in front of the stage at the later rehearsals, astounded at the power of the performance of the young man now lounging by her side. She remembered his delivery in clipped patrician phraseology and his glorious appearance.

"I think I was a hard task-master. I never praised you as you deserved."

"Don't say that. If you had had less commitment and had been less demanding, we would never have achieved the success, we seem to have had. You had the vision and we were lucky to be drawn into it. You gave us all the chance to take part in something truly outstanding."

"Thank you for saying that. For me it was a memorable experience."

Lit by lamps the atmosphere of the room was intimate and peaceful. Antony felt he would like to stay there forever with Margaret by his side. He looked at her. She was gazing across the room apparently deep in thought. He took her hand. She turned to him, her expression serious, her eyes troubled.

"My dear," she said softly, "we have come a long way since the time of those rehearsals. What I fear most is that you might get hurt. The situation is complicated. We must take care."

"Margaret, I want you to know this. I have never been happier than I am now. In fact 'happy' is too weak a word for what I feel. Perhaps 'ecstatic' might be nearer the mark. I know there are difficulties. I accept that there will be an ending, if that is what you wish. But, however soon or late we may have to part, at least we have had this time, these hours, perhaps we may have days, weeks or whatever. And that for me is worth all the future heart ache that might ensue. I feel blessed that I have known you. So I'll risk any future that turns up."

She tried to smile.

"Don't worry," he said softly as he enfolded her in his arms. "We aren't in this to be miserable."

He felt strongly the enchantment of what was still the beginning of their relationship. Laughing he pushed up the corners of her mouth. He seemed so full of joy that she put aside the doubts and fears that his words about an ending had inevitably raised in her mind.

"I have an idea. Tomorrow, let us drive to the coast. No one from here will see us. We can walk along the shore and feel the wind blowing and hear the sea surging forward on the sand and rocks. Let's have a memorable day before your run up to finals and my return to the daily grind."

"That's a marvellous idea. And before that, a memorable night."

"Come, sweet and twenty," she murmured and they drifted up the wide staircase arm in arm.

Chapter Seventeen

Monday was cold with an easterly wind thrashing the trees and laying low the flowers in the exposed beds that decorated the lawns. They rose early wanting to make the most of the day ahead. Margaret rang the university to cancel the single tutorial she had that day. Antony had a free day and his non-appearance in the laboratories would not be remarked on in a finalist.

They drove to the east coast where wide sandy beaches stretched for miles. High waves broke noisily even far out in the dark grey sea, filling the air with a rushing, seething rhythmic roar. Where the sea met the land wave after wave surged up the beach.

They left the car in the deserted car-park and hastily put on the sweaters and Barbours Margaret had, at the last moment, thrown into the boot of the car. They threaded their way through the dunes and descended to the beach, where the impact of the wind and the ocean's blast made speech difficult. It did not occur to either of them, however, that they had made a bad choice in coming there. The air was bracing. As they walked they felt energised.

When the wind veered to a southerly direction, they found it easier to walk with the wind behind them. As they progressed the curve of the shore gave some shelter. Nearer to the dunes even the sound of the sea diminished. Talking became easier.

"It was a good idea to come to the coast," he said. "I've never been to this particular stretch of beach before. Do you know it well?"

"Yes. We once lodged near here when I was quite a young child. It was one of the happier times before my parents became estranged and my mother so embittered."

As they walked on Antony tried to imagine his delightful companion as a young child, suffering in an unhappy environment of parental quarrels and bitterness. His own experience of childhood had been so different. He found it difficult to imagine. She glanced at him as he walked, head bent, eyes lowered to the sand. They were silent for a while.

"I hate to think of your being unhappy as a child," he said, stopping and turning to face her.

"One recovers," she said, strolling on, "but I think it hardens you. My strategy was to try to separate myself mentally from my parents. I concentrated on school work and I read widely. My main aim from the age of about fourteen was to become independent. I saw that the way to do it was to get the best education I could. I vowed never to marry. More than anything I wanted to be free of all shackles. I wanted to live entirely as I pleased."

"And were you happy, when you achieved this?"

She laughed, "Oh, yes."

"Presumably you left home?"

"Yes. After taking my degree, I never lived in my mother's house again. My father had died when I was seventeen."

"He must have been quite young."

"Yes."

"You once said that you would tell me about him."

157

"Did I?"

"It was when we were talking about acting as a career and I suggested it could be a pretty useless way of passing one's life. Something I said must have brought back memories of your father, or at least, I thought so at the time."

Margaret rarely thought of her father. The subject was too painful. She was surprised that at some time she must have spoken of him to Antony. She stopped and gazed out at the sea. After a while she moved on, walking slowly along the deserted beach. He followed her and saw how unhappy she looked. The state of solitary independence she had craved, had not been entirely successful in yielding happiness.

"I never realised, until it was too late, just how miserable my father must have been. It's very easy for a mother to turn her child against its father. And I was no exception in being influenced. Teenagers can be cruel, totally self-centred and unforgiving. Rather than trying to understand and sympathise with him, I chose to block my father out of my life. When it was too late, I realised I had missed knowing a man full of charm, talent and sensitivity. Oh, he was weak too, but if we, my mother and I, had shown some love and kindness in understanding his misfortunes and bolstering up his confidence, things might have been very different."

He took her hand. The sound of the sea beating against the shore and the cries of gulls seemed intensified as they walked, two lonely figures, along that desolate shore.

"Perhaps it wasn't a good idea to come here," she said. "I don't want to worry you with my past miseries that this place seems to have released."

"If it's any help to you, I don't mind."

"I'm sorry I've revealed the selfish and maudlin sides of my character. What must you think of me?"

He looked down into her eyes. "I don't think you are selfish or maudlin, but I'm glad you felt you could be so frank with me. I never suspected that your background could have had disadvantages. But you overcame them. By your own efforts you have become successful. No one can be blamed for their parents' mistakes. You acted as you did to survive and succeed in your own life. You are not responsible for theirs."

"Thank you. But I'm not the person I would wish to be. I'm selfish and immoral. I hide behind a veneer of sophistication and amusement . . . "

"Stop right there... You are a beautiful, talented... enchantress. And I adore you."

The wind continued to blow but less furiously. They watched as a large vessel loomed on the horizon, steaming slowly southwards.

"I feel hungry. Shall we find a sheltered spot and eat those sandwiches?"

The dunes rose high topped by long grasses. Many nooks offered shelter and the sun, less fitful now, warmed the sand. They ate the sandwiches and drank cold apple juice.

"I wish I'd brought a flask of hot coffee, but these drinks fit so easily into a pocket, that I didn't bother."

"Are you cold?" He put his arm round her shoulders.

"Not really. I just like coffee."

"Do you know what Mae West said about liking coffee?"

"No. I'm surprised you've even heard of her."

"She said, 'I like ma coffee like I like ma men - hot and strong, black or white.'"

They laughed. "Where did you hear that?"

"From one of the Jamaican students, a wonderful chap, with a glorious sense of humour. And of course the joke was obviously funnier when he said it."

"I can remember seeing photographs of Mae West. She always wore a long dress down to her ankles and, as a child, I got the impression her legs were like tree-trunks, with no knees or ankles."

"Poor woman. But at least she was witty and they do say wit and humour entice more people into bed than one would easily believe."

Margaret laughed. "You are always surprising me. And of course you are right. I expect you know Blake's angel who didn't even need to speak.

As soon as I went an angel came.
He winked at the thief
And smiled at the dame,
And without one word spoke
Had a peach from the tree,
And 'twixt earnest and joke
Enjoy'd the Lady."

"I didn't know that poem. And I didn't think angels bothered about sex."

"Yes. It is a bit odd, but then Blake was rather strange."

"There's something very attractive about the idea of angels," Antony tentatively commented. "I've pretty well given up belief in God, but the possibility of all powerful guardian angels really appeals to me. I wish more had been written about them."

"There's 'Paradise Lost', don't forget."

"Yes and 'Tobias and the Angel'. But neither of them, for different reasons, satisfies me."

"You ought to write a novel about your type of angel. Or how about a play? And you could act the main part."

They both found this very funny.

"Would I have to wear a long white dress and grow my hair?"

"Not necessarily. It could be a play set in modern times, with the angel carefully concealing his identity."

"The attributes I'd give the angel would be mainly strength and power and of course goodness, characteristics perhaps better shown on film than on the stage."

"Certainly in the case of miraculous strength."

So they carried on, freely exchanging the inconsequential thoughts that neither had expressed before even to their closest friends. At times in silence they sat watching the distant sea and the clouds moving across the sky.

"I wish I could stop Time moving onwards. I'd like this hour to last forever."

"It's reassuring how at times our thoughts run on exactly the same lines." Margaret smiled at him. "I was trying to remember a poem called 'Le Lac' by Lamartine. He is with his lover and expresses exactly what you have just said.

> 'O Temps, suspends ton vol,
> Et vous heures propices suspendez votre cours,
> Laissez nous savourer les rapides delices
> Des plus beaux de nos jours.'"

Her slow delivery of these romantic lines enabled him to understand most of the sonorous French verse, which, like the Blake, he had not heard before. For a while, they gazed out towards the dark blue horizon.

"You will think me a terrible blue-stocking. It's just that my head is often more crammed with quotations and snippets of poetry than it is of reality. And now when we have a miraculous reality to enjoy, I start quoting other people's thoughts."

"I think it adds an extra, wonderful dimension. I like to think we are tuned in to all those lovers in the past or in literature who felt as we do."

She gazed into his eyes. "I am beginning to think that in you I have found my soul mate."

The sweet words, spoken softly, in a moment when the wind lessened and the sea sparkled below them, brought such ineffable joy with them that Antony could only gaze at her speechless. She smiled. "That night at the ball, when I found you leaning on the bar, looking so devastated, I knew we had to come together. The time that had passed since we had talked, on that bitterly cold night, after the play's last performance had not allowed me to forget you. I knew that if I ever saw you again, I would be unable to dismiss my feelings as I had earlier been determined to do. When I first knew you, I did struggle, but gradually as the rehearsals continued, watching you perform became like a drug. I was obsessed and I suppose, as a sort of self defence, I began to dislike you. I couldn't stand your sudden frivolity. I thought you were too influenced by the adulation of the others. It was as if, aside from the play, there was nothing either of us had to say to the other. Then one night, after a rehearsal, we were alone and you asked me incongruously about Anglo Saxon, and we seemed to be able to talk together at last, up in my room."

"I remember. And of course you knew I was smitten?"

"Yes. And there were those in the cast who let me know,"

"Really? Who?"

"Pasco was one. I was quite angry with him. He seemed to want me to confide in him. Anyway that was sorted out."

"I think Sloan knew. I never admitted anything but he's always been able to read my mind."

"Is he still here? Or has he gone back to London?"

"He'll be here till tomorrow."

"Good. You'll be able to see him before he goes. We will part this evening. We won't meet again until your exams are over. You don't want any distractions."

"Shall we speak on the phone?"

"Let's not."

His heart lurched as he heard this. He looked at her trying to understand this uncompromising reply. Her expression was grave but kind.

"Trust me. This is for the best. You must put your mind on finals. Knowing we won't meet or speak to each other, will make the situation much easier to manage. I shall think of you."

"Think of me all the time!"

He held her in his arms. Their lips met and as the sky darkened they lay secluded in the dunes on that lonely beach. Their passion was undaunted by the few heavy drops of rain that heralded the coming storm.

Chapter Eighteen

As the days went by Antony became more and more engrossed in his Chemistry revision. He had in his first years at University found the subject a tedious bore. That had changed. He had to admit how sensible Margaret's suggestion had been, not to see each other until Finals were over. Had he not known that there was no chance of their meeting, and all that that might lead to, he would have been in a permanent state of distraction. As it was, he gave his full attention to those parts of the syllabus he knew he had earlier neglected. He found, somewhat to his surprise, that he enjoyed the work. His excellent powers of concentration came to his aid now. His confidence grew. The love he shared with Margaret provided a background of joy, comforting as a sweet air barely heard but deeply reassuring.

On the day when Finals began he went with some relief into the examination room. He felt nervous but on reading the paper he found the predictability of the questions encouraging. As always in exams he enjoyed the challenge and felt buoyant as he progressed through the three hour paper. Nevertheless during that first week he was not free of nightmares that jerked him awake. In these dreams he had to answer questions in a foreign language about subjects he had never studied. Mercifully he was able to go back to sleep after these odd, traumatic interruptions and dismissed them as merely the result of subconscious anxiety.

When the last paper had been completed and all the practicals were over, the euphoria he had expected to feel was missing. He felt drained and flat. This seemed a normal reaction, shared by most students. They wandered aimlessly from building to building, too lacking in energy or initiative even to go into the town to see a film.

Students' letters were delivered to racks of pigeon holes hung outside the formal dining rooms in the Halls of Residence. Margaret's letter arrived at Holmwood on the Friday after the exams finished. He knew at once from the crisp white envelope and sprawling handwriting that it was from her. Annoyingly there was insufficient time, before the dining room doors opened, for him to find a quiet corner where he could read her letter in privacy. He put it unopened in his pocket and read the letter from Geoff that he had also picked up. This was a brief note expressing the hope that his exams had gone well and confidently predicting a good result. In a post-script he had added, "I trust there were no repercussions re-Susan."

"Good old Geoff," he thought as he went into the dining hall with the other students, his mind centred on the letter in his pocket.

An hour later, sitting on his bed, he opened it.

Dear Antony,
Would you like to join me for lunch, here, on Sunday?
Say one p.m.?
Sincerely Margaret.

He had hoped for a longer letter, even a love letter, or at least one expressing some feeling. On reflection, however, he thought as he usually did, that she was right. What need was there to write what they could say to each other so soon? He decided to send her flowers.

When he saw the display outside the florists the next day, he was glad he had not telephoned but come in person to the shop. He gasped as he looked at the beautiful arrangements and the array of unusual flowers. It seemed to him that he was being welcomed back into a radiant world full of scent and colour after the dull seclusion of exam rooms, laboratories and his own study-bedroom. He passed through the banks of flowers ranged in containers outside the shop and entered a cool space where delightful odours assailed the senses and various hues dazzled the eyes. He gazed, in silence, at the exotic displays.

A young woman came forward to greet him.

"This is fantastic," he enthused.

She smiled.

"I'd like to buy some flowers - but I've no idea what to choose."

"Are they for some special occasion?" she asked.

"Well, yes, in a way - a celebration?"

"And are they for a young lady or perhaps for your mother?"

A smile began in his eyes and curled his lips. How to describe Margaret?

"Let's settle for a beautiful enchantress." he said.

Surprised at this odd reply, she smiled and said, "A lucky lady! What are her favourite colours?"

He remembered the gold and blue drawing room. "I think blue, white and yellow. I like those delphiniums."

"Shall I put together a variety of blooms and see how they meet your wishes?"

"A good idea."

The florist soon put together a mixture of blue agapanthus, white stocks, both dark and pale blue delphiniums, pink and purple sweetpeas and other flowers whose names Antony did not know. Green fronds were added and finally tiny yellow rosebuds.

"They are beautiful," he said. "Is it possible for them to be delivered this afternoon?"

"Certainly. Would you like to write a card to send with them?"

She led him to the office at the rear of the shop where there was a display of cards. He chose a plain white one and wrote on it, "Longing to see you, Antony." He placed it in a small envelope that she attached with a clip to the flowers. He gave Margaret's address, paid and, smiling thanked her for her help.

On his return to Holmwood, he wrote to Geoff.

Thank you for your letter. I'm sorry I didn't see you before you left but quite understand that you wanted to leave for London that morning rather than hang about waiting for me. You asked whether there had been any developments in the Susan business. Thankfully no. I haven't set eyes on her since that last evening.

I've been doing nothing but revision. I forced myself to work hard and in fact became engrossed. I found it, i.e. Chemistry, more interesting than I ever did in the first two years, when I regretted my choice of subject and wanted to change my course. It wasn't only the relief of being rid of Susan that enabled me to concentrate, but something deeper.

Margaret Gerrard and I are together. I have never felt happier in my life or more 'centred' - if you understand what I mean. I don't expect you to approve of this, but I believe you will not be surprised. I think you have known for a while how I felt about her, and suffered, when I thought there was no hope for me. It is because you have always been such a good friend that I am revealing this now. We have told no-one yet. Everything happened very quickly. In fact three days were all we had together before necessity decided us to keep apart until Finals were over. Tomorrow I shall see her again and I can't express what that prospect of bliss does to me.

As ever, Antony.'

On Saturday morning, Margaret received two letters. They were from Elaine and Douglas. Elaine wrote to ask if she could spend the weekend with Margaret arriving on Saturday afternoon and staying till Monday morning. This unexpected request surprised and annoyed her, as she had invited Antony for lunch on Sunday.

She picked up the phone and dialled Elaine's number. It was nine-thirty. She hoped Elaine would not yet have set off. The phone rang and rang. It was not picked up. She tried again fifteen minutes later, with the same result. She thought of the several options open to her. She could try to reach Antony to postpone the lunch date. She could take Elaine out for the day on Sunday and send Antony a telegram or she could go out herself now, leaving the house until evening, by which time she hoped Elaine would have gone. None of these plans appealed to her or seemed feasible, so she decided to let events take their course. She would greet her friend as graciously as she normally would do and pass off Antony's coming to lunch as casually as she could. She knew she could rely on his discretion.

Now, she could sit down and read Douglas's letter. It was dated ten days previously.

Dear Margaret,

This is probably the most difficult letter I have ever written. Several earlier versions of it I have torn up for various reasons. But these previous attempts made me realise that honesty and brevity would be my best options in expressing what I have to say.

Africa has affected me deeply. My fascination with this continent began a long time ago and, as you know my studies of its history and its present state have occupied my mind for many years. I now realise that I knew nothing and that my planned work on the upper Nile area and the changes there since the nineteenth century was basically trivial. I am not alone in being bowled over by the conditions here. Poverty, sickness and starvation are the norms. The smell, the dust, the insects and the over-crowded camps of course we knew about, but actually to experience these things is something else. I feel impelled to try to do what I can to alleviate the desperate situation that the people find themselves in.

I have been in contact with V.S.O. and they have asked me to set up a school, organise a teaching programme and recruit a group of teachers to run it. I don't know how long I shall stay in Africa, nor whether I shall succeed in what will be an uphill struggle, but I must try.

Please do not regard my decision as in any way a desertion. My love for you is constant. If you need me, I will return. It has always been accepted by both of us that neither will seek to limit the life of the other. I ask your generosity in understanding my present overwhelming need and graciously accepting it.

In the weeks before I left I believe you were troubled by something deeply personal that you had no wish to share with me. Perhaps you will welcome the time and freedom that my absence will grant you. Please take both, particularly the freedom, with my blessing.

Ever yours,

Douglas.

For a long time she sat with the letter in her hand. She read it again, hardly able to comprehend the solemnity of Douglas's decision. She tried to picture him in the alien environment familiar from TV newsreels of Africa. Gradually she began to have positive feelings about his decision and to grasp the inevitability of his going. She knew he would gladly sacrifice the comfort and ease of his life in England to serve those he believed he could help. The toil and discomforts would be nothing to him. He would be dedicating his life to a soul-satisfying endeavour. Douglas, so steadfast, brave and good. Tears filled her eyes as she contemplated life without him. She read again the closing words of his letter. 'Take both time and freedom with my blessing.'

"Yes, Douglas," she murmured, "take your time and freedom too."

She went upstairs to prepare the guest room for Elaine. Mechanically she made up the bed, put fresh towels in the adjoining bathroom, then went to stand at the window. This was a room she loved for its quaintness. It was supported on stilts and the bay window was set at an angle to the rest of the room to overlook the garden to the west and of course the setting sun.

As she stood there she wondered what Douglas had meant when he wrote that he knew she was troubled by something deeply personal. Had he guessed anything about Antony? Had she called out in her sleep? Certainly she had had disturbing dreams about him in the early mornings when sleep at last came after exhausting wakeful nights. Douglas had never mentioned anything like that. But then, would he ever question her? They had always respected each other's privacy. It had never occurred to her to ask if he had been unfaithful to her during his various absences. If he had been, that was his business, she had no wish to pry. Similarly, he never so much as hinted that his trust in her was not absolute. No, she did not think he was referring to Antony. He was perhaps thinking about her writing, surmising that it wasn't going well.

She went downstairs to pick some roses from the garden to put in Elaine's room. She thought her friend would arrive about three. She decided to have a quick lunch, before preparing a casserole for their evening meal.

The flowers arrived minutes before Elaine drove up the drive past the front door. Margaret's first thought was that they were from Douglas, who had, somehow, managed, with great ingenuity, to have flowers sent to arrive on the same day as she received his letter. A moment's reflection convinced her that this was highly unlikely.

"Thank you, they are gorgeous," she said to the young woman who delivered them. "What a wonderful scent!"

Carrying the flowers she went to greet Elaine.

"Hello, did you have a good journey?"

"Fine, thanks."

"They embraced and Margaret led her into the house.

"What super flowers! Who sent them?" Elaine asked her when she put them down on the kitchen table.

"I don't know."

Margaret looked for a card. "Ah, this will explain them," she said as she opened the small envelope attached to the flowers and read the message inside.

"Longing to see you,

Antony."

She hid her delight, saying nothing, and turned away to fetch vases from the high kitchen cupboards. To distract Elaine's attention she asked her advice on arranging the flowers in the variously sized vases she had produced. It was a pleasant task and owing to the numbers and variety of the flowers more containers had to be found to do their arrangements justice. A tall thin blue glass vase held three gladioli so exquisitely that Margaret vowed never to call such flowers vulgar again. Alstromeria filled a large stone jug. The yellow rose-buds, with shortened stems, were arranged with foliage in a cut glass bowl. When all the flowers were in water, they carried them to different rooms in the house and admired them afresh, in the places they had carefully chosen.

Margaret made tea and they sat to drink it at the kitchen table.

"You have quite a knack for arranging flowers, Elaine. Thank you so much for your help."

"I once worked in a florist's when I was a student. I picked up a few ideas there. It was a nice job, but I was paid a pittance."

Margaret had thrown away the wrapping paper and trimmings of the flowers before she made tea, but she kept the card. It was lying on the table. She reached for it and saw that Elaine was watching her.

"It isn't your birthday is it?"

"No."

Margaret wondered how she could explain the flowers. It was tempting to pass the card over. The word 'longing', so revealing and emphatic, would not be lost on Elaine. Should she tell her the truth about Antony? She acknowledged the relief there would be in revealing her love for him to such a friend. She knew she could rely on her to respect the confidence, but she was not prepared for her disapproval. Why had Elaine come so unexpectedly, with so little warning? It must have something to do with Douglas. The coincidence of the timing of her visit and the arrival of Douglas's letter was compelling. There also remained the necessity to explain the flowers, although that was fairly easy. What was more difficult was to warn Antony of Elaine's presence. She wanted to ensure that their first meeting was either not observed or else controlled by the realisation that they were not alone.

Elaine's thoughts were complicated. Burdened with knowledge she had yet to share with Margaret, regarding Douglas's decision to remain in Africa, she suspected the flowers might have a romantic explanation. Was Margaret concealing the existence of a lover? Privately, she believed Douglas had known or at least had suspicions that this was so.

Margaret broke the silence. "The flowers are from a grateful student who's just finished his Finals and whom I have invited to lunch, tomorrow."

"Oh, how nice. What a generous offering."

"Yes. It's a bit over the top, but then people do feel like celebrating when Finals are over."

"He must be quite well off, Was he a favourite student - likely to get a First in English Literature?"

"He is exceptionally talented," Margaret replied, "and very well-read."

Elaine imagined a bespectacled, studious young man, round shouldered and possibly spotty who would bore them to death at lunch, the following day.

Margaret stood. "Now I'll show you to your room and you can freshen up, whilst I get on with our meal."

When she came downstairs she went into the study and took a folder from a drawer in the desk. She opened it to reveal a black and white photograph of Antony as Coriolanus. She had not looked at this photograph for a long time. His disturbing beauty was compelling. What would Elaine surmise when she saw him?

That evening after dinner they sat in the drawing room drinking coffee. Elaine thought the time had arrived when she should explain her visit. She had half hoped that Margaret might have spoken of Douglas, but she had not. Was it possible that she had not received the news of his intention to stay in Africa? If that were so it would be unacceptable for her to mention it. Douglas had quite clearly stated that he had already written to Margaret and wished Elaine to visit her, after she had received the statement of his intentions. Diffidently he had expressed the wish that his wife should have the support of a close friend, if she became overly upset at his revelation. He had written that he believed she would accept his decision with equanimity. It was just reassurance he asked for and he begged Elaine to write to him and describe how Margaret had taken the knowledge of what would be his prolonged absence.

"You've been gazing at your coffee for about five minutes," Margaret remarked. "Is there a fly in it, or something?"

Elaine laughed apologetically. "Sorry. My mind was miles away.

"I know.

Elaine took a sip of coffee, trying to think of how to open the subject. She thought she would edge up to it slowly. "I expect you were surprised to receive my letter, inviting myself to visit you."

"I was rather." She was not going to second guess the reason, lest she reveal more than Elaine needed to know.

"By the way, have you heard from Douglas recently?" Elaine asked as casually as she could.

So that was it. "Yes. I have."

"He wrote to me. I received his letter on Friday morning."

"Ah, so you were a day ahead of me in learning his news? My letter came today."

"That would be a postal delay. Douglas would never have intended your letter to arrive after mine."

"No, of course not!" Margaret relented, sensing Elaine's dilemma. "I expect he told you that he is joining V.S.O. as a teacher and will stay in Africa for sometime. And he asked you to come and see how I was taking it."

"Yes."

"I'm glad you came."

"I was concerned for you. It must have come as a shock. From what he wrote to me, I understand that his decision was a very recent one."

"Yes. I had no warning. But in many ways I think it was inevitable. Knowing Douglas's altruism, I think it was likely that in Africa he would find the perfect field for action. I shall miss him, naturally, but I would never try to deter him from such a self- fulfilling course."

Seeing Margaret's expression, Elaine had no doubt that her friend spoke from the heart. She felt that her reaction in its unselfishness balanced her husband's self-sacrifice.

The evening slipped by in reminiscing and considering a future that was suddenly unfocussed and unknowable. At Margaret's suggestion they went to bed quite early. Neither had referred to the 'student', but when Margaret was in her own room she quietly planned how best to avoid arousing suspicion as to her true relationship with Antony. With some amusement she planned her opening strategy. Even as she did so, she had a mental picture of their meeting if Elaine were not there. He would leave his cycle where it fell and, smiling, fling his arms around her, before kissing her again and again. No-one watching would be in any doubt about their feelings for each other. She needed to prepare him. She would make sure that he saw her guest first. This decision made, she prepared for bed and slept soundly.

Chapter Nineteen

Sunday was warm and sunny. One of those days when the world outside beckons and uses all its tricks to draw one out. The ears are wooed by bird-song and the eyes seduced by flowers whose fragrance delights the senses. Margaret decided they would have drinks before lunch in the garden.

"Whilst I take the chairs out, will you be ready to answer the door when the 'student' arrives?" she asked Elaine.

"Certainly. If you're sure you don't need my help."

"I can manage, thanks. Take the opportunity to read the paper - it's in the sitting room."

It was about 12.40.p.m. Antony was due to arrive at 1pm. After putting out the chairs, she arranged glasses on a tray in the kitchen and put various bottles ready. She had set the table in the dining room earlier, but wandered in to check that she had forgotten nothing. A ray of sunlight back-lit the beautiful white flowers placed as a centre-piece on the table. She touched them briefly, acknowledging her pleasure in them as tokens of love.

Five minutes before he was due to arrive, she went upstairs. She ran a comb through her hair, sprayed on some perfume and contemplated her appearance in the full length mirror. She wore a simple pink linen dress. It was difficult to relax. She was longing to see him. Ah, yes. That was *le mot juste*. She heard bird-song through the open window that over looked the garden and then the quiet purr of a bicycle free-wheeling up the drive. She smiled waiting for him to knock. The door was furnished with a large cast-iron knocker. As she lingered upstairs she reflected on how people revealed their characters by the way they knocked. She hated the peremptory, unnecessarily loud, knocks, and even more the rapid burst of knocks that one of her acquaintances employed, as if to say, "I am important- waste no time- open the door at once." Antony gave two knocks, the quiet controlled action of the supremely polite. Elaine seemed to be in no hurry to open the door. Margaret listened wondering if she had not heard or moved elsewhere perhaps into the garden. Then the front door was opened. Antony spoke after a short delay.

"Hello. I'm Antony Lodge. I – er – was invited to lunch."

His beautiful voice revealed no surprise or embarrassment, although the slight hesitation suggested a sort of modest diffidence. There was a pause. Margaret wished she could see Elaine's expression.

"I'm Elaine, please come in. You are expected."

Margaret forced herself not to rush, not to run downstairs, not to smile too broadly. She heard them go into the sitting room and listened at the turn of the stairs to their voices. She breathed deeply, trying to calm her dancing heart, then descended, crossed the hall and through the open door, saw him. She had forgotten how elegant he always was. He wore an expensive, light wool jacket and beautifully pressed trousers that draped elegantly on to his highly polished, brown leather shoes. He rose and stepped towards her. She held out her hand which he took, squeezed briefly, then released.

"Antony, I'm so glad you were able to come. I see you've met Elaine, a very dear friend of mine." She turned to where

178

Elaine sat but avoided her eyes. "As it's such a lovely day, I thought we'd have drinks in the garden. I've put some chairs out all ready. Now, if you would care to go out, I'll fetch the drinks. Would you like wine or gin and tonic, Elaine? And what about you, Antony?"

They both chose gin and tonic. Margaret led the way through the conservatory and indicated the chairs and table on the lawn nearest the house.

"I'll be with you in a moment."

"May I help?" Antony asked.

"Thank you. You can pour whilst I find some ice and lemons."

"And I'll act the lady of leisure and go and sit in the garden," said Elaine with a smile.

They moved into the kitchen.

"It seems ages since I saw you," he murmured.

"I only learned yesterday that Elaine was coming. I thought of cancelling the lunch. I wondered how I could get in touch with you - never an easy thing to do at the last minute. Then I couldn't bear not to see you and thought we'd brazen it out. I told her the lunch was to celebrate the completion of finals."

"Right. And am I allowed a celebratory kiss?"

Smiling, they moved together and their lips met in a long lingering kiss. Antony was the first to pull away.

"I've missed you so much," he said softly, his hands holding her upper arms. Then he kissed her forehead and stepped back. "You were right about our separating for a while. I could never have concentrated properly if I had been thinking all the time of our next meeting."

"That's what I thought!" she said. "Now let's get the drinks." They started the ritual of combining ice, lemon, gin and tonic.

He carried the tray into the garden, where Elaine sat at an iron table. She faced the lily pond, her back to the house

"That's a welcome sight," she said, "Thank you."

"I've brought a few nuts and tit-bits," Margaret offered. "First of all though, "Here's to the end of exams, and best of luck, Antony, on the results."

"Yes, indeed. Here's to a good degree!" Elaine said raising her glass.

"Thank you, ladies," he replied, smiling. "I couldn't celebrate in better company!"

They sipped the ice cold delicious drinks, a cooling, perfect choice for the warm sunny day.

"How were the papers?" Margaret asked.

"They were less difficult than I had feared and I had been able to cram in a lot of revision." He glanced at Margaret. "Your advice helped enormously. I just put everything on hold and lived and breathed Chemistry."

"Chemistry?" Elaine asked. "Is that your subject?"

"Yes." He wondered why she seemed surprised. He noticed her quick glance at Margaret.

"And now it is time for me to thank you for the superb flowers. They are absolutely wonderful and we had great fun arranging them. There are vases of flowers all over the house. I must show them to you later."

"I'm glad you liked them. I got rather carried away at the florist's. I just let the lady choose what she thought appropriate and I couldn't bear to reject any of the 'blooms' as she called them to make a less exotic offering."

She laughed, "I loved them. Thank you again."

"My pleasure," he said with a dazzling smile.

"That florist has a wonderful colour sense. And blue and white flowers are my favourites and the touches of yellow and pink are so pretty," Margaret enthused.

"Yes. I thought so." He did not mention that the choice of colours had been his, nor that it had been based on the decoration of her drawing room. Perhaps Elaine might have been led to think that this was his first visit to the house, he was not going to disabuse her. He wondered if his presence there had been adequately explained to her. Obviously she had known when she opened the door that he was expected for lunch. He tried to guess what reason might have been given for his being invited. He looked at Margaret, hoping for a clue. She looked amused as if enjoying a private joke. All he could do, he thought, was to be as non-committal as possible. He realized Elaine had asked him a question.

"Did you say you were reading Chemistry?"

"Yes, although there were times in the last three years when I have questioned my choice, even regretted it."

"Really? Why was that?"

"I think my real interests lie in the arts. However at school I opted to take Physics, Maths and Chemistry at A level. So you might say, 'the die was cast'."

"Ah, yes, it's not an unusual story," Elaine sympathised. "It would be so much better if a student's options could be kept open longer. They should be allowed to study a much wider range of subjects at a higher level. In your case Foreign Languages perhaps and History and Latin as well as Maths and Sciences."

"Yes, in fact you can't read English Literature without Latin in many universities. And that subject would have been an ideal choice for you." Margaret spoke as a tutor might. He began to feel very much the young student being advised by his elders.

Yet it was quite entertaining, like playing a game, or acting in a play. Margaret's obvious amusement did not quite fit a tutor's role, but Elaine's sympathy seemed genuine.

They continued to chat about various career openings and the sacrifices each had made in making their final choices. Antony was surprised that Margaret regretted giving up Maths - she had never mentioned this to him. In the next thought, however, he realised there was a great deal he did not know about her. Elaine's wish to have been a veterinary surgeon he could understand. There was something kind, practical and humane about her. She seemed to him much more down to earth than Margaret who was primarily an intellectual.

"Why didn't you become a Vet?" he asked with genuine interest.

Elaine smiled rather bitterly. "Where do you want me to start? First I was educated at a girls' school where Sciences were neglected. I did not have even the basic qualifications. I wrote to various Veterinary Colleges for advice and it was quite obvious in their replies that even had I obtained the necessary qualifications by further study, as a woman I would be at a grave disadvantage. Probably I would never be accepted to pursue such a course, which incidentally, they always pointed out, was extremely long and arduous, and even if I succeeded in becoming a qualified Vet., as a woman I would find the job difficult and employment unlikely."

They were silent. Margaret of course knew what Elaine's ambition had been, but she was moved by her succinct account of the obstacles that had prevented her from fulfilling her dream. Full of sympathy, Antony now regretted asking the question. He felt it had been intrusive.

"I'm so sorry..." he began.

"Don't worry. I'm over it."

Trying to lighten the atmosphere and able to joke about even her serious concerns, Margaret said, "And I wanted to be a writer!"

"Well you can be!" Elaine spoke with some exasperation.

"Ah, but you see I'm so lazy, so easily distracted and too self critical to fulfil my dream." She grinned at her friend. "But I'm not too lazy to refill your glasses. And, meanwhile, you should ask Antony what he would like to be."

He waited, uncomfortably aware that Elaine was watching him. She said nothing. She was certainly not going to question this courteous young man on a whim of Margaret's whose behaviour was worrying. Her edginess was possibly a reaction to Douglas's decision. She invariably found relief from tension in joking or mischief-making.

"Another drink will be very acceptable, I think. Don't you agree, Antony?"

"Definitely," he replied, relieved she was ignoring Margaret's suggestion.

Only two glasses were on the tray when she returned.

"I hope you can amuse yourselves whilst I finish off in the kitchen. Lunch will be in about ten minutes."

Although a breeze stirred the top branches of the trees, the multi-coloured lupins that filled a long raised bed nearby, remained undisturbed.

"I love massed flowers," Elaine remarked. "I think Margaret raised those from seed. Isn't it a splendid idea to grow so many together like that?"

"They look terrific," he agreed.

Soon they were summoned in to lunch and ushered into a small dining room that Antony had never seen before. The walls were papered in plain dark red, a colour echoed in the round table-mats on the polished mahogany table. White flowers beautifully arranged in a cut glass vase supplied the centre-piece. White china, white linen napkins and silver cutlery were set on three sides of the table.

"Will you pour the wine, Antony?"

He couldn't help grinning as he dismissed the wish to ask her, "Full to the brim?" which he would not have resisted had they been alone.

Elaine observed his amusement and wondered what was so funny.

She watched him as he moved round the table pouring the wine. He was extremely good-looking and had a natural elegance. What was he doing here with them - or at least with Margaret? Surely someone so attractive would have a girl-friend to spend his Sunday afternoons with? His build and bearing seemed those of a natural athlete. To break the silence and to satisfy her curiosity, she asked, "Are you a sporty person, do you play any games?"

"Yes. I play rugby in Winter and I like tennis. How about you?"

The last words took her by surprise. Most young men would have seized the chance to talk of their prowess on the games field, never thinking that women too might enjoy physical activities. But this young man she realized was unusually sensitive. It seemed to come naturally to him to include everyone equally in the conversation.

"Mostly I enjoy fell-walking these days. I still play the odd game of tennis - but that's about all."

"I love walking in the hills too," he enthused.

Margaret joined them.

"We've just been talking about the games we play," Elaine commented as they began to eat.

"Has Elaine told you she used to play hockey for her county?"

"No. That's excellent. What position did you play?"

"Lord, it seems ages ago. It was school-girl hockey. I used to play right-inner mainly."

"So you were fast?"

"Yes, she was."

"Did you go to the same school?"

"No. Margaret remembers when we were together on the staff of a girls' school and we played against the sixth form."

"And we beat them!" Margaret cried with exaggerated delight.

"So you play rugby?"

"Yes. It was my height that got me involved, but I've never been heavy enough to be a seriously good player. Geoff was always a first rate player," he remarked, glancing at Margaret.

"I can see he would be," she agreed. "Geoff is a good friend of Antony's. They both acted in 'Coriolanus'!"

"Oh, really. I heard it was a brilliant production. A great success. I deeply regret not having seen it, but I couldn't get away. What parts did you play?"

"Geoff played Aufidious and I was Coriolanus."

The statement hung in the air. For Elaine it seemed to clarify several things that had been puzzling her. It was likely a friendship would develop between the actor who played the main part in such a successful production and its director. It explained his being invited to lunch. Even the gift of flowers seemed natural enough in the circumstances. Then unwished for and surfacing slowly in her mind, came a memory of Margaret checking her mascara and laughing. "I'll tell you something funny - one of the cast has a crush on me!" And Elaine knew it must have been Antony.

"They made an impressive pair of warriors! Antony was particularly brilliant and brought the audience to their feet." Margaret smiled at him. "One of the things I wanted to talk to him about today was his future - the possibility of his going to Drama School and becoming an actor."

So she explained his presence at the luncheon.

Although she never professed to be a good cook, in fact Margaret was proficient at producing meals that were both delicious and well presented. After an entree of melon and raspberries there followed roast lamb with mint sauce, new potatoes and an assortment of vegetables. The pudding was apple-pie and cream. Wine flowed freely and as they relaxed the conversation flowed. They talked, not surprisingly, of the theatre, their favourite films, actors they admired and also flops they had seen. Elaine remembered seeing a Carmen whose face, owing to some make-up error, was bright orange. She was also middle-aged and fat but her glorious voice and vivacious acting swept the audience away, so that her appearance became irrelevant.

"I was once in a dilemma at an outdoor production of 'A Midsummer Night's Dream' " said Margaret. "Heavy rain forced us to take shelter. The audience was packed into a large marquee and seated on benches very near the actors. Puck forgot his lines and I knew them. For a while I waited for the prompt to help him out - but he or she had gone missing. I debated with myself on whether to intervene. Finally I called out the next line and the play proceeded. To my great relief Puck wasn't at all put out but blew me a kiss and bowed at the end of the scene and the audience applauded both of us."

"It's your turn now Antony," Elaine suggested. "Have you known any disasters?"

He smiled. "I think the worst, or the best, was when Macbeth's head bounced off the stage in a local school's production. My own worst experience was in 'Julius Caesar' when Brutus and Cassius are quarrelling before the battle. We had rigged up an awning to suggest a tent. Just after Brutus said,

'The name of Cassius honours this corruption
And chastisement doth therefore hide his head.'

the awning collapsed hiding us both. The audience of course loved it. We sort of crawled out and tried to put the awning up again. Then our English master snarled from the wings, "Bloody carry on! Leave the fucking tent!" It made a big impression on us because we had never heard him swear before."

"I know just how he must have felt," Margaret said when she could stop laughing.

When the meal was over, Elaine offered to make coffee which they decided to have in the garden. Margaret and Antony went outside. They sauntered down a path by the far wall of the garden and then crossed to the pond. Its surface was covered by the pads of water-lilies with two or three pink-tinted flowers still in bud rising up out of the water.

"Shall I go soon?" he asked. "You must want sometime alone with Elaine."

"Not really. We've already discussed what she came here about. But it's a bit awkward. She's going tomorrow. Will you be free on Monday evening? And, if so, would you like to come then?"

"Yes." He looked back at the house. "Can she see us here?"

"Not if we go into the orchard."

They passed through an arch-way into the orchard where there was a wooden bench. They sat and immediately his arms were around her and his lips were on hers. He kissed her for a long time and drew her closer. She could hardly breathe. She pushed him away.

"I think we'd better stop. I'd hate us to be observed. Come tomorrow, and," she added in a whisper," stay the night."

He leaned away from her, breathing heavily. He grinned. "That was a bit thoughtless. I've just been so longing to see you."

They heard the rattle of china. Without speaking, they stood and strolled slowly through the orchard, not touching, casually making their way back to the table where Elaine was lifting the cups from the tray. An hour later, Antony left. Elaine watched as he rode his bicycle down the drive. "What a beautiful young man!" she commented when Margaret joined her.

"Yes. He is." There was a finality in these words that Elaine accepted. Margaret was not going to talk about him.

In the evening they sat in the drawing room, always one of the coolest rooms in the house. They chatted for a while then read the papers. As Elaine wanted to leave early the next day, she decided to go to bed at about ten-thirty.

Margaret reread Douglas's letter and thought for a long time about its implications. It was certainly a turning point in her life. His absence she knew would be prolonged. He would never have written such a letter if he intended to remain in Africa for a limited time - a year, for instance, or even five. No, unless some unforeseen event occurred, he would, she believed, spend the rest of his working life there. She shuddered thinking of what his daily struggles there might entail: the gruelling heat, the likelihood of sickness, the emotional strain of trying to relieve suffering on such a scale, the immense effort needed to educate children whose concentration must be impaired by their poor diet, the long distances they would have to walk to reach the school, their frequent illnesses. She pictured him as he might be in a few years' time - gaunt, bearded, his skin burned by the unrelenting sun, thinner certainly. Then she forced herself to remember that he had chosen that life. He would find fulfilment in it. He would be happy.

At last she felt composed enough to go to bed and try to sleep. As sleep came her thoughts drifted to the flowers that adorned her room. Their sweet scent soothed her and she saw again in her imagination Antony's dazzling smile when she had thanked him for them.

Chapter Twenty

After Elaine had gone she filled the morning with necessary household tasks, such as washing the sheets from Elaine's bed, preparing an evening meal to share with Antony and checking the flowers distributed about the house. They looked as beautiful and fresh as they had done yesterday. She carried the yellow roses into the room she now regarded as 'theirs', which she had prepared three days before. She placed them on the dressing-table. The buds were a little more open and emitted a sweet smell that she inhaled appreciatively.

She waited for him in the garden. It was a warm, still afternoon. She had brought out the poetry of John Keats, intending to reread some of his shorter poems whilst she waited. On the table was a bottle of Chardonnay, cooling in an ice-bucket, and two glasses. She became engrossed in the sonnets. Her favourite, she thought, was still 'On the Sea'. She touched the bottle of wine. It was very cold and she was tempted to pour herself a glass. Sipping it slowly, she began to read, 'La Belle Dame Sans Merci.'

> *O, what can ail thee, knight-at-arms*
> *Alone and palely loitering?*

She knew it by heart but enjoyed reading it from the page. Soon she automatically refilled her glass and continued reading. She did not hear Antony's arrival and was startled by his voice.

"I hardly dare to interrupt you," he said, smiling. "You look so engrossed!"

"Sorry. I didn't realise you had arrived."

She rose and walked with him to the garage where he left his bike.

"I hoped you would be in the garden. It's a sort of magical place to me." He kissed her. "You taste of wine and smell delicious."

"Come and have a glass - it's nice and chilled," she said with a smile.

He drank. "It's really good. And, may I say, you look stunning in pale green. That colour emphasises the green of your eyes...if you'll excuse the cliché." He gazed into her eyes with a slight smile on his lips. It was a look of love and longing.

She reached for his hand, needing to touch him. "You'll have to use your left hand to hold your glass, I can't release this one," she said after a while.

"I guess I'll manage." He drank, then added, "You could have provided straws so we would each have had two free hands."

She sipped the wine hoping to cool the feverish ideas his remark had provoked in her. Desire filled her being. When she put down her glass he reached for her waist and pulled her close, kissing her open lips. One of his hands was in her hair. He bent to kiss her throat and her chair tilted backwards. She thought they would fall but he held her with a strength that surprised her. He lifted her and they stood clinging to each other, kissing again and again.

"Let's go inside," she urged.

With arms around each other they moved towards the house. She locked the conservatory door and holding his hand led the way upstairs. Fully clothed they fell on the wide bed. Their lips seemed glued together. Then their hands, at first stroking clothed flesh, began unfastening buttons, hooks, belts and zip-fasteners until they reached warm, soft skin and the road to rapture. Passion devoured them. Neither had known before such a powerful feeling, and if they had no time to recite the poetry of love, all its sweetness was there still, but in a strength that intoxicated them and left no room for words. Later they lay, with limbs entangled and eyes closed in the bliss of oblivion.

Covered by a duvet, half-sleeping, half-waking they gradually realised that the sun had moved further to the west and the room was in shadow. Antony raised himself to lean on one elbow.

"Have you noticed the time?" he asked.

"What has time to do with us?" she sleepily replied.

"Nothing at all."

They lay facing each other for a while. Margaret sighed.

"What is it?"

"I have something to tell you. But not here. Let's get dressed. I'll see you in the study in about fifteen minutes. I'll use the shower in my room. You'll find all you need in there."

The study was as he remembered it. He wandered around, reading the titles of the books on the shelves, occasionally pulling one out and reading scraps of text or looking at the illustrations. Some of the books were familiar to him - even the editions were the ones he owned himself. Other shelves were filled with what he realised were books of literary criticism, like 'Longinus on the Sublime', Aristotle's 'Poetics', 'The Sublime and Beautiful' by Edmund Burke and 'Laocoon' by George Gissing. Seeing these books made him realise for the first time what a vast range of works the study of English Literature entailed. He was impressed. Moving on, he saw what looked like a full set of the Arden edition of Shakespeare's plays, the pale blue hardbacks easily recognised. In the next shelf he saw the poems of Herbert, Donne and other Metaphysicals. Two vast book-cases held novels - Fielding, Dickens, the Brontes, Hardy, Conrad and Meredith. He passed over the modern novels of Waugh, and Virginia Woolf and found himself opposite the old map of the world where Margaret had pointed to Africa and said, "He is there!"

The feeling of disquiet came back, as it always did when he thought of her husband. He tried to dismiss the uncomfortable notion that he was wronging the man. After all Douglas had left voluntarily. He had not been forced to go. He had gone because he wanted to. Antony could not imagine any situation when he would voluntarily leave Margaret. Their recent brief separation had been painful enough, and that had been mutually agreed upon, for a purpose. Also its duration had been fixed and so bearable. It seemed that Douglas might be gone for months. Perhaps that would be all the time he and Margaret would have together. Stoically he would accept the necessity for them to separate on Douglas's return, if it was her wish. Always at the back of his mind he was resigned to that, but it would be like death to him. He knew he would never love anyone else as he loved her. She was his soul-mate, he believed.

He turned as Margaret came through the door. She was smiling and came rapidly to embrace him.

"Sorry to keep you waiting, but I was just doing the last few bits of preparation for supper."

"I love you," he said.

"I know."

She went to the desk in the large square bay-window. From the top drawer she took out the letter she had received from Douglas on Saturday. Her first inclination was to hand it to Antony so that he could read for himself the shattering decision Douglas had made. But it was, she thought, too easy an option. She held the letter for some time before she spoke.

"I received this letter on Saturday. It is from Douglas. He has decided to stay in Africa."

Antony's eyes were fixed on hers. He said nothing.

"He has given up his project on the Nile and has decided to join V.S.O. He will, at their request, set up a school, recruit teachers and educate the children. His motivation is to do what he can to alleviate what he refers to as, 'the desperate situation the people there find themselves in.' " She stopped. Still Antony said nothing. He stared at her for a long time. A frown deepened between his brows.

"This is my fault," he said so softly she could hardly hear his words.

"What? Why do you say that?"

"Guilt. Did he know about me?"

"I don't think he did."

"You never spoke about . . ."

"No. And yet there was something in his letter that made me wonder."

Unnaturally still, he continued to gaze at her, waiting.

"It was in the last part of the letter." She looked at it and then read, " 'In the weeks before I left, I believe you were troubled by something deeply personal, that you had no wish to share with me.' That's all - as vague as that."

He considered this for a while. "I don't want to pry, but was there something worrying you then, that he would register?"

"I've been wondering what he could have meant. Maybe he thought it was my writing going badly- which it was. I never discussed that with him, but I certainly never enthused about it."

"I'm so very sorry. You must have been shocked by this news."

She merely nodded. 'So,' Antony thought, hating himself for so quickly allowing such an idea to come into his mind, 'he has left the field clear for me.' He wondered how upset she was. Would she regard this as a permanent separation? Would she divorce Douglas? Would she join him in Africa?

Suddenly the room felt claustrophobic. He wanted to get out into the fresh air. He stood. "Can we go outside? Go for a walk or something?"

"Let's take the car."

'Obviously she fears we might be seen,' he thought. Then on consideration he accepted that it was sensible not to set tongues wagging yet.

She drove fast, as if she wanted to escape the thoughts and doubts that were filling her mind.

About ten miles north of the village was an area of open woodland. She drew in to an open space at the side of the road and got out of the car. He followed. The air was cool. They took the widest of the paths that led into the wood, walking side by side, not talking. They came to a place where a stream crossed the path and stepping stones had to be negotiated. After glancing at her sandals, he took her hand to help her balance and did not let it go when she was safely on the path again. They walked more slowly now. He looked into the distance.

"I had thought we would have drifted on for a while, getting to know each other, coming gradually to a realisation of what we would do with our lives. Now suddenly, everything has accelerated. I feel both stunned and excited. It seems that obstacles are being cleared away for us - and yet I am afraid to hope too much." He broke off and drew her close. He could feel her tremble.

"Are you cold?"

"Yes. A little."

He took off his jacket and placed it round her shoulders. He laughed.

"Now, after urging you to come for a walk, I want us to go back. I want to hold you while we talk."

It was almost dark when they reached the lay-by. She switched on the headlights and turned the car. Lit up, the leafy branches looked like a stage-set. She glanced at her companion and simultaneously remembered an almost forgotten dream. She shuddered.

"What is it?" he asked.

She switched off the engine. "I called out your name," she said.

"When?"

"Oh, God," she murmured, "he knew."

She stared unseeing out of the window. Baffled Antony tried to read her expression in the dim light. She looked horrified and then unutterably sad.

'What a strange reversal,' she thought. With Douglas she had wept for Antony; now with Antony the tears came for Douglas. But it was not the same emotion. In the dream she had ached with longing for Antony, now she grieved guiltily for Douglas. Noble and generous he had written, 'take particularly your freedom with my blessing.' She surreptitiously wiped away a tear, hoping he would not see the gesture. Of course he did.

"Let me drive you home. You shouldn't be sitting here in the cold."

He got out of the car and moved round to her door. He helped her out and with his arm around her, took her to the passenger seat. He tucked his jacket around her and kissed her forehead as if she were a young child desperately in need of comfort. He drove them, then, back to her house.

A delicious savoury smell greeted them as they entered the conservatory and they realised how hungry they were. The slow oven of the Aga had fulfilled its purpose. The meal, a chicken casserole, seemed perfect to them. Margaret's gloom diminished and, as she looked more cheerful, Antony's spirits rose.

"I'm sorry about that," she said referring to her anguish in the car. "I suddenly remembered something. I think Douglas might have heard me saying your name, when I thought he was . . . wasn't listening."

Antony looked uneasy. She had avoided saying 'asleep', as if he didn't know, only too well, that she would have been sharing a bed with her husband.

She continued, "I used to have nightmares, and sometimes I would wake up, calling out . . . various things. One night I dreamed I was driving through a forest. It was so beautiful, quite magical, and in the dream I believed you were there with me in the car. When I looked for you, the whole scene melted away and you with it. I felt utterly bereft. I called out your name and woke up weeping."

"I've brought you a lot of grief. I'm so sorry."

"No, don't say that. I had those dreams because I was in denial. I wouldn't accept that I'd fallen in love with you. I am the guilty one."

He shook his head. "You tried to put a stop to it. I didn't."

She remembered how he had pleaded with her, on that icy cold night, to admit she loved him. She remembered their first kiss and even then she had told him there could be no future in a relationship between them.

"I was unkind. I thought feelings could be switched off at will. And I suffered for it."

They sat in silence, each remembering the months apart from each other.

In denial, Margaret had persisted with her novel, creating an arid portrait of a narrow society given over to clever witticisms and immoral affairs. She had become more and more dispirited. What did such writing say about its author? She wondered if she was as empty as her characters. Her spirit cried out against the vacuous society she had created. Perhaps it was based on reality - but she had selected the parts of it she would portray. Self disgust finally forced her to stop writing it. Freed from its demands on her time, she was able to look outward, to interact more with her students and colleagues. However, one painful encounter, she remembered vividly. She was in the Senior Common Room sometime in March when Miles Radford joined her. They had become friends, each quietly admiring the other's talents. In fact she had bought one of Miles's paintings at his last exhibition. Suddenly, not prompted by anything in their conversation, Miles had commented, "Your noble Coriolanus character is becoming pretty obnoxious."

"What?" Margaret's horror surprised him.

"Well, perhaps I'm exaggerating but one or two of us in the Maths and Science Departments have been rather surprised by his behaviour recently. He's been obviously drunk on a few occasions and involved in a lot of rows with other students. He's also going out with a rather unpleasant girl."

"I can't believe it. That sounds so unlikely. He was always so very polite and controlled."

"Maybe he was missing the self-importance or adulation that the play gave him."

Margaret remembered sitting there, warming her hands on her cup of coffee, deep in thought. "I don't think that would be the reason."

"Perhaps you should have a word with him. You used to be pretty close, didn't you?" Miles suggested innocently.

"I never see him, and I don't think he would appreciate any advice from me."

She dreaded meeting Antony almost as much as she wanted to see him again. She had not found it as easy as she had expected to put him out of her mind. Fortunately their subjects kept them in quite different areas. She never entered the Science Block and he had no reason to visit her department in the Arts Block. She was certainly not going to seek him out. But adamant as she was in this decision, she could not help wishing that, perhaps one day, soon, they might meet by chance, walking across the quadrangle or entering the library. This did not happen.

Her life became solitary. Douglas had left for Africa and she had given up writing her novel. Unwished for, her memories of Antony grew more vivid. Miles's comments had led her to imagine him involved in bizarre acts of drunken violence. As for the girl. Who was she?

Antony, sitting at the other end of the room, considered how badly he had reacted to her rejection. He tried not to think of how stupidly he had behaved but his memories of regularly getting drunk persisted - and what that led to. He felt Susan was as responsible as he was for their sordid affair but he could not throw off his feeling of guilt. He should have behaved better. Also Douglas had been betrayed and he was to blame.

Margaret was unhappy, and, although she wished to take on all the guilt of their affair, he feared she would feel less for him and regret ever having met him, as she now realised the result. He sighed. He wanted to comfort her but did not know what to say. He rose and went to her where she sat near the window.

"What are you thinking?" he spoke softly and drew her towards the sofa.

"I was remembering how I missed you."

"It was a dreadful time for me. I behaved like an idiot," he admitted.

She smiled. "And then miraculously, we met at the Ball. You were with Geoff Sloan. I saw him first and he welcomed me like an old friend." She paused, remembering how Antony had turned and looked at her. She had forgotten just how handsome he was, how dangerously attractive.

"That was the happiest hour of my life. I had gone to the Ball, hoping to catch a glimpse of you. But when you came and spoke to us, I was so shocked and yet so deliriously happy, I could not speak."

"You soon recovered."

"Well, Geoff helped. If he hadn't been there to invite you to stay with us and have a drink, you might have left, thinking I was an imbecile."

"A very handsome imbecile!" she joked, stroking his cheek. "I wonder, did we fall in love again that night? Or was it just a reawakening?"

"I never stopped loving you!"

She smiled. "But there was a girl," she teased.

He frowned, embarrassed and annoyed. The memory was still painful. He hoped Margaret would have forgotten her, regarded her as too unimportant ever to mention. He was filled with chagrin and believed there was nothing he could ever say that would adequately express his regret and shame. Perhaps a brief, even blunt statement of his present view of her would be the least damaging course.

"She meant nothing to me," he said coldly. The words of course condemned rather than exonerated his behaviour. Was there any way he could make her understand? He wasn't going to explain his behaviour as being the result of his misery at her rejection. That was too pitiful and weak. He would offer no excuse, for basically there was none.

"I'm sorry. I shouldn't have teased you like that."

"I just can't stand the thought of her. I'm so ashamed of my behaviour."

"Let's say no more. We are neither of us blameless."

She kissed him tenderly on the cheek and for a while they sat side by side in the dimly lit room.

"This is my favourite room," he said, looking round at the laden book-shelves. "It makes me realise what a tremendous amount of reading English students have to do. Have you really read all these books?"

"That's a pretty naive question. The answer is, only in part. You find what you need in a book and leave the rest. But having them here means I can always go back to them and find new things."

"I wish I'd read English!"

She smiled.

"The great thing is that it's a subject anyone can take up - at any time - unlike Maths or Physics or your own subject, where it would be very difficult to progress without tuition."

"Yes. I suppose so. And you could always blow yourself up in a lab. if there were no Chemistry guru to put you right."

She laughed.

"Have you got Chemist's hands?" she asked. "You know - able to pick up hot things, and stained with chemicals?"

He held out his hands for her inspection and when she touched them, jerked back as if her fingers were red-hot.

"You've singed me!" he cried.

"Wait till I get you in bed, I'll do more than singe you!"

"Yes, please!"

Chapter Twenty One

The next morning, after breakfast, Antony could no longer suppress the fear that had been gaining more and more strength in his mind.

"I have a question that I must ask you," he began. "I don't want to hurry you, or press you to make a decision. In fact I don't need or expect any answer at once. I just have to let you know what I'm constantly thinking about."

His troubled expression and restless movements, as well as the rather confused build-up to what he wanted to ask, puzzled her.

"Just ask your question and I'll try to give you an answer."

"Ever since you told me that Douglas intended to stay in Africa, I have wondered whether you would join him there. Will you go to Africa?"

"No!" Her answer was delivered with explosive force.

He felt he could breathe again. There was no doubting her sincerity. The one word gave him back his life.

"Oh, thank God," he murmured.

She laughed. "I can't believe you would dream that I was likely to play the loyal wife and give up everything here that I value to do that. I would loathe the life Douglas has chosen. I admire his altruism but I know myself well enough to be sure that I could not stand that life for a week, never mind a life-time.

I'm not the self-sacrificing type. I couldn't endure the conditions. Just the flies would drive me berserk. And as for giving up teaching at degree level for the elementary education needed there – that I would not contemplate."

She paused and reached across the table for his hand and said simply, "Also I could not bear to leave you."

He squeezed her hand. "Thank you for saying that."

Antony knew his parents were expecting him to go home when the term ended and he felt obliged to do so. Recently so much had happened to complicate his life that it felt strange to be going back to the world of his childhood and adolescence. His parents knew nothing of what was the most important aspect of his life, his relationship with Margaret. He wanted to tell them about her, but, always, when he had almost decided to do this, he was filled with misgiving. He wondered if he should avoid, at first, telling them she was married, and wait before revealing this until they got to know her and like her. But would Margaret agree to such a deception? He would not lie and introduce her as a student, yet when they learned she was a lecturer, they would at once be curious as to her age. She looked young, but he knew she would never pretend to be younger than she was. She was right to be uncompromising. In the turmoil of trying to decide what to do, he clung to the essential facts about her, for he loved her exactly as she was. His parents must accept her or not; she was his choice.

During the days he stayed with her, they talked at great length about his future career. She was convinced that he would have no difficulty in being accepted by a prestigious drama school, but he had as yet not fully committed himself to a life in the theatre.

"I remember you as Coriolanus. You can't tell me that that performance meant nothing more to you than a passing success in an amateur production of a University Drama Group."

He said nothing so she continued. "You are very talented you know. Not everybody can mimic accents as you can. And you understand difficult texts. Also you can express your thoughts without uttering a word by your facial expressions alone. You would do very well as an actor."

"Don't you think there is an element of luck in achieving anything on the stage?" he asked.

"Of course there is. But you ought to try."

She remembered how mesmerising she had found him as she watched night after night at the rehearsals and saw the sometimes minute alterations and then the great leaps forward he made in seizing the role and making it his own. The rest of the cast seemed engrossed by his performance and tried to follow where his inspiration led.

He sat now deep in thought. She wondered what was holding him back. Months ago when they had first spoken about acting as a potential career, in general terms, he had seemed to dismiss it as a trivial occupation. Was he, because of a high seriousness, temperamentally unfitted for such a way of life? She had only to recall the times of uncontrollable laughter they had shared to dismiss this idea.

"Are you afraid of becoming a 'heart-throb'?" she asked suddenly.

At once his solemn expression vanished as he laughed.

"I think you might be in danger," she continued, smiling. "You won't have to get your teeth fixed – they are perfect. You won't have to get your nose straightened, ditto. You are tall – so no leading lady is likely to tower over you. You move well. You look athletic. Your eyes are dazzling." She laughed. "And if you can't get a job as an actor, you could earn a living as a male model, with ease."

He found this very funny, thinking of knitting patterns illustrated by pipe-smoking, middle-aged men, cosily dressed in cardigans.

"Don't tell me that acting means nothing to you. Admit that delivering that performance of Coriolanus made you live more fully in an hour than most people do in a year. A gift like yours should not be wasted."

She eventually convinced him. He decided to apply for a place at RADA.

"By the way, why did you not invite your parents down to see 'Coriolanus'?"

"I did, but my father was too involved in some legal business in London to get away and my mother was exhibiting her work in the West Country and had planned to spend some time there with an old friend. So, I played down the importance of the play and, to tell you the truth, my feelings were so involved elsewhere that it didn't matter to me that they missed it."

She gave him a long hard look.

"He nodded. "Yes. It was your fault."

"I was thinking that if they had seen the play, your parents would have been half-way convinced that a career in acting would be a logical outcome. Do they know that Chemistry no longer holds much interest for you?"

"I don't really know."

"I'm going to make some coffee," she announced.

She wanted to be alone to think over an idea that she thought might help him to convince his parents. If they intended, as many parents did, to come and pick him up and transport home all the books and stuff he had accumulated over the years as a student, it was possible she could meet them. He could introduce her as the director of the play in which he had triumphed. She would be in a strong position to reassure them that his decision to become an actor was a sound one.

When she suggested this to him, he frowned. "I'm not keen on that idea. It seems a bit contrived."

"But it is a way for them to meet me. And, who knows? They might like me. I'm not suggesting we tell them about our relationship. It can be left to dawn on them that we are a couple."

He was gratified to hear the word 'couple' applied to them. But what did it mean? Had she resolved to part from Douglas completely? She had never actually said she would do so, although this was implied in her belief that he had gone to Africa for good and in her decision not to join him.

"What do you see for us in the future?" he asked.

"That's rather a strange question. I suppose you are referring to the practicalities of our relationship?"

"Well yes."

"I think that whilst you are at drama school you could regard this as your home and spend weekends here, if you wished, whenever you could. And let the tongues wag if they will!" she added mischievously.

"Would your job be threatened in any way?"

"I think not. Many couples live together these days. It's becoming quite acceptable."

"It's a marvellous thought that I could live here with you."

Chapter Twenty Two

It was two miles from the station to Antony's home. He left his luggage to be picked up later and joyfully set out on the well-known route to Forest Lodge, his parents' house. It was good after the train journey to breathe fresh air and walk at his usual fast pace along the lanes he had known intimately for years. The landscape seemed peopled with his young friends. He could almost hear their shouts in the nearby woods and the crackling of twigs and branches as they made camp fires. He remembered the impatient barking of his setter, Ross, and saw him again in his imagination looking up from the bole of a beech tree, frustrated that he could not climb up to join his young master. Antony sighed and smiled bitterly at the memory. Deliberately he thought of later times when, singing loudly, four or five of them walking abreast would return from the pub, spread across the lane in the dark.

Forest Lodge was on the edge of the village. Built in the 1920s, it was a large white-stuccoed, rambling house set well back from the road. It was beautiful and imposing and after taking it for granted for years, Antony had recently become aware of its unique charm. Three years of living in a hall of residence, however pleasant, and having only one small room of his own, had made him value the spacious home of his childhood. At the wrought-iron gates he paused. The gravelled drive curved past the double garage and east wing of the house to where his mother's Volvo was parked by the front door. He was glad to see it, to know she was in. He had come on a whim, not even phoning to let them know of his intended visit.

He rang the doorbell and waited, wondering where she might be in the house. He guessed she would be in her studio, painting. Her appearance showed he was right. She wore a smock spattered with oil-paint and there was a streak of Prussian Blue on her chin.

"Antony!" she called out, delighted to see him, her arms open wide to embrace him. He held her tightly and kissed her cheek.

"My darling, how wonderful to see you!" she exclaimed. "Gosh, I hope I haven't smeared you with paint." She took off her smock and dropped it on the tiled floor of the porch.

"I hope you don't mind my turning up like this. I thought, as I had so much stuff, I'd make a start getting it home. I've left a couple of bags at the station."

"I'm delighted you're here. So you walked from the station?"

"Yes. I fancied walking after the train journey."

"Come in. Let me look at you." She took his hand and drew him into the hall where she stood facing him. "You look so well. No one would believe you had just taken your Finals. I hope you did some work!"

"Oh, yes. I was a real swot for a while."

"How did they go?"

"OK I think."

"Oh, my dear. It's lovely to have you home. Give me a hug now I'm not covered in oil-paint."

Laughing, he wiped his finger on the blue streak of paint on her chin and showed it to her.

"Oh, that wretched blue gets everywhere."

He put his arms round her and gave her a bear- hug, lifting her off her feet as he did so."

"Idiot, put me down!"

They went through the hall to the kitchen where she put the kettle on.

"What are you painting at the moment?"

"It's a sort of weird picture - an experiment. You can see it later. I think I should have done more rough sketches and planning before I started the painting. It's not going too well. On the other hand, sometimes, after a struggle on the canvas and lots of over-painting, a picture suddenly materialises that quite surprises one."

As they drank from the large mugs she had made the tea in, she looked at him again. He looked different, older or more mature. But above all there was a joyousness about him - a settled happiness that was new. She suspected that he had come to break some news, to tell them something that was important to him, that filled him with some secret delight. If that were so, he seemed in no hurry to tell her what it was.

"Is my father well?"

"Yes. He'll be rather late in getting back tonight, but he's not staying in London, so you will see him."

"Good."

"Would you like to take my car and pick your bags up at the station? I'll get changed and then we can have a real drink before supper."

"Thanks, I'll do that. Are the keys down here?"

"Yes, on the hook."

He took the keys and smiled at her. "See you soon."

He adjusted the seat and the off-side wing mirror of the Volvo and drove to the station. His bags were in the office. The ticket collector had moved them inside to keep them safe.

"Whatever have you got in these bags?" he asked. "They weigh a ton."

"Books," Antony told him.

"I'm glad to hear it. I thought you'd been nicking lead off the church roof."

"You didn't think it was a body then?"

The ticket collector shifted his hat to scratch his head. "Have you finished your schooling, at last?"

"Yes. Three years of it."

"And what was it you were studying?"

"Chemistry."

"Ah." His thoughts on this, if there were any, he kept to himself. "There's a trolley on the platform," he suggested. "You don't want to be putting your back out for a load of books."

Gratefully, Antony followed his advice and wheeled his books to the car where he heaved them into the boot. As he drove home he anticipated with pleasure the time he would spend with his mother, seeing her latest paintings and hearing recent news of friends. She was an easy person to be with, full of charm and interested, it seemed, in everything one told her. She had changed into an attractive dress, and put on makeup, as if her son's home-coming were that of a favoured guest.

He lugged his books upstairs, had a quick shower, found a clean shirt then ran down the familiar stairs, as he did when a boy, to join his mother. He found her in the kitchen.

"I think we'll have trout for supper, with peas and new potatoes. It will be quick so I can spend more time with you. There's beer in the fridge, or would you like a G and T? That's what I'll have."

"Beer would be good. Shall I get them?"

"Please."

They carried their drinks out to the terrace where they lounged in supreme comfort in the well upholstered garden chairs.

"So you did lots of work for Finals?"

"Yes. I did. I worked really hard and strangely became more interested in it than ever before."

"That's good. Have you done anything about your future yet? Have you had any careers advice, researched opportunities?"

She spoke in a leisurely fashion, as of a subject of general interest. She didn't sound particularly eager for him to get a job. He did not answer for a while, wondering how he should break the news. As far as he was concerned his Chemistry Degree, which he was now confident of obtaining, would be a useless piece of paper. He had no intention of spending his life in a laboratory.

"One of the reasons I came home early was to tell you I don't want to make a career in Chemistry; I want to go to Drama School. I want to do something creative - like acting."

He felt his statement was rather blunt. He had meant to describe how exciting and fulfilling he found acting. He had meant to tell his parents about 'Coriolanus' and how enriching taking part in such a production had been. He wanted them to know what Margaret thought and to try to tell them about her ability as a director and about her knowledge and skill. Her belief in his abilities had played a big part in his decision, but he found it difficult to speak of this.

"You want to be an actor?" She smiled. "Goodness. That's quite a surprise."

"Is it? Remember all those plays I was in at school!"

"Yes. You were always very good."

"At University I was also involved in acting. You actually saw 'The Rivals' in my first year."

"Yes. It was extremely funny. I remember it well."

"But you didn't see 'Coriolanus'. As a production it was in a different league. We had one of the English lecturers as our director. She was superb and taught us all a tremendous amount. It was inspirational. When we performed it, I felt I was truly alive like a vehicle being used to transmit the spirit of Coriolanus as Shakespeare created him. She thinks I could be successful as an actor," he concluded.

As he spoke his features had become lit up. He had the absorbed expression of one who remembered exceptional events and was carried away by his recollections.

"Has this lady a name?"

"She is called Margaret Gerrard."

"Tell me more about her."

How to begin?

"Well, she's young, very clever. She knows a tremendous amount about acting. She's obviously very well read. Her subject, as I said, is English Literature."

"What does she look like?"

He had not expected this question and was struggling to find an answer when he remembered the drawing he had made of her.

"Just a minute," he said, and dashed indoors.

She was rather puzzled, then imagined he would bring out a photograph of the cast and others associated with the play. He returned with a book from which he extracted a piece of card. He handed her the drawing of a young woman.

"This is Margaret," he said in a surprisingly tender voice.

He stood behind her chair as she looked at it.

"Did you draw this?" she asked.

"Yes."

"Is it a good likeness?"

"Pretty good, yes."

"She's very striking. The eyes are beautiful. This must be the best drawing you've ever done. The economy of line and yet the detail . . . I'm impressed."

"You're impressed with the drawing. What do you think of her?"

"Oh, Antony, how can I say? In the drawing she looks very controlled. Maybe it's something to do with the mouth. One wishes she could speak. But the eyes are so alive, and there is a glint there, almost as if she were laughing at a private joke."

She looked up at her son who still gazed at the drawing. He wasn't looking at it with the objective concentration of an artist evaluating his work but rather as a lover who can't take his eyes off the picture of his beloved. She returned the drawing to him.

"Is it because of her that you want to be an actor?"

"No. I'd thought of it before, but she encouraged me to believe it was possible. That is that I could succeed. I had always thought it was a matter of luck or of knowing the right people."

"Did she suggest you should go to Drama School?"

"She thought it would be a good idea."

"So you have felt like this since Christmas?"

"No, not really. It was later when we talked about it."

"But 'Coriolanus' was in December?"

"Yes. We've talked about quite recently."

He wondered if he should tell his mother about his relationship with Margaret. She seemed, as they spoke, to be about to ask him pertinent questions, then, as if out of politeness, veering away from them. He looked at her across

214

the table. Her eyes were on the book that contained the drawing.

"When you came to see us just before Easter you were very miserable. Now you almost glow with satisfaction. I'm so pleased to see you are happy, whether this is to do with your decision about acting or not." So his mother backed away from asking the questions she intuited he was not yet ready to answer. He loved her for her tact and sensitivity.

"Your father and I wondered if you would like us to come and collect the rest of your stuff? We could come on Friday."

"That would be great. I have a bike and trunk and yet more books."

"The Land Rover will cope with them."

"Could you get there in time for a late lunch? There's a village pub that has pretty good food."

"What a good idea!"

"I'll ring them up and book a table for one thirty p.m."

"Can you stay here till Friday and travel back with us?"

"Sorry. I have a few things to do. I'd better go back tomorrow, as I planned."

"Now. Come and see my latest paintings. I've promised six to a gallery that's just opened in Thaxton. I've done four, and I'm struggling with the fifth."

Her studio was upstairs. It was a fairly large room with a big window facing north-east. Its large bookcases were crowded with art books and several piles of art magazines. Racks for unsold paintings and new canvases filled one wall. On their spacious surfaces was an eclectic assortment of ceramics that Caroline had collected for use in still- life works. Tubes of oil-paint lay in plastic trays on a table near her easel and brushes stood in an assortment of jars. The ones she had been using when Antony arrived waited to be cleaned, next to her palette.

Four canvases were propped against the wall under the window. They were sea-scapes, mainly of Scottish shores, depicting windswept clouds over boisterous seas. In two there were lighthouses built on the top of cliffs. The others were of dark-blue seas streaked with purple and green surging towards rocks where white breakers crashed.

Antony admired them, knowing how well they would look in the wide off-white frames his mother usually used.

"And this," she said, "is the one I'm struggling with."

The picture was dominated by a ship's figure-head that reared out of a rough sea. In the background tall cliffs rose behind rocky stacks where broken spars littered the sea's surface."

"Gosh, it's rather macabre."

"I know. It's nightmarish." She laughed. "Shall I scrap it?"

"No. It's powerful stuff. Go on working on it. If it's truly hopeless you can always over-paint it, perhaps using knives - its texture will be interesting."

"By the way, why don't you frame your drawing? I'm sure I have a frame here that would suit - and I have plenty of card for you to cut a mount.

"Oh, I don't know. I've never shown it to anybody, except you. It was never meant to be displayed."

"Hasn't she seen it?"

"No."

This seemed to perplex his mother. She picked up the book that enclosed the drawing and said, "I'd like another look at it, if I may."

She stayed in her studio, ostensibly to clean her brushes, and he went to his room to unpack his books. He soon filled the empty shelves and decided to store the Chemistry text books in cardboard boxes that he found in the cellar. He spent some time rummaging through drawers and then idly glanced at the framed school photographs on the walls. As he moved from one to another, he realized he hadn't really looked at them for years. There were two photographs of the whole school taken when he was in the fifth and sixth forms and several of cricket teams with everyone dressed in whites, holding their bats. Many of the same boys were also in the rugby photographs. He looked for his particular friends, and was amused at how young and vulnerable many of them looked. Some of the photographs were five or six years old. He laughed to see himself looking so lanky and thin - why on earth he was in the rugby team he could not imagine. Geoff looked good sitting in the centre of the front row as captain.

He removed the photographs from the walls and put them in the bottom of the wardrobe, out of sight. The walls looked strangely empty and seemed to be crying out for pictures, a need, which in such a house could easily be filled. He went to his mother's studio. The door was open he saw that she was busy at a large table.

"I've taken down those old school photographs and the walls look pretty bare - have you any paintings I could borrow to fill the spaces?"

"Certainly. Choose what you like from the rack, there."

"As he moved across the room, he saw she was putting together a small picture. It was his drawing of Margaret, now surrounded by a dark green mount and she was fitting it into a narrow black wooden frame. She held it up.

"Doesn't it look splendid?"

It was a shock to see his secret drawing of Margaret framed. She saw his discomfort.

"Oh, dear. I'm sorry. I think I've blundered."

"No, it's all right. I was just surprised to see it like that."

"I'll dismantle it."

"No. It looks very good - much better framed."

He took the picture from her and saw how the small drawing had taken on a power and importance it had never had in his eyes before.

"Are you sure you don't want to go to Art School, rather than become an actor?" she joked, hoping to lighten the atmosphere.

He laughed ruefully and went on gazing at the drawing.

"She means a lot to you doesn't she?"

He nodded. It was tempting to tell her about his relationship with Margaret. It would be so easy but he really wanted them to meet first. The possibility of a meeting seemed more likely now that he knew his parents would be coming to Covlington to help him with his luggage. He decided to ring Margaret that night and arrange a way of introducing them to each other.

His mother started to pull various paintings from the rack and prop them up for him to choose what he wished to hang in his room.

"Take what you want. I'm going downstairs. Your father will be home soon."

He chose three pictures. Two he remembered seeing before that he had particularly liked. The third a new one that his mother had been working on during his last visit. It was based on Yeats' 'The Song of Wandering Aengus'. It was mysterious and fascinating. It had been his mother's intention to paint a series illustrating the poem. He wondered if she had done so.

He carried his choices to his room and tried to utilise some of the hooks where the photographs had hung. He liked the paintings immensely and would adjust the position of the hooks later, when he had more time. He heard a car approaching the house and watched from the window his father's Saab

218

sweeping round the curve in the drive. From the top of the stairs he heard his mother greet his father and saw her in the hall below reach up to kiss him.

"Robert, guess what, Antony is home!"

His father looked over her head to see his son descending the stairs and, with one arm round Caroline, held out the other to shake his son's hand.

"Welcome. We weren't expecting to see you for a few days. What brings you home, today?"

"I came on a whim, and also to start getting my stuff home."

"It's good to see you."

Later, after the evening meal, Robert asked his son to accompany him on a walk round the garden.

"It's still light enough to see where we are going and I feel the need for some fresh air."

They walked across the extensive lawn and followed a path through rhododendron bushes into a copse where silver birches predominated. It was darker here. Robert slowed down and looked at Antony.

"From your unusual taciturnity, I am beginning to think you have something on your mind. What is it? Do you think you've flunked your Finals?"

"I hope not." Antony was amused at his father's use of the American term 'flunked'. "Actually, I worked pretty hard. I'm sure I did enough to pass."

"I hope you do not use the word 'pass' to indicate you might scrape a third."

"That was not my intention. I just wanted to say that I do not believe I have failed."

They walked on. Antony waited for the next question. His father glanced at him. "You know I never have understood why you chose to read Chemistry. Your interests never seemed to lie in that direction. What are you plans now?"

Antony could not believe his luck. His father had given him the ideal opening and, strangely, even encouragement to admit how he wanted to change the direction of his career. "You are right. I made a mistake. I've known almost since I started the course that I'd made a wrong choice. I contemplated giving it up, or changing my subject, but I couldn't see a way out. So I stuck to it,"

"I admire that. It takes courage to follow a path that no longer seems the right one. The question is what do you wish to do now? There are opportunities in Law where a science background could be advantageous. Have you thought of taking a two-year conversion course? Your acceptance in such a course, however, would depend on your achieving a good degree."

As Antony listened, he felt deeply moved and grateful. His father's calm acceptance and understanding of the situation was more than he deserved. He was so wise and, unbelievably, had already produced a possible and very acceptable solution to the dilemma that he believed his son found himself in. He was reminded of the parable of the prodigal son who, expecting condemnation is forgiven and welcomed home.

"Thank you, father, for your understanding. Had I not a very different career in mind, I should have been delighted to follow your advice and take up Law. As it is I have set my heart on a career that you may find difficulty in accepting. I want to be an actor."

Antony waited, expecting an explosion, even from such a controlled man as his father.

"I know such a choice is unlikely to meet with your approval. I have, believe me, considered it carefully. I accept it is a precarious profession, in which many fail, or live from hand to mouth. But I want to try. I believe I can succeed."

Robert considered his son's words. "What makes you think you can succeed in this?"

It was not easy to answer this question without appearing to boast.

"It was taking the leading part in 'Coriolanus'. The play was an acknowledged success. The director, a lecturer in English Literature, told me I should take up acting. She believed I had talents that should not be wasted. She suggested I should go to drama school."

"And you believed her? You think you should follow this person's advice?"

"It is what I personally want to do."

They had by this time emerged from the trees and begun to cross the lawn towards the house.

"What is the length of a course at a drama school? And what qualification do you work for?"

"I don't really know how long the course is. It is a very recent decision. I intend to make enquiries."

They re-entered the house and joined Caroline in the drawing room.

"Has Antony told you that he wants to take up acting?" Robert asked his wife. His voice expressed neither approval nor opposition.

"Yes," she replied, looking from one to the other. "I believe we missed a very important event in his life. He has described the great success they achieved with 'Coriolanus'. If only we had seen it. I know we were both very involved with our own careers but it was unforgivable not to cancel our own arrangements to see him perform in that play. At least one of us should have gone."

"Oh, please, don't blame yourself," Antony urged. "It might have been a flop!"

"Somehow, from what you have said about Margaret Gerrard, there was never any doubt about its being a success."

"Who's Margaret Gerrard?"

"She was our director."

"I see, and she is the one who believes you should become an actor?"

"Yes."

Caroline reached across to touch her son's arm. Speaking softly she asked, "Will you show Robert your drawing?"

His mother could never keep anything from her husband so this was not a totally unexpected request, although embarrassing. He got up. "OK. I'll fetch it." He left the room and they heard him run up the stairs.

It was on the tip of Caroline's tongue to reveal her suspicion that Antony was in love with Margaret, but she resisted the impulse and waited for him to return. Before he did so, he had imprinted a kiss on the lips of the portrait, but that would definitely remain a secret.

He handed the picture to his father and returned to his place on the sofa next to Caroline.

Robert had not known what to expect. It seemed rather bizarre to be looking at his son's drawing of a lecturer who had happened to produce a play, and, also odd that Caroline should have asked Antony to show it to him.

"I think that is the best drawing he has ever done!" she said. "That is why I wanted you to see it."

Antony watched his father as he examined the drawing. He could see that he was impressed. He raised his eyebrows fractionally and looked at his son. What he saw in Antony's expression, he kept to himself. At last he spoke.

"It is a very accomplished drawing. Did you frame it, my dear?"

"Yes. He was using it as a book-mark. I thought it should be treated with more respect."

"I agree with you."

Antony felt the moment was right to put forward the idea he had discussed with Margaret. "I wonder if you would like to meet her? I believe you are coming to Covlington on Friday. Perhaps we could have lunch with her? She would, if you were interested, perhaps tell you why she thinks I should take up acting."

He spoke with some hesitation. His mother smiled encouragement and nodded her approval. "What a good idea," she said. "I'd enjoy that. Don't you think it's an excellent plan, Robert?"

"I can see it's already as good as decided. Yes. Let's meet her. Can you book a table for us, somewhere decent, where we can talk properly."

Antony rejected the idea of taking them to the pub he had mentioned as a possibility to his mother and decided 'Woolton Park' would be preferable.

"Yes. I know a country house hotel that would be perfect. I'll book a table and invite Mrs Gerrard, tomorrow, to join us."

He realized his slip at once. He had not meant to reveal her marital status yet. It was nervousness that had led to the lapse. He had tried to avoid suggesting his closeness to her before they had met her and so, accidently he had revealed something else that he would have preferred to keep quiet about - that she was married. It was out in the open, now, so, he thought, philosophically, that was one difficulty made clear.

He glanced at his mother. She was looking very thoughtful and slightly disappointed.

"So, she's married. Silly me. I was thinking there was possibly a romance brewing there."

Antony laughed. There was no hiding anything from Caroline, but she would have to wait, for the time-being.

Chapter Twenty Three

Woolton Park, about eight miles from Covlington, once a stately home, had been converted into a hotel about ten years before. Built of stone at the beginning of the nineteenth century, it was a noble building with high-ceilinged, spacious rooms set in pleasant grounds.

"You chose well, Antony. I like this place," Robert said, looking appreciatively at the large, tastefully furnished lounge of the hotel.

They had arrived early as had been his father's intention. His impeccable manners could not countenance a lady, arriving alone, having to wait for them. Earlier the trunk, bicycle, various bags and boxes of books had been stowed in the Land-Rover.

A waiter appeared and took their orders for drinks.

Caroline had been looking at the paintings. She seemed impressed to see they were original oil-paintings; mainly landscapes. Antony half-expected her to go around the room studying them at close-quarters. She resisted the temptation, remarking only on the good taste of the owners.

Antony was nervous waiting for Margaret's arrival. On the telephone two days before, she had seemed pleased that he had arranged the meeting so soon and so conveniently.

"What have you told them about me?" she had asked when he rang her.

"Oh, the usual, that you are a battle-axe and will frighten their socks off!"

"Fool!"

"I told them that you had directed 'Coriolanus' and that you believed I could succeed as an actor."

"Anything else?"

"Not really, but I'm afraid I inadvertently referred to you as Mrs Gerrard. It slipped out. I told them nothing about Douglas being in Africa."

At one-thirty, Antony's restlessness got the better of him. "I'll just pop out and see if she's arrived," he told his parents.

"They know at reception that we are expecting a guest," his father reminded him. "They will show her where we are."

"Right." Although he desperately wanted to go out and greet her, to challenge his father in this seemed unnecessarily rude. He sat down on the edge of an armchair near his father. His mouth was dry. He took a long drink and realized his glass was now empty. His parents had hardly touched their drinks. With a glance Robert summoned the waiter. "Another gin and tonic, please," he indicated Antony's glass, amused at his son's show of nerves.

Five minutes later she arrived. She came with the man from reception, chatting to him easily, and after he had indicated where they were sitting, she smiled her thanks and walked unhurriedly towards them.

The men rose and Antony went to her side. "Hello," he said, "I'm so glad you were able to come, today. I'd like you to meet my parents, my mother, Caroline, and Robert, my father. This is Margaret Gerrard."

The waiter attended them and brought fresh drinks, this time accompanied by a second waiter bearing menus.

"Did you have a pleasant drive here this morning?" Margaret asked. "I saw a huge Land-Rover in the car park. I assume it's yours."

"Yes. It's a good vehicle to have to transport bulky items," Robert glanced at his son, "and also in winter it can deal with most conditions."

Antony wondered if she was comparing it with the much smaller, older vehicle Douglas had had.

"Do you both drive it?"

"Yes. I have to cart paintings about the country. It is invaluable for that. And of course with assisted steering it's not difficult to manoeuvre. You just have to look out for spacious parking spots."

"So, you are an artist?" Margaret asked.

"Yes. Of sorts. Painting keeps me out of mischief."

"We understand you lecture at the University in English Literature," Robert commented. "That must be a fascinating subject to teach."

Margaret warmed to him. "Yes. It is. It's like being able to earn your living by indulging a favourite hobby."

"And you also direct the plays the students put on?"

"Yes. More indulgence!"

"It's jolly hard work, too," Antony interjected.

"Yes. And for the cast," she smiled at him, then turned to his father. "The wonderful thing about students is that they have enormous energy and commitment so working with them, on an enterprise they enjoy, like putting on a play, takes on its own volition and everybody becomes slightly frenzied if not almost mad."

Antony laughed, "Oh, come on, you can't be suggesting that we all went barmy!"

Her expression as she looked at Antony was impenetrable. She was remembering the long rehearsals, her deepening feelings for him, the sleeplessness that she feared impinged on her sanity.

"No, of course not."

"It was a great success, I believe," said Caroline.

"Absolutely. And your son was superb as Coriolanus."

"And it was this performance that suggested to you he should take up acting as a profession?"

"I'm sure you know that he isn't keen to make a career in science."

"Yes," Robert agreed, "we know that. But acting is a risky alternative. As parents we naturally want our son to be happy in his choice of career, but we would not like him to follow a course leading to disappointment and penury. One hears all the time of out of work actors spending their lives washing up in dingy hotels. I have also been thinking of actors going to audition after audition and failing to be chosen for the parts they crave. How does anyone cope with rejection on such a scale and go, full of enthusiasm, to the next audition?"

Margaret herself could have delivered such a speech. She agreed with everything he said.

"It is a precarious profession. However, many actors make good. I believe Antony's talents are exceptional. You would have been convinced of this had you seen him playing Coriolanus."

She paused, watching for the effect of her words on his parents.

"He has the appearance, the voice, the intelligence, the athletic ability that will go far to ensure his success on the stage."

Her tone seemed practical rather than enthusiastic. She felt inhibited talking about Antony to his parents in his presence. She glanced at him. He was looking out of the window, his face expressionless.

A waiter approached to usher them into the dining room. They were shown to a table in a window embrasure. Caroline sat opposite Margaret. She saw her son had achieved a remarkable likeness, in his drawing, particularly in capturing the liveliness and intelligence of her face, expressed particularly in her eyes. What of course he had not been able to suggest was her voice. It was low-pitched and expressive. When she read poetry to her students, Caroline imagined, they would be entranced, seduced by her beautiful enunciation, never wanting her to stop. She saw her turn to address Antony.

"This is a lovely place. Was it your choice?"

"Yes. I'm glad you like it."

For a brief moment, as they exchanged smiles, they seemed to be enclosed in a circle of intimacy and sweetness that excluded even those sitting in close proximity. Caroline felt sure Robert must have noticed how the facade of social correctness, they had until that moment kept intact, had slipped. Her husband, however, was well practised in concealing his thoughts and with polished equanimity he added his own praise of the venue to Margaret's.

They began to speak of the area generally. Margaret told them about the village where the Students' Halls of Residence were situated and of her house there and its garden.

"It's quite a fascinating building, rather quirky in its way. One of the previous owners added several small extensions to the rooms which give it an individuality which I find quite charming."

Listening, as she described the house, Antony wanted to add his own comments on the elegance of the decoration and the many beautiful objects on display. He remained silent, however, and saw how his parents were fascinated by her description of the house. He felt sure they liked her; but then, she could always charm people effortlessly.

As the luncheon proceeded, Antony was relieved and gratified that the food was as excellent as all the other arrangements of the hotel had been. The conversation, enlivened by the well-chosen wines, drifted easily from topics of general interest to the particular concerns of each of the party. Margaret was eager to hear about Caroline's latest paintings particularly the one Antony described as 'macabre'.

"I love painting sea-scapes, but I thought I ought to try something new- hence the floating figure-head."

"You do paint other things. What about those based on 'The Song of Wandering Aengus' by Yeats, that you had just started at Christmas."

"I have almost finished three of those, but it is difficult to achieve the correct balance between telling the story and keeping the magic and mystery. It makes me admire Yeats' work more and more as I struggle to express in paint what he accomplished effortlessly in verse."

"I hope you complete the series, I should love to see them," Margaret enthused. "Yeats is one of my favourite poets."

"Be careful", warned Robert, "she'll be after you to buy them!"

He went on to describe some of the shady deals perpetrated by various painters that he had come across, as if warning Margaret to be on her guard. He was an accomplished raconteur, who could mix wit and instruction with ease, when he had an audience he considered intelligent. Lawyers, Antony thought, had an unfair advantage as conversationalists, furnished as they were daily with the incredible details of their clients' lives. He was glad to see his father was so relaxed in Margaret's company that he would speak so easily and freely.

They had coffee on the terrace and, afterwards, at his father's suggestion, walked in the grounds. They paired off naturally, Robert to walk with Margaret and Antony with his mother.

Walking at a brisk pace, Robert and Margaret soon drew ahead. They walked in silence for a while, both aware this wasn't the time for trivialities. She knew what he would say.

"Now that Antony is out of earshot, I should like to ask you to give me your honest opinion about his taking up acting. Be quite ruthless in what you say. I'd like a cold clear opinion of his chances. I see that you and he are friends and, I wonder if you may be unwittingly more encouraging than he deserves because you like him. Please give me an objective assessment."

"I understand your doubts and hesitation. I know the pitfalls of a career on the stage but I say to you absolutely sincerely that your son is phenomenally good. I have seen him deliver a performance that was better than many professionals at the top of their game could achieve. He has star quality."

Robert was impressed by her words, and felt deep pride in his son. He believed she meant what she said and sensed in her an objectivity he could trust.

"Thank you. I needed my lingering doubts to be obliterated-which you have done." He smiled, "I have enjoyed meeting you, Margaret. I'll support him through Drama School. Then it's up to him."

Antony and his mother sauntered along, admiring the flowers in the well-stocked borders. They watched a red-squirrel climbing jerkily up a vast beech tree and remarked on how tame the birds were in that quiet garden.

"What do you think of her, Mother?" he asked at last.

"I like her immensely. As I think you do."

He smiled. "Is it so obvious?"

"To me? Yes."

They walked on, wondering how much to say or not about the situation that beguiled them both.

"I've been wanting to tell you about her for a while, but there are complications."

He paused.

"You referred to her as Mrs Gerrard. She is married, isn't she?"

"Yes. Douglas, her husband, has gone to Africa. He means to stay there."

"Really? So, he's left her?" She seemed surprised.

"Yes. To all intents and purposes." He was silent, wondering how to explain Douglas's sacrifice. He decided not to try. It was not after all certain that he knew anything of his wife's love for a student. Perhaps her belief that he did was due mainly to her feelings of guilt.

"Why did he go to Africa?"

"He is evidently fascinated by the country and was exploring the area in the upper reaches of the Nile when the plight of the people there caused a change of heart and he gave up his research to join V.S.O.."

"Do you know him personally?"

"I've never met him. I can only tell you what I've heard from Margaret."

"Are you and she in a relationship?"

"Yes."

"How long has it been going on?"

"It started for me almost as soon as I met her. A year ago. But we've been together just since May."

"When you say 'together'?"

"I mean we told each other how we felt. That we loved each other."

Caroline looked into his dark, shining eyes. So, her son, after apparently ignoring girls for years and, as far as she knew, never particularly liking any of them, was now in love with a married woman quite a few years older than himself. It was certainly not an ideal situation. As regards Margaret, herself, she could not dispute that he had chosen well. She was a beautiful woman, full of charm and highly intelligent. But how old was she? How did she come to fall in love with someone so much younger than herself. Perhaps she had found him irresistible in those rehearsals, where his ability had obviously surpassed all her expectations. And yet, apparently, they had waited, after the play, for about five months before declaring themselves. This suggested it was not a passing fancy but something deeper.

His mother's silence began to feel a little uncomfortable. He wondered how he could reassure her. He was about to speak when Caroline, realized how long she had been silent.

"I'm sorry. I am taking too long to answer. I was thinking how you never bothered about girls when you were growing up and, now, suddenly at twenty-one you choose a married woman, who must be at least ten years older than you are. It takes a little time to get used to the idea."

"Yes. I can see it must be a shock to you. I can only say that when I first met her, it was like a revelation. She seemed so special. I wanted to be with her all the time. It was as if the sun shone more brightly when she was there. I knew that to her I was just another student, but gradually a sort of connection grew between us. After the play, I told her I loved her. She said it was an impossible situation and that nothing could come of it.

I kissed her. And she responded. I was deliriously happy and I ignored her ban on our seeing each other again. After Christmas I went to find her and she snubbed me. Her decision had been final. I felt suicidal."

"I remember you came home for a couple of days and you looked dreadful. We were very worried but we wanted to respect your privacy, so we said nothing and waited for you to tell us what was wrong. Did we let you down?"

"No. I let myself down."

"So how did you get together?"

"We met at the Spring Ball and she took pity on me." He smiled. "She took me home. And we became lovers."

So it was out. He felt surprised at his temerity in declaring this to his mother. Yet it seemed such a natural thing to do. Why should he hide the most overpowering event in his life?

The others had turned back and now joined them. It seemed to Margaret that mother and son were sharing, not a joke, but a delicious secret. She was a little taken aback, later, by the warmth of the hug Caroline gave her as she murmured, "It's been delightful meeting you," and kissed her.

Antony took a small bag from the back of the Land-Rover which he carried over to her car. They had told his parents that she would give him a lift back to the village so they could proceed on their journey home straight from the hotel.

Robert asked Antony to go with him into the hotel. First he paid the bill and complimented the staff on the excellent lunch and service.

"I just wanted a quick word, before we go. I want to tell you that I shall be happy to finance your drama course. Margaret has convinced me that you ought to give it a shot."

"Thank you. That is so generous. But I hadn't intended to ask for help. I could find a temporary job and I've managed to save quite a bit of money from your generous allowance."

"Stop! We can afford to support our only son in what he wants to do. And why not spend your savings on a car? I gather you are going to stay down here for a few days?"

"Yes. I need to say goodbye to my tutor and a few friends."

"Right." His father held him in a brief hug, then, together, they went out to join the others.

Robert shook Margaret's hand and thanked her for meeting them.

As the Land-Rover disappeared down the drive, Antony wondered how much of what he had told his mother she would pass on to his father, and what its effect would be. He turned to Margaret. "My father is going to pay for me to go to drama school."

She was silent, looking at him with an expression he could not read. Gone were the smiles that minutes before had been directed at his parents. Her face showed no warmth. Her lips were compressed, her eyes cold. He waited, not moving, feeling an icy chill. At last in a low voice she snarled, "I know. My God, do you know how lucky you are to have such parents?"

He frowned. It was like hearing a sudden false chord in a lyrical song of joy. He felt diminished.

"Sorry. That was not what I meant to say."

"But it's what you think. You see me as a spoilt rich kid, dependent on his parents when at my age I ought to be out there earning my own living."

"They are your words, not mine."

She walked to her car and got in. He looked after her. Embarrassed he saw his bag on the gravel behind her car

235

where he had left it. Angry, yet able to see how ridiculous the situation was, he stood, demeaned, uncertain of what to do. She did not switch on the engine nor did she look at him. He hesitated.   Irritation drove him to action. He walked back into the hotel. He ordered a whisky at the bar. If she waited, he would apologize and everything would be all right. Then, horrified at his behaviour and full of dread, he drank the whisky in one gulp, threw some coins on the bar and ran out.

The car had gone. His bag remained.

Chapter Twenty Four

Furiously he strode over to the bag and kicked it. What an idiot he was. He felt like knocking his head against the stone wall of the hotel, until he saw a nearby gardener was watching him curiously. He slung the bag over his shoulder and stomped off down the long drive. It was eight miles to Covlington. He walked the first three miles at a furious pace, driven by anger at his stupidity. The road wound through farming country. There was little traffic. He was impatient to reach Margaret and began to wish he had 'phoned from the hotel for a taxi. Several tractors passed him.

"Is there a 'phone box near here?" he called to one of the drivers.

"There's one about two miles down the road," was the reply.

He took off his jacket and went on walking.

About a mile further on he heard a great rattling and a filthy van drew up beside him.

"Want a lift?"

A dog stuck its head out of the side window. Beyond the dog he could see a young man, wearing a cap on the back of his head.

"Yes. Thanks a lot."

"Move up, Skip. I can't put him in the back, it's full of sheep. Jump in."

Antony got in and the dog promptly licked his face and leaned against him.

"Where you off to? I'm going as far as Covlington."

"That's great."

"You seemed in a bit of a hurry."

"Yes. I am."

"Got a train to catch?"

"No. I just have to see somebody."

"Oh? Is that right?"

His curiosity amused Antony. He began to relax. It was fair payment for the ride to entertain his deliverer. "I had a row with someone and I want to make it up."

"Lady trouble, eh?" asked the driver, grinning broadly.

Pushing the dog's nose away from his face, Antony smiled, "Yeah."

"They need careful handling, women. Best to take the blame for everything and then give them a kiss. They usually come round."

"Thanks for the advice."

"Skip seems to like you!"

"Yes," said Antony, looking down at the hairs and spittle on his shirt. "He's a friendly dog."

Where a track left the main road, the driver dropped him off. It was about five hundred yards from Margaret's house. He walked slowly down the familiar road. The gates to Margaret's drive were open and her car was parked in front of the house. He hesitated, wondering what sort of a reception he would receive. He was puzzled by her behaviour and angered at his own. It occurred to him that she might be in the garden, but he saw no trace of her there. He went to the door and tapped twice using the iron knocker. As he waited the advice of the young farmer bizarrely came into his mind. It seemed an over simple remedy for what he feared was a complicated situation.

She opened the door. For a while they stood looking at each other. She seemed upset.

"I'm so sorry," he began.

"Sorry I drove off!" she said almost simultaneously.

"I was at fault, I shouldn't have walked off like that!"

She half-smiled. "Come in."

He grinned, "Not until you quote something fitting!"

"Come into the garden, Claude."

"I expected something harsher than that."

"Nothing suggests itself. You look as if you need a shower - right away."

"I know. I got a lift and an over-friendly dog drooled over me for the last couple of miles."

"So you walked most of the way?"

"Yes."

"Go up and have a shower. I'll fetch us a drink."

Her brisk manner suggested he had some explaining to do. He went upstairs and showered.

Later he found her in the study.

"I didn't know what you would like," she explained. "I was trying to decide between tea and Scotch."

"Can we talk first?"

"Certainly." She waited for him to begin.

"I think I got a bit over-wrought today. It meant so much to me that you would like my parents and that they in turn would like you. The whole lunch party I thought had gone so well. And when my father approved of my going to drama school and offered to pay the fees, I was delighted. I believe you convinced him that it was the right thing for me to do." He paused, finding no tactful way of saying that her remark had spoiled the whole thing. "I was surprised when he offered to pay the fees. I told him that I was prepared to get whatever job I could, that I never wanted him to go on supporting me. He insisted."

After this explanation, he broke off, not wishing to repeat the interpretation he had already given to what he thought was her sneering comment.

She looked at him for a long time and then spoke sadly. "You never thought that my reference to your luck in having such parents had a very different and a much worse explanation than the one you gave it?"

"No. It seemed clear enough to me." He looked puzzled.

"What I thought was how much I wished I had had parents like yours. My remark was due to envy. How despicable is that?"

She saw that he was surprised, almost shocked. "I am ashamed that I could say what I did. It had been such a lovely day. I really liked your parents. Your father's generosity was the icing on the cake or if you like the final straw. The memory of my, oh so different, parents just overwhelmed me and I spoke words that I regretted the moment they were out of my mouth!"

"Why did you drive off?"

"Shame. Anger. Stupidity. Take you pick!"

He nodded. "The same feelings made me go back into the hotel."

He did not say that he had gone into the bar, nor did he mention ordering and downing a Scotch. He could not explain his behaviour. It had been an almost automatic reaction to getting upset - just swill down alcohol. Where did such behaviour come from? He knew when it started, but there was no excuse for it now.

"I think we might both have been on edge. After all it isn't everyday one's parents meet the person one loves, and you must have found it exhausting being interrogated."

"They couldn't have been nicer. I like both of them immensely. What came over me I don't know. It was like being slapped in the face by a resurgence of memory - of bad memories. For a while a cloud of such bitterness overwhelmed me. I could only see the contrast between your life and mine. And I hate myself for that. I want only to rejoice for you and your good fortune, not to diminish it."

It was difficult for him to understand fully how the past lived on in her, spreading its poisonous tentacles into the present, for she was outwardly so controlled, apparently so well adjusted. Of course he remembered her brief references to her early years, but their present relevance in her life had not really impressed itself on him. As he considered her explanation, he was forced to realise that her outward polish and control covered a very damaged psyche.

"I'll make some tea," she said and went to the kitchen.

As she waited for the kettle to boil she thought of Douglas and longed for his burly comfortable presence. She wished she could step into his encircling arms where she used to feel so secure. Tears filled her eyes. Blinking furiously, she forced herself to concentrate on setting cups and saucers on a tray, filling a jug with milk and pouring boiling water on the teabags in the teapot. Then she dashed upstairs to her bedroom and locked herself in the bathroom. She examined her face for traces of the tears she was still forcing back. She splashed her eyes with cold water to reduce their redness. She was appalled not only at what she had said but at her own vulnerability.

It won't work, she thought, I have been fooling myself. He is too young, too much the golden boy. I have no right to let him ruin his life with me. Seeing him with his parents, who did not seem much older than she was, had forced her to concentrate on his youthfulness and her own unsuitability. When she had walked with his father in the grounds of Woolton Park, it seemed to her that Robert was more like her contemporary than the father of her lover. She wondered how much his parents had guessed about her relationship with Antony. She had been thinking as she drove back about his mother's warmth as she said goodbye and wondered if Antony had told her about their relationship. She believed he had.

She went into her bedroom and sat before the dressing table. She brushed her hair renewed her lipstick and studied her reflection in the glass. Slowly she rose and went downstairs. She found him standing at the window in the study. He held a book open in his hands but was staring out at the garden, not reading it. For a while from the doorway, she watched him. Soon he would be embarking on a new life, meeting new people; young people of his own age. He ought to go to this new life unhampered by any ties to his recent past. She must release him. She suddenly remembered she had made tea and hurried off to the kitchen. He heard her and turned in time to see her go. He put the book down and followed her.

"Shall we have it here?" she asked, ignoring the way he was scrutinising her face. "It's probably stewed," she added, pouring out the dark liquid into the cups. "Help yourself to milk and sugar."

They sat at the kitchen table drinking the strong dark tea, which wasn't too bad when well-sweetened.

"Are you all right?" he asked quietly.

"I don't know. I feel very unsettled."

"Tell me about it."

"When you go away," she began, "I want you to feel free."

"Free?"

"Yes."

"What do you mean? Free of what?"

"Of me. Of this relationship. I don't want you to feel tied down."

"I can't believe this. I don't want to be 'free'."

"But you might. You will be starting a new life, meeting new people. You are too young to be tied to anyone."

"Oh, not this age business. If you were the same age as me, you wouldn't be saying this!"

"Perhaps not."

"What has brought this on?"

"I suppose when I met your parents I was made aware that I was nearer their age than yours."

"My father is forty-eight."

"Exactly. Do the maths."

"But when we are together we seem the same age. We are both adults. We are soul mates."

"You are just at the start of your career. Still a student. You will change. You may travel - anywhere. I cannot be a mill-stone round your neck. You must feel free."

Anguished, he gazed at her.

"Are you sick of me? Is this your way of breaking it off?"

She shook her head. "Of course I'm not sick of you. I love you. You know I do. I just want what is best for you."

"Then don't scare me like this."

"I'm trying to be realistic."

"What is real is our relationship." He put his hand over hers and spoke earnestly. "We are fortunate in having no real obstacles to overcome before we can be together. My parents like you, I'm sure." He hesitated. "Douglas has gone. We are individually financially secure and I see no difficulty in our being together here, whenever we can, as you suggested."

"Do you think your parents accept our mis-matched relationship?"

He smiled ruefully at her words.

"In fact, do they know we are together?"

"I told my mother and she will, almost certainly, have told him. But we don't, in any case, need their permission."

"In a sense you do, if you are going to be dependent on your father to pay your fees."

"I needn't be dependent on him. And anyway he won't change his mind. His decision was not contingent on my remaining alone."

"But if he disapproved you would be, to say the least, embarrassed."

"My father is not a petty-minded man. Nor is he likely to take a negative attitude to what means so much to me. If he has doubts about us, he will keep them to himself."

"You make him sound quite saintly!" she joked.

"When you know him better, you may find that description is not far off the mark!"

His words silenced her.

Chapter Twenty Five

Before Antony left for home, he went to say goodbye to his tutor, Alan Smythe, with whom his relationship for three years had been at times fraught with difficulty. In the first year his tutor's irritation at Antony's lack of interest in and commitment to his subject had sometimes boiled over into anger. The youth's unfailing courtesy and ready acceptance of all his criticism did not lessen his annoyance but, at the same time, strongly endeared the lazy student to him.

"I'm sure you have the ability to do well, if only you would put your mind to it!" was a common refrain at their meetings.

He suspected that Antony's real interests lay elsewhere. This seemed confirmed in the student's final year when he had a brilliant success acting in 'Coriolanus'. Then he noticed that Antony's manner had changed. The cheerful smile that acknowledged his shortcomings disappeared. Sullen hostility and silence met all his attempts to find out what worried him. He began to fear that Antony was on the verge of a nervous breakdown. Then although he remained off-hand and miserable, there was a change. He began to work hard. His marks improved. He spent hours in the laboratory as if trying to make up for two wasted years. He could work fast and even, as the weeks passed, seemed to enjoy what he was doing.

Between Antony and his tutor there developed a truce. They respected each other and a diffident liking grew between them.

Now Antony waited at lunch-time outside Smythe's laboratory. They exchanged amused glances.

"I've come to thank you. I know I've irritated you and I've been pretty impossible at times, but I always felt you were on my side. I thank you for that. I just wanted to say goodbye. I won't forget your patience, which I didn't deserve."

His tutor smiled. "Oddly enough I think you are going to get a good degree. I shall be very interested to see how you get on in life. People like you sometimes achieve incredible things. I ask myself if you will discover something in Chemistry that we hard- working academic types would fail to do in a hundred years."

"That's pretty unlikely. I'm not going on with Chemistry. I've just sent off an application to RADA. I believe my true vocation is acting."

The hard stare, that Antony had become used to over the years, transformed Smythe's features. "Right. So that's three years wasted!"

"Sorry. I made the wrong choice of subject three years ago."

"Ah, well, if you ever get to play the part of a mad scientist, say Frankenstein, at least you will know what your lines mean."

Antony laughed. "Can I buy you a drink? I'll really miss all your pep talks."

Three unbroken days which they could spend together seemed a wonderfully long time to Margaret and Antony whose meetings had been rigidly curtailed in the past by the demands of studying, examinations, lectures and secrecy. Now they could relax and talk for hours, or lie blissfully in each other's arms letting the hours drift by. The weather was kind. All day the sun shone from a cloudless sky. Sometimes in the long sultry afternoons they read outdoors lounging in garden chairs.

"Have you really decided not to go on with your novel?" he asked, late one afternoon.

"Yes. It was going nowhere. I didn't like the characters either."

She continued reading. After a while he spoke again. "Have you thought of writing anything else? A different sort of novel?"

"Not really."

"Would you ever consider writing about your own early life?"

Surprised, she looked at him. It had never occurred to her to discuss her writing with anyone. He was serious, she saw, as he waited for a reply.

"No. I never felt the urge to write about myself."

"I'm surprised. When you think of the novels you have most enjoyed, you find they are usually based on the writer's own life. Think of D.H. Lawrence's 'Sons and Lovers'. You can't put it down. Dickens of course made excellent use of his own early experiences." He broke off. "But you know all this. I just think it might be a good idea to have a go. See how you get on."

"You're right. A lot of powerful writing is confessional. I'm just not sure that I want to go down that road."

They sat in silence, thinking about the autobiographical elements in novels they admired. It seemed to them that the most powerful writing was usually based on sad or even tragic experiences.

"I know very little of your childhood, but what you have told me or hinted at, I always found intriguing. I never wanted to pry but what you did say fascinated me. I wish particularly I could have known your father. I should be intrigued to read the story of your early life and I'm sure, fictionalized it would be gripping."

"Is this a sudden idea you have had?" she asked smiling.

"Not exactly."

They remained silent. The languor of the late afternoon and the warm sun slowed their thoughts as they sat in the quiet garden and let their musings drift as they would. An idea had however been planted.

Antony was surprised that events in her childhood could be recalled with such bitterness, even in happy times. He suspected when he considered the latest revelation that she could never relax completely into the comfortable contentment that most people enjoyed and took for granted. He saw that the calm surface she presented to the world was hard won. She hid so much of what she felt under a tight discipline and joked to hide her real feelings. Douglas's departure he believed had hurt her more than she would ever admit. When he had gone too, he worried that the loss of the constant reassurance of his presence might seriously affect her. What she needed was to expunge the awful memories of her past. The common belief that writing about unhappy events was cathartic he was familiar with and tended to believe. He hoped she might follow his suggestion and so release herself from the past.

They did not speak again about Margaret's writing before he left for home. It was there that he would wait to hear from RADA and also learn if he had earned a degree. It would be easy for them to keep in touch by telephone so they made no plans as to when they would next meet.

Chapter Twenty Six

Caroline met him at the station in the early afternoon. He watched her as she drove.

"You look awfully pleased about something," he remarked.

"I'm pleased that you are home and will stay for a while. What else do you expect?"

"Thanks for that. It's good to be home."

"How is Margaret? Have you seen her since we had lunch?"

"Yes. I've been staying with her."

"Really?" she glanced at him and the smile left her face. "Did the college know you were there?"

"Well, we didn't exactly broadcast it, but things are a bit disorganized at the end of the year, people leave at different times."

Soon they arrived at Forest Lodge. Caroline drove through the open gates and stopped behind a rather battered Ford.

"Oh, good! Geoff's arrived. He rang up last night and I invited him over for supper this evening. I thought you would like to see him."

"Excellent. But where is he?"

"He's probably in the garden. Just help me in with the shopping and then you can go and look for him."

He found him on the terrace behind the house stretched out on a lounger. He was asleep with an open book balanced on his chest. Antony picked up the book, curious to see what his friend was reading. It was 'War and Peace'. He had not got very far with it. Antony was amused at how soon such a wonderful book had sent him to sleep. He returned to the house after replacing the book.

"He's asleep," he told his mother. "It seemed a pity to wake him."

"I think he was very tired. He told me on the phone last night that he might find it difficult to keep awake driving up today. He's been called out several times during the week in the early hours. I've never understood why solicitors have to go to police stations to see new clients in the middle of the night. Is it to stop the police from beating them up?"

"I shouldn't think so, but ask Geoff."

"Shall I make some tea? That would revive him."

"Yes, that's a good idea. Meanwhile I'll take my bag upstairs out of the way."

He was pleased to see that the pictures he had chosen on his last visit and hung rather haphazardly, on hooks already there, had been repositioned on the walls with some care. He looked at them admiring them again with fresh eyes.

"Thank you for hanging those pictures," he told his mother. "You have such a good eye for placing them in just the right spot."

"I've had years of practice," she replied. "Now let's rattle the cups and wake Geoff up."

When Geoff opened his eyes he saw Antony, holding his book and laughing down at him.

"It's probably the greatest novel in the world and yet 'War and Peace' sends you to sleep!"

Geoff grinned. "Sorry I fell asleep. I was just exhausted." He swung his legs round and stood rather unsteadily.

"Don't get up!" Caroline protested. "Have some tea. That will revive you!" She smiled as she offered him a large mug. "I'm sorry there was no one here to welcome you. I did some shopping earlier and then met Antony's train. I'm glad you made yourself comfortable."

Gratefully Geoff drank the tea. "I knew you wouldn't mind, and was I glad to stretch out!"

"How's it going? Are you still enjoying life in London?"

"Yes. It's hectic but there are some great people working in the practice and we socialise quite a bit. Several are young and single so we have become like a big family."

"I'm so glad for you. Now, if you will excuse me, I have a few things to do inside." Caroline left them.

"Do you need any help?" Antony called after her.

"No thanks, stay with Geoff. You and he must have lots of catching up to do." She went into the house.

"Have you had your results yet?"

"No. They'll probably come in tomorrow's post. Why not stay the night here then you can shout at me if I fail, or rejoice," he added nonchalantly, "if I pass?"

"Are you expecting to fail?"

"Not really. I worked pretty hard, but you can't ever be sure you'll get through. Anyway it's not really all that important. I'm not going to become a Chemist."

"What are you going to do?"

"I'll give you one guess."

"How should I know? Don't tempt me. I might make some insulting suggestions."

"Such as what?"

"Never mind! What are you going to do?"

"I'm applying to RADA."

Although initially surprised, Geoff soon realized the inevitability of this course of action.

"I'm glad," he said. "You should never have taken up science. You have always been more interested in literature and art and you have real gifts as an actor. I'm glad you are going to go for what really turns you on. When did you decide?"

"It's always been a possibility at the back of my mind. And talking with Margaret, after finals were over, convinced me I should give it a go. She's been so supportive, and very flattering about the likelihood of my succeeding as an actor. She helped to convince my parents that it wasn't a mad scheme, but that I had some ability."

"So, they've met her?"

"Yes."

"Gosh. Things have moved quickly."

Geoff waited for Antony to say more about his parents' meeting Margaret. He also wondered, recalling Antony's letter, if they were 'together' still and if his parents knew or approved of their relationship. He asked nothing and minutes drifted by.

"How's the Ford going?"

"OK. It's had a couple of knocks. Parking in London is dire. Driving about at night, looking for Police Stations in rather shady areas is time-consuming and risky and you tend to dump the car as near as you can get to the station, without taking much care about its position. I know it looks battered and badly needs a clean, but it serves its purpose."

"Gets you from A to B. Fair enough."

"I've thought about changing it, but it goes well and it doesn't break my heart if it gets the odd prang."

"My father thinks I should get a car," Antony remarked. "It would be convenient for driving up and down to London. That is if I get accepted. I should hear from them soon about conditions of entry."

"But surely you would get lodgings or something in London?"

"Oh. Yes, but I'd spend the weekends with Margaret, whenever I could."

He met Geoff's prolonged stare with a serious, closed expression on his face.

"You would miss a lot of the life in London, if you did, just as students who lived at home missed half the life of university. Have you thought about this? You should be making new friends, associating with the other actors, going to theatres."

"I can do that during the week."

Geoff wanted to warn him, to urge him to give himself some space. At the back of his mind he had hoped the relationship with Margaret had cooled off. He considered the age difference between them with misgiving but he kept his thoughts to himself. Antony could read the disapproval in his face and was irritated by it. There was so much that Geoff just did not understand. He did not want to leave Margaret on her own for weeks. He feared she was more fragile than he had ever supposed when he first knew her. Also, he wanted, needed, to be with her. She was the most important person in his life. He loved her completely and was already missing her.

He picked up the mugs. "Would you like a beer or something?" he asked.

"Thank you. I'd love a beer!"

Caroline joined them on the terrace for drinks and the mood between them improved as she chatted happily about some newcomers to the village.

At about five p.m. Robert came home and the party was complete.

It was a lovely warm evening. Roses bloomed at the edge of the terrace adding their fragrance to the charm of the late afternoon.

For Antony it was one of those times which, even as they are happening, take on the misty aura of memory. He knew he would in the future always be able to conjure up this scene, where, lit by the golden glow of the sun, people he loved chatted and laughed in a blissfully happy present. He himself existed between two lives. His student days were still fresh, he hadn't quite stepped out of that life, which included his relationship with Margaret, new and fresh and full of the expectation of happiness. The next part of his life he contemplated with both excitement and apprehension. Even tomorrow he might learn the steps he must take to enter the life he longed for. As for his degree the expected result, whatever it was, would just draw a line under the last three years. Glancing at his mother, he caught her eye and smiled and later when she returned to the house, he followed her. Geoff and his father, he knew, were happy to talk and, as he left them, they seemed to settle more comfortably into the well-upholstered chairs. He replenished their drinks and returning to the house poured himself a large Scotch.

"It's good to be home!" he told his mother.

"Well, don't let the whisky go to your head. I want you to set the table."

He laughed, "It will take more than a couple of Scotches to affect me!" he boasted.

"I dare say. But it's nothing to be proud of."

"I know. Please don't get all moral about it. It's my first day home."

"Yes. And that's worth celebrating. I love having you back." She reached up and kissed him.

Together they set the table, decorating it with candles and flowers. Antony opened a bottle of claret and put two bottles of white wine in the fridge. The dining room faced north, so they lit the lamps on the side tables to brighten the room which seemed dark in comparison with the blazing light at the back of the house.

"Tell them we can eat in about twenty minutes. Geoff will probably want to freshen up so fix him up with a fresh towel and whatever else he wants," she advised her son.

Antony took his friend upstairs.

"Have a shower if you like. Do you want to borrow a shirt?"

"Thanks, if you have one that will fit me. Sorry to give you this trouble. I should have gone straight home and just returned for the evening."

"No you shouldn't. And I think you should stay the night. The guest room is always ready, and you don't want to drive after drinking."

Geoff agreed to stay. Antony found him one of his father's shirts after his own were found to be too small. When ready he went downstairs leaving Antony to finish dressing. He joined Caroline in the kitchen. He noticed she glanced over his shoulder to see if Antony was behind him.

"He'll be down in a few minutes," he told her.

"I was hoping for a quiet word with you," she said softly. "A couple of weeks ago when we went to pick up Antony's trunk and bicycle, he introduced us to Margaret Gerrard. We had lunch together and we liked her very much. You know her of course."

"Yes."

"Did you know that she and Antony . . . ?" She broke off not knowing how to put it.

"Yes. They are, to quote your son, 'together'."

"I think he's moved in with her."

Geoff wondered why she was discussing this with him.

"Oh, really?"

"You didn't know?"

"No."

"What I'd like to know is what you think of it."

Geoff was embarrassed. He felt he was being put in an impossible position. He felt a fierce loyalty to his friend but he also sympathized with his mother.

"What he does is his own business. It isn't up to me to have an opinion." He spoke quietly with some resignation.

"Do you like her?"

"Yes, I do. I admire her knowledge and expertise and she is a very charming woman."

"Yes, we thought so. I'm just concerned that she is married and also older than he is."

Geoff nodded.

She went on. "I'm glad he's found someone after all this time. It's just ironic that his choice is . . ." She broke off. "I don't mean to say 'unsuitable', but there are obstacles, and these cannot be ignored."

"I agree. But I don't think I've ever seen him so happy as when he is with her nor so devastated as when she seemed to have rejected him, last January."

Caroline remembered how ill her son had looked when, with no explanation for his visit, he had arrived home in February.

"Yes, he seemed ill when he visited us. I've since wondered if we should have tried to get him to confide in us. Although I don't know what we could have done."

"I don't suppose there was anything."

"Do you think they have a future?"

"Who can say?"

"Is she as keen on him, do you think?"

"Yes. I believe so, but . . ." he broke off.

"You have some doubt. Please go on."

"I think she is very complicated. I think she is probably tormented by misgivings. It won't be an easy relationship and, although her husband is in Africa and may well stay there indefinitely, he will remain a threat to Antony. I met him once, in my first year, when he gave a lecture at the University. He had a very powerful presence. There was a benign strength in him that you recognized at once in his manner of speaking and in his physical appearance." He paused as he contemplated the situation. What a tragic dilemma Margaret must find herself in. He believed she was genuinely in love with Antony, whose physical beauty and grace she must have found irresistible, when added to his intelligence, ability and devotion. He was the perfect romantic lover. And his weaknesses, which Geoff recognized and disliked, he knew did not really compromise his underlying goodness.

Caroline realized that he would not elaborate on what he had said. Perhaps she had been wrong to try to learn what he really thought about their relationship. His description of Margaret's husband offered no comfort and increased her fears for her son's happiness. She had not told Robert that Margaret was Antony's lover and was now both glad and sorry that she had not done so. She tried to find relief in the idea that their separation, if Antony went to London, might weaken their feelings for each other. Geoff's words also reminded her of what a powerful tie the marriage bond was, not easily or readily broken.

Geoff wandered into the garden. His exhaustion had returned. The conversation with Caroline had revived the feeling of dread that he had had since knowing the extent of Antony's feelings and dreams about Margaret. He felt some anger too at her husband's apparent opting out of all responsibility for her. In this gloomy mood he met Antony.

"What's up with you?" he asked, laughing at Geoff's morose expression.

"Nothing."

He noticed the full glass of whisky in Antony's hand. "Aren't you celebrating a little early?"

"Oh you're as bad as my mother. It's the end of university and the end of swotting up chemistry, thank God. Surely you don't begrudge me the odd drink?

"No. Not the odd one."

Robert summoned them into the lamp-lit dining room and Geoff soothed and entertained by the pleasant conversation, forgot his tiredness and put aside his doubts about Antony's future. They were a delightful family, he thought, as he laughed at their jokes and shared in the celebratory mood that lasted throughout the meal. He could even imagine how well Margaret Gerrard would fit in and almost wished she were there with them.

When at last he lay in bed, drifting towards sleep, he recalled the last time he had seen them together at the Ball, glowing with joy and devastatingly beautiful.

Next morning when Robert sorted the post, he found two official- looking letters addressed to Antony.

"I think the results have come!" He told Caroline. "Shall I wake him?"

"Yes, do!" She smiled broadly, optimistic that both letters would bring good news.

Robert went upstairs, knocked quietly on Antony's door and receiving no response went in. His son lay sprawled across the double bed, sound asleep. "The post's come!" he announced fairly loudly. Antony stirred and opened his eyes.

"What?" he murmured sleepily, then realized why his father was there holding up two envelopes. He sat up and Robert handed him the mail. He opened the one from the university first. He took a small booklet from the envelope and looked through several pages of lists of names. He paused when he found his own name and checked the words written at the top of the column. Class Two, Grade One.

"I've got an upper second!" he announced with as much amazement as delight.

"That's excellent! Congratulations!" His father smiled broadly.

Geoff appeared in the doorway, in borrowed pyjamas.

"What did you get?"

"A 'Two One'. Can you believe it?"

"No, I can't. Did you bribe somebody?"

Hearing their laughter, Caroline called from the landing, "What did he get?"

"An upper-second," Robert told her.

"I'm delighted."

Antony ran out of his bedroom to hug her, grinning broadly. It was immensely satisfying, against the odds, to have gained such a good degree. For a while he forgot the other letter that he had in fact been more eagerly anticipating. He returned to his room where it lay on the bed.

He opened the large envelope and read quickly the letter acknowledging his interest. His suitability for the course would be investigated and he would be invited to attend for an interview and an audition. At this he would be required to perform a piece of his own choosing and also read passages chosen by the academy. The accompanying booklet gave a brief history of the academy and its aims. There was a short list of previous students who had achieved success in their subsequent careers. Three years of study could lead to a degree.

He went downstairs to join his parents and Geoff for breakfast.

Chapter Twenty Seven

The long vacation had begun. A memorable year had ended. Margaret could hardly believe that it was only a year ago, in the last few weeks of the previous Summer term, that, at the auditions for 'Coriolanus', she had first met Antony. She tried to recall the impact he had made on her at first, when he was to her just another student. She remembered noticing his voice and his height and then his smile when she offered him the main part. But that was all and during the time she was in Italy that summer with Douglas, she had never for a moment thought about him. For a while she contemplated what her life might have been had he not presented himself at the auditions. It was difficult to imagine. Whether present or not, he now occupied a place in her heart and thoughts that expanded into every aspect of her life. She loved him desperately - much more, she believed, than even he realised. She sometimes wished she could discover some flaw in him, something to dislike, but there was nothing.

Yet perfect happiness eluded her. She could never forget how much younger than herself he was. She feared this difference in age would inevitably impinge on their relationship. No matter how often she tried to dismiss her fears and to remind herself of Antony's constant denial of any importance in their age difference, she could never convince herself that it was unimportant. When she was fifty, he would be younger than she was now. Suppose they were photographed together and she looked like his mother? She could not bear the thought. Inevitably their interests and perceptions would reflect their ages. Would she pretend to be younger than she actually was? Or was it foolish not to regard each other just as adults - an idea Antony had actually voiced.

To try to escape these thoughts, she went outside and wandered about the garden.

Often in the last days of his stay, they had lounged in the garden, talking of literature, acting and writing. He had wanted her to write a novel, based on her own life. Idly, she contemplated the idea. She imagined showing him a first draft and listening with amusement to his opinion of it. Gradually, with nothing else to do, she became fascinated by the idea and began, rather frivolously, to consider how the story might begin. Would she start with her very early years when she remembered times of joy and laughter or would it be better to begin with the later period of unhappiness and use flashbacks to explain it? Too many old films of the forties and fifties used such devices which she suspected had brainwashed a generation to accept a sentimental handling of the story and mechanical plotting. She was irritated to think she had even considered it. She reminded herself of Aristotle's advice, *'A whole is that which has a beginning, a middle and an end.'*

That afternoon she began to write. Her memory of the dashing figure of her father, emerging from the sea, was as vivid as her recollection of the icy cold drops of water trickling from his hair on to her chest as he clutched and lifted her up into the sky. She remembered laughing uncontrollably as he ran into the sea, balancing her on his shoulders. The rolling waves, the blue sky, the screeching of the gulls and her tiny fingers grasping his wet hair summed up for her the ecstasy of living. As she wrote she forgot the time and was surprised when she looked at her watch to see it was nine p.m.

She read through what she had written making a few alterations as she did so. The prose flowed with an ease that surprised her. She thought it was a good piece of writing and decided to continue the next day. She had not eaten since lunch time and realised she was quite hungry. She felt no inclination to cook so made herself a cheese sandwich and poured a glass of red wine, which she carried into the study. On the arm of one of the chairs she had left open Maupassant's 'Bel Ami' that she was reading in translation. She had reached the chapter where Georges Duroy (Bel Ami) with his new wife, Madeleine, visits his peasant parents, an unattractive couple. Engrossed in the novel, she felt some irritation when the phone rang. She answered without anticipating who might be calling.

"Hello, Margaret!" It was Antony's voice. He sounded happy. "Is everything OK?"

"Yes. How are you?"

"Very pleased with myself. Get ready for a shock. I passed! In fact I got an Upper Second!

"That's so good. You led me to believe you would be lucky to scrape a Third, although I never believed that."

"You should have. Geoff was here and said I must have bribed the examination board."

"Well you and he are so very different. I don't suppose he ever did much last minute cramming. He's not a risk taker at all, whereas I think you might thrive on it."

"I also heard from RADA and when I rang them up, they offered me an interview next Friday. There will also be an audition. In fact more than one. The candidate can perform some passages of his own choosing and they will pick the others."

"What will you choose?"

"Something from 'Coriolanus' seems the obvious choice. What do you think?"

"Yes. Shakespeare must be good. I expect they will give you something modern as a contrast. It will probably be something you know. It's fortunate you've read so much, my dear book-worm."

"Is that what you think I am?"

"Certainly."

He laughed.

"That's one of the attractive things about you. You've read everything!"

"That's what Geoff used to say. Oh, by the way he's reading 'War and Peace' and guess what? It sent him to sleep! I found him in our garden snoozing away with only about two chapters read!"

"And I expect you read it at twelve and found it an easy read!"

"Yes, but I was about fifteen not twelve."

She felt a sudden overwhelming rush of love for him.

"What have you been doing without me?"

"Scribbling."

There was a moment's silence.

"Scribbling? What have you been scribbling?"

"My life story."

"Really? That's great."

"I was in the garden and I remembered our conversation and, suddenly, I thought it might be amusing to have a go. And you can pass judgement on it - from the breadth of all your reading."

"I wouldn't dare criticise anything you might write. Don't forget I'm a mere Chemistry Graduate."

"Oh, don't you enjoy that title. Are you by any chance wearing a hood and gown?"

"Seriously, will you let me read it?"

"Why not? I'd be interested to hear your opinion."

"Really?"

"As long as you promise to be honest and tell me if you think it's rubbish."

"I promise," he said, knowing he would find it fascinating.

"How is Geoff - despite his exhaustion?"

"He's fine. He gets on very well with my father. They discuss minute aspects of the law and seem genuinely engrossed by it all."

"And your mother?"

"She's great, thank you, and asked me to give you her best wishes."

Before they finished talking Antony asked if she had any advice to give him about the audition. She suggested he should choose passages from 'Coriolanus' of widely differing moods and concentrate, as she knew he would, on their meaning, intellectual and emotional, and forget his judges and not try to impress them. As regards the passages they would require him to read, she thought it would be a good idea to work out the period the work was set in, or when it was written, so that he might read them in a historically suitable manner. Clipped or casual speech for example, if chosen correctly, could add immensely to the creation of the correct mood.

"I wish you could be there!" he said, reminded by her words of how knowledgeable she was. He recalled how her presence had inspired all the students to rise above the mediocre and give their best performance.

"I'd love to be a fly on the wall. It's a while since I heard you perform. Anyway I'll look forward to hearing how you get on, and what they said."

"I'll give you a ring as soon as I get back."

Chapter Twenty Eight

When Margaret was quite young they lived in a cottage near the sea on the Yorkshire coast and she loved riding on the donkeys that trotted up and down the wide sandy beach, their big heads nodding, their bells tinkling. The days always seemed to be sunny. The sand was hot and the sea was warm. She loved to dig her toes into the wet sand and watch the flat surface of the ocean that no breezes disturbed. One day when the sea was still and calm she walked down the gradual slope of the beach, until the water lapped against her chin. She felt no fear and loved being in the water. Then she heard the quiet voice of her father, half-laughing as he said, "I think that's far enough to go until you learn to swim." Hand in hand they had returned to the golden sands where her mother was setting out the picnic on a dark blue rug. They ate tinned-salmon sandwiches and somehow hers became gritty with sand.

She remembered her mother, still youthful at thirty, wearing high-heeled sandals, even on the beach, and a rather shapeless cotton dress. She tried to remember what her parents talked about but recalled nothing. They seemed happy and her mother was laughing at something her father had said. It seemed that laughter had filled their days. She shrieked with delight when her father suddenly pounced on her where she hid in the heather in a game of hide and seek, up on the moors, or when he gave her an unexpected push on the swing and she rose high in the air.

He told funny stories too and gave to all the characters in these and in the fairy stories she loved, strange outlandish voices. She could still hear, in imagination, his Rumpelstiltskin and remembered how scared she was when, realising his cunning had failed, the villain stamped on the floor. Odysseus's duplicity was however invariably successful. She was fascinated by the account of how he deceived Polyphemus, the Cyclops, and saved most of his men. Such guile her father imparted with breathtaking finesse. She perceived, at a very young age, that he was clever as well as entertaining.

One of the best times was when her father put her to bed and read to her. He had a collection of fairy tales retold by Andrew Lang in Blue, Pink or Red Books. The superb language they were expressed in she absorbed without realising what it was that so delighted her. Her father also recited poetry. She remembered one about Old Nod that he said was by Walter de la Mare. How safe she felt, tucked up in bed, listening to his soft, slow delivery.

> *Softly along the road of evening,*
> *In a twilight dim with rose,*
> *Wrinkled with age, and drenched with dew,*
> *Old Nod, the shepherd, goes.*

Soon she would drift to sleep with phrases like 'steeps of dreamland' and 'waters of no more pain' meandering through her mind.

When the summer ended and the visitors departed, the theatre, where her father was playing a main part, closed. He had auditioned at the end of August for the part of Hotspur, in Henry 1V, Part 1, in a production at a prestigious Birmingham theatre and was daily expecting to hear whether he had been chosen to take the part. It was a role he knew he could excel in. When the news arrived that he had been successful, his delight was overwhelming. He immediately read the play again and acted his part especially for Margaret. The northern accent, the reckless torrent of words, Hotspur's cavalier attitude to his wife welded into a convincing whole. Although she could not understand it fully, Margaret was enthralled. Her mother tried for a while to rejoice with her husband but eventually her dismay and fear became too much for her to conceal. From the garden, one day, Margaret heard her parents arguing.

"You will be much more comfortable here than in lodgings in Birmingham," her father said.

"But I don't want to be alone here where I know nobody, not while I'm pregnant."

"I'll come home every Sunday and . . ."

"That's not good enough."

"We'll never be able to find a place in Birmingham half as nice as this cottage and whatever we find will be desperately expensive, if it's at all decent. I don't mind roughing it on my own but for you and Margaret it's better to keep this place. There's a garden and you can walk on the beach. Margaret loves to play there."

"I know and she loves to run into the sea. How do I know that I can keep her safe?"

"Oh, you will. She's a good kid and will do whatever you say."

"You can't go. You can't leave me."

"I have to. This is an important break for me. I must take it up."

"You think more of your acting than you do of me!"

"It's my job! It's our livelihood. You should be thankful that I've been offered this part."

"Well, I'm not."

That was the gist of their many rows before her father left. The news that she was to have a baby brother or sister was broken to her by her father with anxiety and joy fighting for expression in his features.

Without her father the days seemed very long and the weeks interminable. Her mother preferred to spend more and more time in the cottage or the garden, rarely going out and always avoiding the beach. Each Sunday her father came home and life was joyous again, but the hours sped by and on Monday afternoons he left taking the train back to Birmingham. The play he told them was a hit. Lots of young people went to the matinees and some came to the stage door to meet the actors. Margaret loved to hear the comments some of the school-children made and longed to go to the theatre and see it all for herself.

In November her mother's health rapidly deteriorated. She had headaches, felt nauseous and her ankles became swollen. One day she stayed in bed and told Margaret to go next door and ask the neighbours to ring for an ambulance. Terrified she did so and later watched her mother being carefully lowered down the stairs on a stretcher and then driven away in an ambulance. The neighbours, an elderly couple, took Margaret in.

"Where is your father?" they asked.

Margaret remembered telling them about the play he was acting in that she called 'Hotspur'. Then she said he was in Birmingham. The old couple, with the help of a Sunday newspaper found out at which theatre 'Henry IV' was being performed and telephoned the box-office. At six o'clock in the evening her father, having been contacted, returned their call. He told them he would come at once and asked about Margaret. Learning she was with them, he asked to speak to her. She remembered calling "Daddy, Daddy!" into the phone and hearing his reassuring voice - but what he said she could not recall.

Her mother was suffering from severe pre-eclampsia. She had convulsive fits and nothing the doctors gave her to lower her blood-pressure managed to save the baby. She became deeply depressed and blamed her husband's 'desertion' for the loss of the longed-for child. Nothing he could say or do placated her. He gave up the part of Hotspur, knowing the damage this would do to his career. From being a promising young actor he would in the future, he feared, be dismissed as an unreliable risk. It would take a lot of living down. Her parents' relationship never recovered. As a result of the depression, her mother's personality changed. She became taciturn and morose, often hardly polite to her long-suffering husband, whom she seemed now to despise.

He managed to get roles in the provinces in shallow comedies that were as depressing to one of his ability as they were facile and badly written. He never again suggested that they should live separately and so they moved regularly from sordid digs to unpleasant rented rooms in the small towns where he found work in shabby theatres.

As the narrator, Margaret described the reality of their days as objectively as she could. She changed their names, trying to distance herself from their story. Otherwise it felt too disloyal to recount their deep unhappiness. Sometimes when she remembered Antony would read what she was writing she felt inhibited. Some of the emotions were too raw to share with one

271

whose idyllic childhood she could hardly imagine. But if her account was to be worth anything, it had to be true. So she pressed on.

The atmosphere of their shared existence was poisonous. To call their miserable lodgings 'home' became a joke to Margaret. Had there been kindness and love in their small family, the poverty would hardly have mattered, but the prevailing mood of all three settled into antagonism and distrust. Her father spent less and less time with them and, although her mother never had a kind word for him, she deeply resented his absences. Again and again her fury would boil over. Often from her bedroom Margaret would hear their voices raised in anger. Her mother resented the popularity of her husband and what she called his glamorous social life. The names of various women were included in her tirades and it was not long before Margaret realised that her father was spending a lot of time with various actresses or devoted female fans. Looking back she understood how failure, loneliness and the easy morals of theatrical life would lead to his lingering in the congenial company of those he worked with. Why go home to a bitter silent wife and the solemn, unapproachable girl that he had unpredictably sired? What more natural than to spend time in pubs near the theatre? He felt his wife's coldness less with a couple of drinks inside him when eventually the need for sleep drove him back to their digs. Nevertheless, as a young girl, who had been devoted to him, she was upset and saddened at the thought of the women he preferred to them. This made her sulky and unresponsive. She took her mother's side and avoided any close relationship with him. It was a kind of self-defence. She could do nothing to improve the situation so she opted out.

Her parents separated when she was in her early teens. The end came one rainy Saturday afternoon when she and her mother went to the theatre to see the new play in which her father played the lead. They sat in the rear circle. Margaret felt horribly self-conscious. Would everybody, she wondered, know that it was her father when he appeared on the stage? She half dreaded, half longed to be recognised. Uncomfortably she saw the seats filling up. Everyone in the town seemed to have come to see her father in the play. When the curtain rose she clasped her hands tightly together and could not concentrate on the words spoken as she anticipated her father's entrance.

She hardly recognised him when at last he came on. He wore a blonde wig, was dressed completely in white and carried a tennis racket. He looked about twenty, with a young man's eager, ingenuous air. His skin, build and erect carriage enabled him to carry it off easily. The alteration amazed Margaret. Her father had vanished and here was this rich young man, born with a silver spoon in his mouth, about to be engaged to a pretty, dark girl in a pink dress whom he kissed, most passionately, at the end of act one. With the clear-sighted reasoning of the young she thought, 'What a pity Daddy can't stay in that lovely house. What a pity it's only a play.'

The drawing room was revealed in Act Two and her father was engaged in some argument about poaching. What a merry high-spirited fellow he was! Then he and his companion, the vicar's son, went off on some escapade and other actors and actresses filled the stage.

There was an interval. As a treat her mother had ordered afternoon tea and now the usherette brought it neatly arranged on a tiny tray. There were buttered scones and cake. Her mother poured the tea and they smiled at each other, enjoying the unaccustomed luxury of having tea brought to them, whilst others queued for ices or sat without refreshment waiting for the play to continue.

The interval seemed to be prolonged. The tea trays had long been collected from all parts of the theatre. The audience had taken their seats but still the house lights had not been dimmed. People began to fidget, to ask each other why the play did not continue. Margaret turned to speak to her mother, but the words died on her lips, when she saw her mother's face contorted with anger. She dared not utter a word, but crouched in her seat, her heart pounding with dread. She knew that something had happened and that somehow her mother knew what it was. The manager strode on to the stage, picked out by a spotlight.

"Ladies and gentlemen," he said. "We apologise for this slight delay. I regret to announce that Mr. Raymond Palmer has been taken ill in his dressing- room. The part of Gary Eglinton will now be taken by his understudy, Mr. Lew Clarke."

The curtain rose whilst the house lights still blazed. Margaret gazed upwards, watching the glow each light cast on the ceiling reduce in size until only a tiny gleam remained in the light itself. Then she dared to look at the stage. The blonde wig looked the same, but the young man was not her father.

"Ought we to go to Daddy?" she whispered in the darkness.

Her mother made no reply, only squeezed her hand and shook her head. When Margaret stealthily looked at her again, she saw that her mother's angry expression had undergone a subtle change. She saw now cold determination, frightening in its ferocity. Margaret had no recollection of the rest of the afternoon and evening. She learned, but how she had no idea, that her father had left the theatre after his exit in Act Two for a drink in a nearby pub. The stage manager had waited as long as he dared for him to return, before sending on his understudy.

Her father had not been drunk but had with fatal insouciance miscalculated the time. When he was fetched at last by the call-boy he was in time to hear the final frolics of Gary Eglinton, played with all the gusto of a new actor miraculously given a chance at last. Raymond was not really surprised when he lost the part to his understudy and when his contract ran out, a month later, to find it was not renewed.

For her mother it was the final straw. She remembered long discussions between her parents whilst she worked at her homework in her bedroom. There were no raised voices. Their plans proceeded calmly. Both seemed relieved that a permanent break was being arranged. Enough money was available to buy a small terraced house in a Midland's town where there was a good Grammar School. Margaret and her mother went to live there. Her parents separated and later divorced.

He became to her an ambivalent figure, talented and a failure, admired and despised, loved and hated. A nagging wife, incipient alcoholism and a largely unrecognised, wasted ability had been all his life. Her memory of him and his miserable life and her own priggish detachment, that she now despised, caused a sinking of her heart as it always had.

From that time on, she and her mother lived alone. It was not a happy period but it was stable. If joy was lacking in their lives, so too was the uncertainty of continually moving from place to place, and in Margaret's case the dread of continual rows between her parents.

The writing became easier as she described her later schooldays. The grammar school for girls that she joined at fourteen had high academic standards. The teaching was to her inspirational. The study of nineteenth century history, both English and European, opened her eyes to aspects of political and social events that she had known nothing of. She read widely to fill out the facts she learned at school. In English Literature she began to understand and really appreciate Shakespeare, she revelled in Jane Austen, Dickens and Hardy; and a host of other playwrights, novelists and poets thrilled her and fed her soul. She was always reading and buying books second-hand or borrowing them from the library. She still kept the copy of 'Tess of the D'Urbervilles', that she once bought for four pence, despite its bad state of disrepair.

For her this was a fulfilling time and her mother encouraged her to devote her time to her education. She was rarely asked to do household chores and always a quiet room with a desk was available. Exams had never worried her, in fact she enjoyed them and covered pages and pages with her large handwriting. She wrote at great speed and developed a sixth sense regarding timing - always finishing the paper just as the session concluded. Some of the invigilators joked that they would need extra sheaves of paper whenever she presented herself in the exam room.

Her examination results at sixteen were good. She won prizes. It was taken for granted that she would stay on into the sixth-form, when many of the girls left. At 'A' level she took English, History, Latin and French. As she settled into the sixth form the world suddenly became for her a more interesting place full of unexpected delights. She was happier than she had been for years. Every thing she read seemed to point the way to new horizons- new writers, new outlooks on life. She went to the cinema often, usually alone, and, on one memorable occasion, saw 'Les Enfants du Paradis.' The film entranced her and filled her mind for days. 'London Town' she found extremely funny, although, to her surprise, unappreciated by the friend she went with. An amateur group's performance of 'A Doll's

House' led her to read not only Ibsen but also Chekov and Turgenev. Tolstoy's 'War and Peace' she devoured also at this time.

When she was in the Lower Sixth, her father wrote to ask if he might pay them a visit. He was particularly eager to see his daughter. The letter, which Margaret did not read, seemed rather longer than they usually were

"Your father wants to come and see us," her mother told her.

"Really?"

"Do you want to see him?"

"When does he want to come?"

"Next week, on Wednesday."

"I'm going to the theatre with the school, that day."

"I'll write and put him off, then."

"OK."

So she expressed as indifference what, later, she was forced to recognise as teen-age brutality. Her mother's reply, whatever it was, discouraged further attempts on her father's part to meet them. Margaret carried on with her protected, impregnable way of life. She shrank from emotional confrontations, living her life at second-hand through books.

As so often in life, there are no second chances. A month later, they learned of her father's death. The account in the newspaper came under the heading, 'Actor, thirty seven, drowns off the Cornish coast.' The paper gave few details. It mentioned several plays in which he had taken part and concluded with the words, 'an actor who never fulfilled his early promise.'

She remembered sitting opposite her mother, shocked and silent. Both were dry eyed, unable to take in the enormity of the sudden news. When her mother eventually spoke, it was to utter the thought that was in both their minds: "But he was such a strong swimmer."

'Drowning, the gentlest death of all' was Homer's thought on the subject. Margaret remembered this from her reading of 'The Odyssey'. Had her father chosen this 'gentle death'? The inquest was inconclusive. The verdict was left open. His clothes had been found on the beach, he had worn bathing trunks. This gave them some comfort, suggesting his death was accidental not planned. But the doubt remained in Margaret's mind.

Alone, when her mother thought she was studying, she would sit for hours remembering. In her mind he was always young, always laughing. His green eyes, fringed with long, black lashes were always full of mischief when he played with her. Her mother's words, 'He was such a strong swimmer' were etched on her mind. Margaret remembered watching him from the dunes, swimming parallel to the shore, moving rapidly in a powerful rhythmic crawl. To and fro he would swim as if he could never tire. Eventually, however, he would turn towards the shore. Then in her mind's eye she would see him rise from the sea, shaking back his wet hair and wading through the shallows, like a god. He was tall, tanned, well muscled. How could he ever have drowned in the element to which he naturally belonged?

He had taken out an insurance policy on his life, four years before, nominating his daughter as his sole living relation and beneficiary. Margaret received the sum of twenty thousand pounds. She gave half of it to her mother. In effect she was paying off all debts. Her mother would not feature in any of her future plans. When Margaret left home to go to University her mother moved to the south coast where she bought a small apartment. A part-time job in a library and a small circle of friends filled her days. She wrote to her daughter about once a month and received in return sanitised accounts of Margaret's increasingly interesting life at university.

The synopsis of her early life she had written in the third person to distance herself from her story.

When she read it through, she was not satisfied with it and decided to use the first person in the second draft. She made rapid progress, referring frequently to her synopsis. When she came to type and edit the second draft she was surprised at its length. She made two copies. One she would send to Antony, for, after all, its writing had been his idea.

Chapter Twenty Nine

The post came at eight thirty. Antony knew when he felt the weight of the large white envelope that it must contain Margaret's novel. The sprawling hand-writing confirmed the identity of the sender. He went upstairs to his room, eager to read the manuscript. A brief note was enclosed.

Dear *Antony,*
I send you this m/s with some trepidation. It is my second draft. The first was a short attempt to put some of the information down as if it had happened to someone else. I thought it would be easier to write it in the third person. Now, as you will see, I have changed to first person. This seemed more straight forward, more honest. I have not found it easy to write as so much of it is depressing. Nevertheless, having once begun, I felt constrained to tell the truth. The actual writing of it has affected me more than I anticipated. I am going away for a while to try to put it into perspective.
With love,
Margaret.

Antony was dismayed at the implications of her letter. Whatever she had recalled and written about, at his suggestion, had clearly depressed her. He felt guilty. Instead of enabling her to become free of the past, writing about it had apparently had the opposite effect. He found the last sentence of her letter disturbing. Where had she gone to? She gave no address or phone number. Obviously she had no wish to see him or speak to him. It was characteristic behaviour, he thought, for someone as controlled as she had appeared when he first knew her. He had hoped she was becoming much less reserved with him. Now her letter reminded him that any revelations she had made about her past life had been very limited - mere fragments that hinted at but revealed little of a past that clearly still tormented her. He regretted his temerity in suggesting she should write about what clearly upset her.

He began to read.

Chapter one.
'Oh ye! who have your eyeballs vex'd and tir'd,
Feast them upon the wideness of the sea.'

My earliest memories are of vast sandy beaches and the ocean, often flat and calm, where I used to paddle so happily, and play with my ideal companion, my father. We lived my father, my mother and myself in a cottage, in Yorkshire, near the sea.

So much he read, standing by the window, then, hardly moving his eyes from the page, went and sat on the side of the bed.

At first the fact that the novel was about Margaret's life secured his interest, then the story itself took over and he read it as fiction. Her father fascinated him. He felt a deep empathy for him, first as a scholar and then, as the story progressed, as an actor. Gripped by what he read, he did not notice the morning had passed. He lounged on the bed, turning the pages rapidly, totally absorbed. He did not hear his mother calling his name. Eventually, receiving no answer, she came and knocked on his door.

"Come in!" He had at last heard and acknowledged her. She found him sprawled on the bed surrounded by sheets of paper, clipped together and in some sort of order. He was engrossed and barely lifted his eyes from the sheets he was reading.

"It's lunch time. Didn't you hear me call?"

"Sorry. I was reading."

"I can see that."

She looked with interest at the manuscript.

"It's Margaret's novel. It's about her childhood and adolescence and her family."

"Really? I didn't know she was a writer."

"I think that's what she has always wanted to do- to write. This is awfully good. I haven't been able to put it down. It came in this morning's post."

"Can you bear to leave it for a while and come and have some lunch?"

"Sure."

Leaving the manuscript on the bed, he followed his mother downstairs.

Caroline had prepared a cold meal which she served in the kitchen. She waited expecting him to talk about Margaret's novel. He said nothing. He sat opposite her, not eating, just staring out of the window. His interest in the narrative had led him to forget, as he read, that Margaret had lived through the events she described. The story seemed to be building up to a tragedy. He dreaded learning the conclusion to which the events were heading. He could not bear to think of what she must have suffered.

"What is it?" she asked.

He did not at first reply. When he turned towards her, she saw his expression was bleak. He remained silent for a while, then he spoke slowly, as if dredging up thoughts that were painful to him.

"You know when you are reading something and, although nothing is made explicit, there develops in your heart a feeling of dread. Well, it has dawned on me, since I stopped reading that something shocking must have happened in Margaret's life."

He paused. "I feel really bad about this," he murmured. "You see I persuaded her to write about her early life. I thought setting it all out, bringing it into the open, would somehow dispel its power over her."

"Perhaps it has."

"No. There was a letter with the manuscript."

Caroline waited anxiously.

"She said she was depressed and was going away for a while."

"You could finish reading it. Then it might be an idea to get in touch with her."

"I can't. She didn't say where she was going."

"Might she still be at home? Packing, making travel arrangements? Why don't you ring and see if she's still there?"

He had gone before she had finished speaking. She followed him. He had already dialled and was waiting with the receiver pressed to his ear. When there seemed to be no hope of its being answered, he slowly replaced the receiver. They stood in the hall looking at each other.

"Why don't you read the rest?"

He nodded and went slowly up the stairs. Caroline looked after him knowing if he needed her he would come and find her. He obviously would prefer to be alone as he read the rest.

If he had not been so worried, the account of her intellectual and imaginative awakening would have fascinated him. Her wide reading at that time echoed his own experience, as did her love of films and plays. Her academic prowess, revealed in her account of examinations, he passed quickly over, reading at a great rate, not pausing to savour well-written passages or lively dialogue. Many paragraphs he found deeply moving, even shocking. He understood now that her defence of free love must have arisen from her awareness of her father's many affairs and her wish to exonerate him. He began to share her pain in living with rowing parents, never able to relax when they were both present. Her account of their poverty shocked him. He had no experience of wearing cheap worn clothes and being ashamed of his appearance. He had never seen the interior of houses such as she described, as they moved from town to town, renting whatever accommodation they could afford. Detail after detail he absorbed, unwilling to associate such suffering with her.

Eventually he came to the revelation he had been dreading. He shared her shock in reading the newspaper heading, 'Actor, thirty seven, Drowns off Cornish Coast.' He had known that Margaret's father had died when young, but she had never revealed the circumstances. He had felt sorry at the time for her loss, but such information about someone he had never known, he had soon, if not entirely forgotten, allowed to remain at the back of his mind. Now her father's death became vivid to him. Her description of him swimming in the ocean was beautiful and moving. It was clear that Margaret feared her father had committed suicide and blamed herself for his death. Phrases that she had used: 'the gentlest death of all', 'such a strong swimmer', his 'powerful rhythmic crawl' seemed etched on his mind and convinced him that her father had indeed taken his own life. She certainly believed so and had never been able to throw off the guilt she felt for her thoughtless, dismissive attitude to him.

He read to the end of the last chapter. At University she wrote to her mother, not often, but regularly. She mentioned the 'sanitised accounts' of her 'increasingly interesting life'. He smiled at these phrases, imagining just how colourful those accounts might have been. He felt no jealousy; he had always suspected that she would have 'granted her favours lavishly'. The old fashioned expression would have amused her. Then, unbidden, came the thought that, after all, there had been a precursor in her father.

It was late afternoon when he went downstairs to find Caroline. He flopped on the sofa in the sitting room by her side.

"I feel as if I have been on a long journey," he said. "I'm exhausted - mentally."

"Have you finished it?"

"Yes."

"Do you want to try to phone her again?"

"No. I'm sure she will have left. I can understand her wanting to get away. She'll write to me when she's ready."

Caroline saw how tired and worried he looked.

"There was something tragic in her story, wasn't there?"

"Yes. It was her father. I knew he died when he was quite young. Now, I believe, as I'm sure she does, that he committed suicide."

"Oh, Antony, how awful."

"Evidently he was a very powerful swimmer, but he died swimming off the Cornish coast. Margaret was about seventeen at the time. Her parents were divorced by then and Margaret seems to have cut him out of her life. She feels guilty about this and I think she believes her attitude was a contributory factor in his death.

"Oh, dear. What a terrible burden to carry around."

"You'd never believe it, nor suspect all the other things she's suffered, when you meet her. She seems so well-balanced, cultivated etc. and yet much of her childhood was spent in poverty and misery. It's only at times of stress that she reveals her unhappiness and guilt."

He paused, then almost unwillingly admitted, "I suggested she should write to try to cauterise these feelings. That's not the right word - but it doesn't seem to have worked."

Caroline saw how distressed he was. "Try not to feel too guilty. Perhaps writing about her early life has helped her! Facing up to it may eventually have a positive result for her."

Antony sat silent and devastated.

"I'm going to get you a drink!" She said. "You look pretty shot at."

She poured them each a Scotch and they sat together, silently thinking of Margaret.

Chapter Thirty

Margaret was already on her way to Scotland when she posted the novel to Antony. She needed time alone and longed for the wild emptiness to be found there. Even the long drive north she welcomed. She knew several good hotels that were comfortable and spacious. Her intention was to spend days walking in the open air, exploring and thinking. She had brought boots, warm clothes and rain wear and as an afterthought various outfits suitable for evening. It would be good for her morale to make an effort to dress elegantly for dinner. Her luggage included a varied selection of books, mainly novels but also some poetry. She also had her address book, all the maps of Scotland she could find in the house and several A4 notebooks.

Making the decision to go away and packing her things had temporarily made her feel less depressed. Gradually as she travelled further north, there was less traffic and she was able to speed along the straight, well-maintained roads.

She decided to go to a hotel at Ardanaiseig where she and Douglas had once stayed for a short fishing holiday. Set in a large garden full of rhododendrons and azaleas and bordering Loch Awe, it was one of her favourite Scottish hotels. She did not know if the hotel was still owned by the same family, nor if they would have any vacancies. As she drove up the long drive, she saw that it appeared to have changed little. At the reception desk she was pleased to recognise the owner, Richard. He was able to offer her a double room.

"Do you know this area at all?" he asked.

"Yes. I know Ben Cruachan, and I know the lochans where you offer trout fishing to your guests."

The owner's puzzled gaze suddenly changed into a broad smile. "I remember. You were here with your husband. And the gillie could hardly keep up with you, when he took you up the hill to show you the lochans and where he had hidden the oars. He was more accustomed to people who needed a lift on the tractor than to mountaineers."

"I remember you had some interesting guests."

"Is your husband not with you?"

"No. I'm by myself. He is in Africa. Doing some charitable work."

They chatted for a while about his work there, then, Richard welcomed her again. He expressed his delight that she had returned for a second visit and then showed her to her room.

The hotel was even more lavishly furnished with antiques than she had remembered. Her room was large with bay windows on two sides, one over-looking the loch and the other the garden. The furniture was elegant, well chosen and offered plenty of space for guests' possessions. She decided to unpack; it would be a good place to stay for a while.

Conveniently, there were tea-making facilities and soon she was settled in an armchair by the window with a book. The view over Loch Awe was delightful. She sat for a long time watching a small boat where two figures sat, their rods in rests. The tranquil scene was calming and she was glad to be there, alone.

The following days she spent walking, using her maps to supplement the guide books with which the hotel was generously supplied. Taking her boots, a rainproof jacket and a packed lunch, she would leave quite early and drive to the regions she wished to explore. After about a week, walking alone became natural to her. Her days passed in a pleasing rhythm. She did not attempt to climb the nearby Ben Cruachan. Once had been enough. The hydro-electric plant, installed she believed since she had scaled it a long time before, seemed to make the mountain more forbidding.

The tiredness she had felt on completing the novel, gradually lifted. She tried to control the deep sadness it had generated by refusing to think about what she had written. Perhaps it had been concentrating on the detail, forcing herself to be absolutely honest that had so affected her. She felt damaged by her recollections. She did not want to be that person who had suffered; she felt disgraced by the conditions and events that had been her life. What folly had made her write about it? She had been happy enough in the past, pushing it all to the back of her mind. Only occasionally when some event dredged up bitter memories did she falter. Even then she rarely revealed the truth. Her control was practised. Amused, ironical remarks came easily to her.

Now she had revealed everything. She had spilled the beans. She didn't want to see Antony. She didn't want the pity he would most certainly feel. She laughed bitterly as she realised that what she most wanted in life was to be able to feel superior and anyone knowing about her early life would know that was a sham. She accepted that she was not a likeable person; she had no humility, perhaps little charity either. She thought often about Antony, the golden youth of her dreams. The beautiful, talented actor who, until he met her, had led a charmed life. By now he would have read all about the degradation of her childhood and would surely see the unsuitability of their pairing.

Her determination to release Antony grew as the days passed. She tried to think of the kindest way of telling him of her decision. He would not accept it easily. He would argue against every reason she gave about the unsuitability of their relationship. He would scoff, as he always did, at the difference in their ages. He would dismiss the relevance of their so different backgrounds, stressing that all that mattered was their future together, a future he believed in absolutely. And how could she bear to let him go? Memories of him kept flooding into her mind.

There he was, huddled in a dark duffle coat, angrily rebuking her for fearing to admit she loved him, and, minutes later, holding her close and kissing her. Their clinging together on that cold night receded and there he was, lounging in the dunes, above a wind-swept beach, wishing Time would stand still so they could lie there forever. The memory of his cold lips on hers was vivid and disturbing. She thought then of the brief separation, that she had insisted on, so that he could give all his time to revision and how, when the exams were over, he had sent that embarrassingly huge bouquet of flowers. She envisaged him riding his bicycle, often at break-neck speed, through the campus or up her drive. The sight of him on the stage, and the sound of his voice were unforgettable. How easily he could dominate an audience or even move them to tears. Then there was the laughter they shared on so many occasions.

Some memories jarred. How odd it was to see him wearing Douglas's sweater to draw attention away from the evening dress he wore, the morning after the sweetest night of their lives. Then, later that day, when abruptly he had asked, "Where is Douglas?" she had with difficulty kept the situation light-hearted as she pointed to Africa on the ancient map.

The daily exercise and fresh air gave her a feeling of physical well-being. As the days went by, she covered the miles more easily. In the evenings, when she dressed for dinner and studied her appearance in the glass, she noticed the healthy glow of her complexion. On some evenings when she arrived back quite early, she would go down to the bar and talk with the other guests. Most of them were middle-aged or older and enjoyed discussing their day's explorations. Richard was always there and she often chatted with him. He was very sociable and well-informed and took a great interest in people. He seemed to get to know several of the guests well. He laughed at their idiosyncrasies in a kind way and was obviously very well-disposed towards the human race in all its varieties. He had liked Douglas and remembered him well. Particularly he admired his skill in catching fish, supplying trout, one morning, for all the guests' breakfasts from the lochan above the hotel.

One evening Richard produced some photographs.

"Have a look at these!" he said grinning.

She took them and saw the first was of a huge salmon, lying on the grass, with a match box strategically placed to indicate its size. The next photograph was of Douglas wearing his old fishing hat, a Barbour and thigh-high waders. He held, what was probably the same salmon, in one hand and his rod in the other. He was smiling.

It was quite a shock to see the photographs. She kept her head lowered as she looked at the rest. The hotel cat appeared in one of them showing a great interest in the salmon. She saw a hand restraining it. It was held back by someone kneeling on the ground whose face did not appear within the frame.

"Is that the gillie?" she asked.

"It will be. But he didn't catch that beauty. Douglas never needed any help in angling."

She handed the photographs back.

"Thank you, Richard, for showing me them."

"You must be missing him. When will he be back?"

"Oh, one of these days. I'm not sure."

Something in her tone of voice alerted him. He gave her a shrewd glance and replaced the photographs in their envelope.

"He will be coming back?" The question was out before he realised it was none of his business.

"I don't know," she replied.

He was silenced by the blank stare she threw in his direction.

Seeing the picture of Douglas had been a shock. How happy he had looked. She moved from the bar to sit by the window. She looked towards the loch and wished he would come strolling up the lawn, dressed as in the photograph, carrying his rod, fishing bag and perhaps a salmon, or even two, dangling, from his hand, by a cord slipped through their gills.

"That's how I would portray him, if I were an artist," she thought.

She wondered how often in Africa he thought of fishing in Scotland. He had fished both the Tay and the Tweed and had grown to love those beautiful rivers. It was much easier to picture him in Scotland than in Africa. The cold bracing climate of Sutherland seemed a more suitable environment for him. Did he ever think of Loch Naver and Loch Loyal where he was happy to fish all day from a small boat, its outboard motor handled by a gillie who knew the lakes intimately? Even in September it was desperately cold in Sutherland and she preferred to stay on the shore walking and taking photographs and often by mid-afternoon retreating to the warmth of the hotel.

Her thoughts were still with Douglas when she walked, the next day, following a path that rose steadily above Loch Awe. She had never been sure whether Douglas knew about Antony or not. What was unequivocal was his statement, or promise, that if she ever asked him to return he would do so. Although there had been times when she thought she ought to tell him about Antony, she had never made up her mind that that was the right thing to do. She suspected that the door he had left open she had from the beginning been unwilling to close, because deep within her she knew she would one day summon him to return. Her life with Douglas had been happy. There was a harmony in their relationship that had lasted for years. They genuinely liked each other. With him Margaret had been able to live in the present. She had, she remembered with some astonishment, been free of the bad memories of the past then. It came to her gradually that the past had been encroaching on her thoughts more and more as her relationship with Antony had deepened. Had she been walking with Douglas on that beach, that had played such a big part in her childhood, she would never have succumbed to the memories of her father, nor felt so strongly again the horror associated with his death. Even as she asked herself why she had felt such sadness so strongly, when accompanied by Antony, on that beach, she knew in a flash the reason. He had become to her, her father incarnate. His youth, his beauty, his charisma, his being an actor, his loving her - all were characteristics he shared with her father. His dazzling attraction, her recurrent disturbing dreams and lastly and painfully her guilt seemed to be explained.

She stood still, overcome by an agonising sense of loss. With eyes closed she trembled with the effort to gain control.

She felt ill. She staggered to the side of the path and leant against the living rock that bordered the path. She realised the guttural sobs she heard were coming from herself. She became silent. She forced herself to take deep breaths. She remembered she had a flask of coffee and as the hot drink soothed her, she decided to go back to the hotel. She walked slowly making plans as she proceeded.

That evening she told Richard that she would be leaving the next day.

"All good things must come to an end," she said with a smile. "I feel a great deal better for this break. Now I must get home, I have a great deal to do. Thank you for everything. I have benefited enormously from being here."

The first priority was to write to Douglas. This she would do at home. She would ask him to return, certain that this was what she truly wanted. She also knew that nothing less than his return would ever persuade Antony to let her go.

Her heart ached for him. She did not fool herself into diminishing the agony both of them would experience in parting, but, if her life had taught her anything, it was this, that their love unstopped would ruin both their lives.

Chapter Thirty One

Two days later she woke in her own bedroom at home. As always the house had welcomed her into its warm ambience. Last night's refreshing sleep had banished the tiredness she had felt after the long journey from Scotland. Physically she felt the benefit of the time out of doors and the prolonged exercise of her days in the hills. Mentally and emotionally she felt strong. She walked round the house, going from room to room, looking at the familiar pictures and objects that she loved both for their beauty and associations. It was a charming house that today was bathed in sunlight. The garden beckoned. She was glad to see the lawns were freshly cut and the paths swept. Some of the roses needed de-heading so she returned to the house for the secateurs. Later she sat on the bench in the orchard to drink a cup of coffee. She thought she ought to check the mail which last night she had ignored. It was still in the mail box inside the front door.

There was a letter from Antony among the rest of the mail.

Dear Margaret,

I've tried several times to get in touch with you by phone and realise you are probably still on your travels. I'm writing now so that, when you do return, this will be waiting for you.

Thank you for sending me the m/s of your novel. I found it engrossing and very moving. I am, of course, upset that you found it a painful experience and apologise for my part in persuading you to write it. It is, I think, a wonderful piece of writing and I'm sure you must know that your success in this field will be just a matter of time. It is beautifully written and absolutely involving. I read it in a day, unable to put it down.

Please telephone me as soon as you can. I have lots of news, including my acceptance at RADA. I'm dying to tell you all about it.

With all my love, and a million kisses, I'm longing to see you.

Antony.

Her first priority was to write to Douglas. She put Antony's letter back in its envelope. She found an airmail in the top drawer of the desk in the study and then took out Douglas's letter telling of his intention to stay in Africa. She read it through again, as she had done many times since first receiving it, concentrating on the fourth paragraph where he had written, 'My love for you is constant. If and when you need me, I will return.'

Dear Douglas,

Please come home. I'm missing you very much.

Do you remember our holiday in Scotland, near Oban? I've been staying there for the past two weeks. You seemed so near in that environment, that I almost expected you to walk up from the loch, after a successful day's fishing, to join me.

There is no emergency. Come when it is convenient to do so. I should not like to interfere with what I know is valuable work.

With my love, as always,
Margaret.

Now she must write to Antony. She sat for a long time, her pen poised above a blank sheet of white paper. Whatever she wrote had to be convincing. To draw out their separation would be too unkind. She dreaded the effect on him of what she was going to write. She hoped the imminent change in his life and the fulfilment of his ambition would lessen the blow. She regretted the plans they had made for him to spend his weekends with her, virtually to live with her. This had given their attachment a permanence which now it could not have. It would be difficult for him to accept her complete change of heart. Perhaps when she explained it to him, he would understand, but she doubted her ability to do so. What he had said about her m/s gave her some hope. He had been affected by it and would understand so much more about her than he had when largely ignorant of her past.

Dear Antony,

It is over. Douglas is returning home, at my request. I realise that my life is bound up with his.

You have known from the beginning my grave doubts about our having a future together. I believe that you too always accepted that we would have only a limited time to enjoy being together and, in a sense, this made every one of our meetings more special.

It is ironic that it should be you who made the suggestion that has led to my understanding the real, if hidden, cause of our having to separate. From the time when I first knew you, I began to be more and more aware of my father's tragic life. It haunted me and I couldn't understand why, after putting it

297

behind me for years, his unhappy life and death dominated my thoughts. When I began to write, what is actually an autobiography, his presence became ever more real to me and I kept seeing clear resemblances between him and you. I remember him most clearly when he was very young. He was tall, athletic and very beautiful. Even though I was only a child, I knew he was clever. Now I would call him scholarly. He loved books and when he read to me I was transported into a magic world. My own love of literature was obviously inherited from him and it blossomed under his influence and care. I loved him deeply and was the more hurt by what I saw as his falling off.

When you came into my life, I recognised you. Not at the first auditions, but when you found me unpacking books in the high room I had just acquired. Your eyes although a different colour, were like his. I felt there was a link between us, even then, and it became gradually, in my eyes, more and more dangerous. You were after all a student and I was a much older, married woman. Now, even in the age difference, I see an uncomfortable parallel between his youth and the older woman he married, and us, a young student and an older lecturer.

They say that siblings who are separated at an early age and then meet again in maturity, are often sexually attracted to each other. My feeling for you seems to me to be similarly incestuous. I am in love, as it were, with my father or paternal substitute. You will, I know, find this idea ridiculous. I find it so myself.

I believe you felt guilt, as I did, at our deceiving Douglas. But underlying my feeling was the guilt of loving someone who too closely resembled my father. But your similarity to him was not tainted by affairs, such as he indulged in. You were, I thought, pure, and should not therefore be *involved with someone in my position. Then it became clear that you also had some baggage and I let myself off the charge of corruption. For a while I believed that we were soul mates, that we could be happy ever after. Then the realism kicked in.*

I am damaged. Writing about my life forced me to accept this. With Douglas I achieved a balance and came to realise that my traumatic past need not affect my everyday life. Living with him was like being cocooned in a warm safe place.

This is the right time for us to separate when you are starting a new life. You will be happy and, I believe, highly successful in your career and, make no mistake, I shall be happy too, as I was before I knew you, with Douglas.

I nearly wrote, 'God bless you!' Then I remembered you have problems with the Deity, so I'll just say, 'May Angels watch over you and protect you, my dearest.' I hope you still like the idea of angels.

Margaret.

Later that day she walked into the village and posted the two letters.

Chapter Thirty Two

It was Saturday morning. For half an hour the post lay on the tiled floor of the Lodge's porch before Robert, still in his dressing gown, picked it up. He was on his way to the kitchen to make tea. He left the post on the hall table.

Antony, knowing breakfast was always late on Saturdays, was indulging in his favourite pastime, reading in bed. Attentive, yet horrified, he was reading Graham Greene's 'A Burnt-out Case' about a leper colony in Africa. The grim subject matter, gripped his attention and inevitably brought to mind the one person he knew who was there, in Africa.

His father came in with a cup of tea for him and saw what Antony was reading.

"It's interesting, isn't it?" He had brought the book home the evening before and had finished reading it after supper.

"Yes. It certainly brings home the horror of Africa."

Robert drifted off to take tea to Caroline.

Engrossed by the book, his mind on Douglas, Antony forgot his tea after a few sips and was later surprised to find it had gone cold. He drank it nevertheless.

The delicious smell of bacon eventually drew him down to the kitchen.

Margaret's letter was lying on the hall table. He seized it and eagerly tore open the envelope.

"It is over," he read.

His father found him standing in the hall, his eyes glued to the pages of the letter that he held in shaking hands. All colour had drained from his face, that was now a greyish-white.

"Whatever has happened? Come and sit down." His father led him to the kitchen.

Caroline, aghast at her son's appearance, thought at first that he was ill. Then she saw he held a letter. Intuition told her it was from Margaret. She must have ended their relationship. She laid her hand on Robert's arm and, with the slightest shake of her head, indicated that he should refrain from asking the questions that she knew Antony would be incapable of answering yet. Puzzled, Robert stared at his son. It seemed to be taking him a long time to read the letter. When he came to the final sentence, he gulped, ran from the room and dashed upstairs.

Robert looked at his wife. She stood facing the door through which Antony had fled. Dismay and sadness were clearly visible on her face.

"I think you are aware of what that is all about," he said. "Could you share it with me?"

"Oh, Robert, I don't know, but I fear he has been jilted."

"Jilted?" The old fashioned word surprised him. "By whom? What has been going on?"

Caroline had always been open with her husband, never keeping anything secret. Now she found herself in the uncomfortable position of having to tell him that Antony loved a married woman, much older than himself and in a position of authority. She regretted she had not told him earlier, as soon as she had known herself. For him to learn this now when her son was obviously traumatised would be to reveal it in the worst possible circumstances.

"You remember," she began, "when we had lunch with Margaret Gerrard and you and she walked together, ahead of us, in the grounds, well, Antony told me they were lovers. I had suspected that he was smitten by her, earlier. The drawing he had made of her, and the way he gazed at it had roused my suspicions. Did you not think there was something between them, at that lunch? The way they looked at each other, and the way they tried to hide what they felt?"

Robert looked displeased.

"I thought they were friends. I thought she seemed very professional. I must say I am disappointed in her."

Caroline waited, knowing how angry he would be with Antony, but also concerned at his son's obvious despair. In Robert's view, marriage was a sacred bond. No one should come between a man and his wife. He had seen and heard too much of the sordid nature of adultery in his profession.

"As for Antony..." he broke off and shook his head. "I'm going to walk. I want to think."

"You won't stop him from going to drama school?" Caroline asked diffidently.

"I couldn't, even if I tried, and why would I do that?"

"Sorry. That was a stupid thing to say. I'm not thinking clearly. I feel very upset."

Robert glared at her and left the house.

Caroline went to the bottom of the stairs and listened. No sound reached her ears. She returned to the kitchen and scraped the congealed remains of their uneaten breakfasts into the waste bin. She filled the dish-washer and wiped down the surfaces of the counters, then wandered through the house collecting yesterday's newspapers, plumping up cushions and rearranging flowers. The morning wore on. Robert did not return. Worried about Antony, she finally decided to make coffee and take it upstairs.

She tapped on his bedroom door and entered. He stood at the window, looking out. She put down the tray and went to him. He looked at her and tried to smile. She put her arms around him and he held her close.

"Have some coffee while it's hot."

They sat together on a small sofa to drink it. Some colour returned to his face.

"Thank you, I needed that."

"So did I," she said.

After a while it seemed natural for him to speak about the letter that had so shattered him.

"Margaret has finished with me," he said. He spoke calmly, but his face revealed his anguish.

Caroline sat silently by his side. She did not know how to comfort him. She felt anger at Margaret's treatment of her son.

"What happened?" she asked, wondering if Margaret's husband had unexpectedly returned.

"God knows. I don't really understand it. She seems to have been badly affected by writing about her past. Her father was evidently a very glamorous figure in her eyes. They were obviously devoted to each other when she was young. Later, as I believe I told you, her parents separated and she became estranged from him. I think she just couldn't take the rows, the poverty, his women and so she deliberately tried to erase him from her life. When he died, she blamed herself."

He was for a while silent, thinking about the preposterous revelation of her letter. "The rest of what she wrote took me by surprise. I don't know what to make of it. She says that her association with me somehow brought back the tragedy of her father very strongly. Memories that she had pushed to the back

303

of her mind continually resurfaced, when we were together. She thinks I resemble him, in both appearance and character. She even . . . " he paused, "thinks that her feeling for me is incestuous, as if she is in love with her father, or, as she calls it, 'paternal substitute'."

"How very strange."

"And . . . this is the clincher. She has asked Douglas to return."

He got up and walked over to the window.

"You can't fight against that."

"I know. I decided long ago that if Douglas returned I would back off. I'll have to accept her decision."

He turned to look at her and added flippantly, "Anyone know what to do with a broken heart?"

They heard the front door close. Robert had returned.

"I had to tell him about you and Margaret. I hope you don't mind, but he was really worried about you."

"It's all right. I just don't want him to go on about it."

"I'm sure he won't!"

Chapter Thirty Three

Margaret's letter had left Antony stunned. He wandered about, unable to think clearly or act. Much of the time he spent in the garden at the far end of their land. The woodland area here was one of his favourite places. Leaning against the bole of a huge elm tree or sitting on a rustic seat, he let time drift by. He saw nothing of the view beyond the garden and was deaf to the song of the birds.

He accepted Margaret's decision. Always he had believed that Douglas had the prior claim and he had never been completely free of a feeling of guilt in his relationship with her. Even though he had never met him, Douglas had assumed a powerful presence in his mind as an adventurer and benefactor. He thought of him as a towering moral being who was willing to spend his life serving the needy in Africa and, unbelievably, willing to sacrifice his happiness to let his wife have freedom to fulfil her desires.

However, as the days passed, he felt more and more dissatisfied with the way his relationship with her had ended. Her letter, decisive as it was, seemed to him a poor conclusion to their relationship. He had to see her one more time. Not to plead with her to change her mind but to give their parting the dignity it deserved.

He asked his mother if he could borrow her car.

"I want to see Margaret one last time. I have things I must say to her. Do you think I could take the Volvo?"

Caroline nodded. "Yes, you may take it. But promise you will drive carefully."

He knew what she feared. "I will. I just want to say a proper goodbye. I need to see her once more. I won't speed and I won't drive if I can't concentrate properly. Don't forget I have to get to RADA in one piece, soon."

"Oh, my darling." His mother held out her arms and he clasped her tightly.

"I'll drive over tomorrow," he said softly as he released her.

He reached Covlington at midday. He parked the car outside Margaret's house and stood for a while at the gate. The house was bathed in sunshine. As he walked up the drive he noticed the full-blown roses that filled the flower beds. He knocked at the door and waited, wondering if he should have come at all.

The two taps Margaret heard from the kitchen had a familiarity of sound that unnerved her. She went through the conservatory and looked down the drive. He stood by the front door unaware of her gaze. She looked with longing at his profile, his tall elegant physique; moved, as always, by his beauty.

"Antony." She spoke quite softly.

He turned and walked towards her. There was a faint smile on his lips but his eyes were wary. Two yards from her, he stopped. For a long time he studied her face. He noted the healthy glow of her skin. She said nothing but her eyes suggested a dancing joy. He was reminded of how she had looked when he had sought her in her high room and he had first noticed her green laughing eyes.

"I received your letter," he said.

She led the way through the conservatory and in the kitchen gestured towards the table. He sat and watched her fill the kettle.

"I hope you don't mind my turning up like this?"

"Not at all."

She took mugs out of the cupboard and made instant coffee, knowing exactly how much sugar he liked.

"How did you come?"

"I drove here. My mother lent me her car."

"Really. How is she and your father?"

"Well, thank you."

"I'm so glad you got into drama school. Not that I ever had any doubt that you would be accepted. You must be eager to get started."

"Yes."

In silence they drank the coffee. Antony knew he should explain why he had come but struggled to decide how he should begin. It felt so right to be there with her in the sun-filled kitchen.

"I love this house," he said.

"Yes, it's a comforting place to be."

At last, somehow, he was able to begin.

"I have not come to plead with you to change your mind. I know you would not have written, as you did, unless you were certain. I just felt that we had to meet, that we could not . . . Our relationship was too strong to be broken off by a letter. I had to say . . . I had to say 'goodbye' to you in person." His voice faltered.

They sat in silence.

"From the beginning I knew that if you decided to return to Douglas, I would have to give you up, and get over it. I always felt some guilt in the situation, although that lessened when he decided to stay in Africa." He paused. "I told myself that, even if I could be with you for just a short time, it would be worth it. I remembered those words you quoted of Blake's about 'kissing the joy as it flies'. Now I accept my fate. What we have known was, I believe, very special. To me it was life enhancing and the deepest joy anyone could hope to have."

Deeply moved she sat motionless. She was near to tears, unable to speak. Her feeling for him was as strong as ever. She loved him and almost despaired of ever being able to part from him.

His eyes never left her face as if he were memorising every feature, every change in her expression. After a few minutes, he rose. "Perhaps I should go now."

The words came like a death-blow to Margaret. "No," she exclaimed. "Don't go yet."

He looked surprised.

"I have a few things I'd like to say. And you can't go without having something to eat. I'll make a sandwich!"

When she asked him to open a bottle of wine, he remembered the long journey home.

"I shan't have anything to drink - I'm driving," he reminded her.

"Do you have to go, straight away?"

Non-plussed, he eyed her warily.

"I thought you would want me to go."

"I'm asking you to stay."

How he longed to accept her invitation. He searched her face, trying to understand her motivation.

She took a bottle of wine out of the fridge. Mesmerised he watched her open it, take two glasses and pour the wine. When she handed one glass to him, he took it and drank. She found a packet of smoked salmon and made sandwiches with brown bread. Neither of them spoke. When the bottle of wine was empty, she took out another, handing it to Antony to open, which he did.

She washed some plums.

"Let's take these into the sitting room," she murmured, "It's more comfortable there."

They sat side by side on the deep sofa with the plums and wine on a low table in front of them.

"This doesn't change anything," she said. "Douglas is coming home."

She took his hand. "I'd like you to remember that whatever our relationship meant to you, it meant the same to me. I loved and still love you deeply and I expect I always shall." She paused, then with an air of determination spoke again. "But, I was happy in my marriage and I know I can be happy again. Had you not come today, I was going to telephone you to arrange a last meeting- somewhere on neutral territory. But this is better."

She raised her hand and touched his face. He trembled, uncertain of what to think. What was she doing? He was torn between guilt and desire.

"Oh, God, have you no mercy?" He groaned as he drew away.

She took his hand again. "Dearest, what we do now doesn't really matter in the final count, we are, after all," she smiled, "practised adulterers. Douglas can't be hurt any less if we behave like prudes now. No one is keeping score."

She smiled and her laughing eyes mocked him, but she released his hand and moved away. She poured some more wine for them both and raised her glass.

"I think we need a Feste here to sing to us.

What is love 'tis not hereafter
Present joy hath present laughter.

That's a good rhyme isn't it? Laughter, hereafter?" Her smile was catching.

"Yes, so is 'bliss' and 'kiss'," and with these words he reached for her and pressed his lips to hers.

The month they had been apart lent a novelty to their embrace, but the prospect of parting added a bitter sweetness. No words were needed when at last Margaret rose. He stood and opened the door for her to pass through. The way was well known, the bedroom a haven they had thought never to share again.

The rich bliss of reunion joined with the tenderness of a final parting. They made love slowly, lingeringly.

"If this isn't perfection then I don't know what is."

"Forever would be better."

"Don't spoil it. For now Time does not exist."

He did remember to telephone his mother to say he would not be home that night.

"Where are you?"

He looked at Margaret lying next to him.

"In Covlington."

"Where are you staying?"

"At Margaret's house."

"What? Are you and she . . . ?"

"See you soon. Bye."

"What a naughty boy!"

"You've corrupted me!"

They talked far into the night. He told her about the RADA interview. She wasn't surprised to learn that he had been asked to read several passages from the part of Romeo. It was very easy to imagine him in a romantic role.

"I expect you wowed them with that!"

"Those readings were easy enough, but then they asked me to read from "The Caretaker'."

"Which part? Mick?"

"No. The caretaker himself!"

"Oh, what a scream! Can you remember any of it? I'd enjoy hearing, or for that matter seeing you as that disreputable old rogue."

"It was the speech where he describes going to the monastery for his papers and a monk opens the door and tells him to piss off."

"What did they say about you in that role?"

"They found it funny. Probably because I was so hopeless."

"I never imagined they would choose something like that for you to read."

Idly they imagined other roles he might have been asked to read. Antony favoured Peter Pan and Richard III. Margaret liked the idea of Bertie Wooster and Vindice, the Avenger.

"I wonder if you will ever be the first to play a new part in the first production of a play? Some play as yet unwritten, and make the role your own?"

"Perhaps you will write it!"

She laughed.

"I thought your book was excellent," he said, suddenly serious.

"Thank you. But I felt it revealed too much. I don't think I want to have it read. I had to let you see it, I'd sort of promised that I would, but I'll never try to publish it."

"That would be a shame."

He remembered how the character of her father had interested him.

"I wonder if you could write a memoir of your father?" he suggested tentatively. "I was so impressed by your vivid portrayal of him."

"I enjoyed writing about him, not everything of course, but he was fascinating."

"I wish I could have seen him as Hotspur."

"I would love to have seen that, even then when I was a child. That was probably the last good part he had." She sighed.

He thought of her description of her father swimming and the loving account she gave of his reading to her, but he did not speak of these things. He feared to distress her on the eve of their own parting.

After supper they went into the study where Margaret had lit a fire. The cool evening seemed to be a foretaste of autumn's chilly nights. It reminded Antony that it was less than a year ago that they had started rehearsals. His final year at University had been a momentous one. He felt much older now than he had when, at the beginning of his third year, he had sought for Margaret's new room and, finding it, had become enchanted by her. Now, together, before a blazing fire, they sat, their arms around each other, facing their separation. Later Antony would remember how, strangely, their spirits were high, despite the sadness of the occasion, simply because they were together. They enjoyed this last evening. They talked and laughed as if this were the beginning not the end. They dazzled each other. They seemed to be falling in love not saying goodbye.

He left the following morning. In the last moments they had clung together like lovers about to face a painful death. Eventually he had found the strength to break away from her.

He left the house by the front door, leaving her standing in the study. He walked quickly down the drive and got into the car, parked in the road. He avoided looking up the drive to see the house for the last time and did not glance back at the garden. He started the engine and drove away.

Chapter Thirty Four

Their parting had been like a death. The days plodded by as she waited for news of Douglas. The feeling of well-being, the result of her holiday in Scotland, had deserted her. She mourned for Antony. The years ahead stretched out desolate and bleak. Eventually, summoning every ounce of courage that she had, she decided to prepare herself for the life she had chosen without him.

More than anything else, she knew that writing would occupy her mind and heart more thoroughly than anything else. She sketched out outlines for short stories and forced herself to write. Deliberately she avoided using her own experiences and concentrated on creating characters and situations quite divorced from any people or episodes in her own life. In this way she sought to banish the memories which otherwise would have crowded into her consciousness. For a while she plotted tales about unpleasant or villainous characters and then, rather oddly, introduced the supernatural and found herself writing a ghost story. This was a genre she had always enjoyed reading even though the denouement was often unsatisfactory. Looking for inspiration she searched for her copy of the ghost stories of Quiller Couch, but could not find it. She did however hunt down Hardy's 'Wessex Tales' to read again and found they had the atmosphere she sought. Soon she had drafted out three stories that satisfied her. She considered sending them out individually but decided to wait until she had a collection ready.

She began to feel impatient for Douglas's return as September drew to a close. She drove his Land-Rover to the local garage to have its tyres, oil and battery checked. Somehow just sitting in it made her feel very close to him.

She thought of what else she could do to prepare for his home-coming. His clothes perhaps needed some attention. She sorted out what needed to go to the dry-cleaner's and discarded one or two items from his crowded wardrobe. When she opened the top drawer of his chest of drawers, her heart gave a sickening jolt for the first garment she saw was the grey polo-necked jumper Antony had borrowed. She took it out and added it to the pile of clothes she was going to wash.

In the last days of September a letter from Douglas gave her the date of his return. He would arrive at Covlington on the fourth of October, probably in the late afternoon. Margaret checked the time-table and wrote down the times when the likely trains would be arriving. She looked forward to seeing him again.

Chapter Thirty Five

The long journey from Africa had given Douglas a lot of time to think. In her letter Margaret had given no reason for asking him to return. Its brevity was puzzling, as was her having spent time at a fishing hotel in Scotland. Ardanaiseig had certainly been a very pleasant place but it was essentially a hotel for fishermen. Margaret had never been a keen angler. He doubted whether she had ever had more than a passing interest in the sport, rather by accompanying him she had indulged his fascination. Certainly she had enjoyed rowing around the lochans on that holiday, but had never in her life bothered to practise casting seriously. She lacked the patience of the true angler.

It was almost six months since he had seen her. Her letters had been fairly regular but somehow impersonal. She seemed to be merely recording what she was doing, at work, in the garden or listing books she had read, friends she had visited, theatre trips she had made. She could have been writing to anyone, such as a friend she was no longer close to. There were no jokes and no scabrous comments about colleagues. On previous absences he remembered receiving brief notes scrawled almost illegibly on scraps of paper that had made him laugh aloud. The general tone of them had been warm and humorous. He could not believe she had grown dull, but the letters were not the lively jottings he had grown to expect of her. They were the cool missives of a heart grown cold.

He recalled that in the last months of the preceding year Margaret had changed. He believed she was working too hard. She had started to write a novel as well as directing a play and teaching. She had often seemed overwrought, on edge, complaining of sleepless nights, and yet she had never looked more beautiful. With this thought he was back to the suspicions he had had before leaving for Africa. He had never voiced his doubts and despised himself for having them. Trust between partners, he believed, should be taken for granted. The control of one individual by another, a common fault among men, he loathed, and believed it was always destructive. Jealousy he had never been able to understand. To him it was clear that the feeling was usually unwarranted. If it were not, then, should someone you loved prefer another, it was time to go.

Margaret's behaviour had nevertheless caused him concern at times. He remembered the evening they had entertained her friend, Elaine, and her new husband. After eating they had played records and she had danced quite provocatively with Jonathan, holding him close and flirting outrageously. Douglas had been concerned for Elaine, and was surprised that Margaret's behaviour did not seem to worry her in the slightest. He supposed that she knew her friend so well that she could see it meant nothing, as he did himself.

That evening, Margaret had worn a new dress. She had been sorting out her clothes, at this time, taking sacks full of discarded garments to Oxfam and replacing them with more glamorous alternatives. She took more care over her appearance than she had formerly. Sometimes she looked lit up from within and was dangerously beautiful.

317

One evening he found her sitting at the desk in the study with several large photographs spread on its surface.

"What do you think of these?" she asked smiling. "I've just got them back from the photographer's. Enlargements from those contact-prints."

He remembered seeing the scroll of tiny prints she had been studying the week before.

"We are going to use these, blown up further, as posters."

He was surprised at the clarity of the enlargements. They were close-ups either of small groups or individuals, dressed in costume for 'Coriolanus'. One of them held his attention.

"Who is this?" he asked.

"That's Lodge. He's playing Coriolanus."

The actor's expression was full of pride and aggression, his stance athletic and powerful. He was dressed in the tunic and armour of a Roman warrior and carried a plumed helmet under his arm. He looked dangerous and majestic. He was also, extremely good-looking.

"I'm impressed. Do you make a habit of calling them by their surnames? Isn't it like reducing them to schoolboys?"

"No. I usually call them by the names of the characters they play. He's called Antony."

Of course that had to be who he was.

Douglas looked at the rest of the photographs, but his eyes were continually drawn to Coriolanus, who appeared in most of them. He handed them back to Margaret. So that was the one she dreamed about. It was an intriguing situation.

They saw little of each other in the early weeks of December as Margaret's evenings were filled with ever-lengthening rehearsals. Then Douglas was called away to take part in a series of lectures at a university in the south of England. He was unable to return in time to see the play

318

performed. Margaret affected disappointment, but, he could tell, she was more concerned about the play's success than his viewing of it.

Their Christmas was quiet. She seemed subdued, which he put down to exhaustion. His expedition to Africa increasingly occupied his mind and time. No longer did he fear to leave her for what would be a considerable time. The fragility that she had revealed in their earlier years together, no longer gave him cause for concern. If she had been a little unbalanced in the last few weeks, he believed it was entirely due to overwork not to her memories of the unfortunate past that used to haunt her thoughts. She was, he believed, as strong now, inwardly, as she had always outwardly appeared to be.

One evening, just after the Spring Term had begun, he found her in the study with the photograph of Antony Lodge in her hand. She sat at the desk, quite still, her eyes fixed on the photograph that had so impressed him. She did not hear him open the door and he stood, not knowing whether to go or stay. Whatever her motivation for looking at the photograph, he decided, was her own business.

Their last weeks together before he left for Africa passed smoothly. Their habitual friendly dealings with each other seemed to suggest that all was well.

Africa was a shock even to Douglas who had always tried to keep up to date with developments there. He enjoyed the explorations that he had planned so carefully, but came to feel impelled to try to alleviate, in whatever way or to what degree he could, the appalling conditions that affected him so deeply.

Margaret's letters he found increasingly disturbing. Not in what she wrote but in how she wrote it. He was convinced that what he had earlier suspected was indeed the truth. She had fallen in love with Antony Lodge. He believed she needed space and time. He still loved her and believed he always would. But he would never force her to give up someone she was in love with, in a mistaken gesture of loyalty to him. That was how he came to write as he did about his intention to remain in Africa.

He was careful to make it clear to her that he loved her still and would return to her whenever she needed him. He dreaded the idea that she might feel deserted and he wrote to Elaine, asking her to visit Margaret and try to assess her state of mind. Elaine's reply was interesting. She assured Douglas that Margaret was well and happy and had accepted his decision to work in Africa. She told him how gracious she had been in accepting his need to help the people suffering as they did and admired his self-sacrifice. Then, as if to emphasise Margaret's equanimity, she had told him how pleasant her visit had been. She had been welcomed enthusiastically despite the short notice and they had enjoyed a lively lunch-party with one of Margaret's students. He had just taken his finals in Chemistry but really wanted to be an actor and as he had taken the leading part in 'Coriolanus' with great success Margaret was encouraging him to apply to drama school. He was an absolutely delightful young man, Elaine added.

Finally, his long journey home was over. He arrived at Covlington Station. As he unloaded his baggage from the train, he glimpsed her at the end of the platform. She hurried towards him.

"Welcome home," she said.

She had driven there in his Land-Rover to transport his luggage more easily. She handed him the keys.

"You can drive it home, then you'll see what an old rat trap it is."

"Thanks. I love that ancient vehicle. I wish I'd taken it with me!"

"And left it there, hopefully!"

"It's good to see you're still on form. By the way, you look great!"

"You too. Sunburned, thinner and your hair is three shades lighter. You put me in mind of Sir Henry Curtis in 'King Solomon's Mines'.

His loud laughter attracted the notice of several passengers disembarking from the train. They saw a tall upright figure, surrounded by the battered baggage befitting one who had travelled from far places. Smiling broadly he hugged the young woman who had so amused him.

"I see I'm back in the land of stories and legends," he joked.

"Yes," she agreed, "where everyone lives happily ever after," and her smile seemed to offer a promise that for them this would be so.